'*We Were the Salt of the Sea* is anything but a conventional whodunit. Every man in the village seems to have been in love with Marie and awaiting her return. The plot exposes the rivalry and feuds that exist in a small community. Who is related to whom? And why do they behave as they do? Everyone seems to have suffered through the drowning of relatives at some stage … They are absolutely fascinating and well-drawn characters, from the fisherman, to the priest, to the restaurant owner, to the undertakers' TripFiction

'The writing is absolutely stunning, its lyrical narrative draws you in from the start as the words just float from the page' Have Books Will Read

'Anyone who enjoyed *The Shipping News* by Annie Proulx will love this one! I couldn't put this lovely book down. I've lived by the sea for most of my life, am endlessly fascinated by it and this book was a real treasure to read … Enchanting and beguiling … I hope there is more of the same from this author' Mrs Bloggs Books

'*We Were the Salt of the Sea* is a superb crime piece hidden in a story about the meaning of life and love. A page-turner which leaves salt on your fingers and sand between your toes' Chocolate 'n' Waffles

'This is a novel that straddles genres, and that made it a refreshing and gripping read … In large part a crime novel – a woman, Marie Garant, is found dead in the ocean and the new detective Morales is pulled in to investigate – it's also a mystery with an outsider, Catherine Day, turning up looking for her birth mother and trying to find herself in the process. It can even be described as a love letter to the sea; it's clear that the author has a love of the ocean herself and this comes through so beautifully in her writing. I swear I could smell the ocean and the fishing boats as I was reading. I could hear the sea waxing and waning throughout the novel – the sea is as much a character in this novel as the people are' Rather Too Fond of Books

'It's moving yet funny, it's a poem of a crime novel, it's a sea shanty of a love story, all rolled into one. *We Were the Salt of the Sea* snares you in its nets and cries out to be read all in one go' *La Presse*

'Colourful, authentic characters with the kind of flavour that can only be inspired by real locals. So good it'll make you want to pack your bags and drive straight to the seaside' *Journal de Montréal*

'Need to escape the madding crowds and turn your back on the concrete jungle? Getting the urge to sail away and feel the sea breeze on your face? Just dive right into *We Were the Salt of the Sea*' *Le Devoir*

'There's no doubt the key protagonist in this novel of many secrets is the sea. She's as fickle as she is steady, as unforgiving as she is subdued and as vindictive as she is seductive' *Nuit Blanche*

'A delightful mingling of poetry, mystery and humour amidst some greatly endearing characters' *La Nouvelle*

'These characters ooze so much authenticity you know you'll find others just like them propping up the bar in any of the fishing villages along this coast … *We Were the Salt of the Sea* is a whale of a tale' Quebec Reads

'Lyrical and elegiac, full of quirks and twists – *We Were the Salt of the Sea* is an elegant crime novel that deserves to be a tremendous success' William Ryan

'As rhythmic and beautiful as the waves, with a fierce undercurrent that pulls you hungrily into its depths' Matt Wesoloski

'Within the first pages of this wonderfully atmospheric novel you are immersed into life in a tiny fishing village on the Gaspé Peninsula of eastern Quebec, a place where everyone thinks they know everyone else's business but no one will tell – especially not outsiders. Along comes an enigmatic tourist seeking her mother, just as a body is pulled up in fishing nets and a sailing boat found adrift in a storm. I loved everything about this novel: the stunning descriptions of place, and of the mesmerising but brutal sea, which has taken many locals; the sharply observed dialogue and vocal tics of the characters; and the beautiful clarity of the writing. We are outsiders, observing from the point of view of the outsider characters, and as such perhaps we can never totally understand – yet Roxanne Bouchard still leads us to a gloriously satisfying conclusion. I genuinely couldn't put this book down and I'm sure I will read it again before long' Gill Paul

'Bouchard has managed that marvellous thing: prose that is at once lyrical and fizzing with energy. It's well matched with her story, embedded as it is in a place shaped by the sea, in which the dead are almost as present as the living. We see Marie Garant through the words of those who knew her, but she is forever out of reach. A *tour de force* of both writing and translation' Su Bristow

'*We Were the Salt of the Sea* is another Orenda blinder – Canadian crime fiction that almost feels literary in its execution and with a quiet, gentle humour that immediately tickles the reader and makes them warm to the characters' Biblio Beth

'Roxanne Bouchard has the heart of a poet, the soul of the darkest crime writer, and the gift of perfect prose. This gorgeous novel is not only an ode to the sea, but an exploration of where we truly come from, and a gripping thriller. I became utterly lost in this book, and when I briefly came up for air, I only wanted to dive straight back in' Louise Beech

'*We Were the Salt of the Sea* is a hypnotic read that manages to be in turns quirky, lyrical and insightful. The fascinating story is held together by a cast of characters you will grow to love and such is the sense of place that Roxanne Bouchard conjures up you'll be looking out your passport long before you turn that final page, and booking your trip to this particular region of Canada. A must-read' Michael J Malone

'*We Were the Salt of the Sea* is more than just an investigation into a woman's death. It's the story of a woman's search for the truth about her birth parents, trying to explore secrets from her past. It's also a detective's journey, discovering more about himself, his marriage and human behaviour. But most of all, this book is about the sea – its uncertainty and unpredictability. The vivid descriptions left me with a yearning to visit Canada (again) and experience the natural beauty of Quebec's coastline for myself' Off-the-Shelf Books

'Do you ever start to read a book and then wish it would never end? *We Were the Salt of the Sea* is that book. Part crime novel, part love song to the sea, it is so beautifully, lyrically written that you want to stay forever luxuriating in the language until the sea comes to claim you as its own. All the more kudos then, not just to the author, but also the translator, because this is an awesome job' Live and Deadly

'This is a magical, ethereal, haunting novel that beautifully captures the essence and landscape of the Gaspé Peninsula. The setting is the story and the story is the setting' The Book Trail

WE WERE THE SALT OF THE SEA

ABOUT THE AUTHOR

Ten years or so ago, Roxanne Bouchard decided it was time she found her sea legs. So she learned to sail, first on the St Lawrence River, before taking to the open waters off the Gaspé Peninsula. The local fishermen soon invited her aboard to reel in their lobster nets, and Roxanne saw for herself that the sunrise over Bonaventure never lies.

We Were the Salt of the Sea is her fifth novel, and her first to be translated into English. She lives in Quebec.

Follow Roxanne on Twitter *@RBouchard72* and on her website: *roxannebouchard.com*.

ABOUT THE TRANSLATOR

David Warriner translates from French and nurtures a healthy passion for Franco, Nordic and British crime fiction. Growing up in deepest Yorkshire, he developed incurable Francophilia at an early age. Emerging from Oxford with a modern languages degree, he narrowly escaped the graduate rat race by hopping on a plane to Canada – and never looked back. More than a decade into a high-powered commercial translation career, he listened to his heart and turned his hand again to the delicate art of literary translation. David has lived in France and Quebec, and now calls beautiful British Columbia home.

Follow David on Twitter *@givemeawave* and on his website: *wtranslation.ca*.

We Were the Salt of the Sea

ROXANNE BOUCHARD

Translated by David Warriner

**ORENDA
BOOKS**

Orenda Books
16 Carson Road
West Dulwich
London SE21 8HU
www.orendabooks.co.uk

First published in the United Kingdom by Orenda Books 2018
Originally published in French as *Nous étions le sel de la mer* by VLB éditeur 2014
Copyright © VLB éditeur 2014
English translation © David Warriner 2017

A catalogue record for this book is available from the British Library.

ISBN 978-1-912374-03-8
eISBN 978-1-912374-04-5

Typeset in Garamond by MacGuru Ltd
Printed and bound by CPI Group (UK) Ltd, Croydon CRO 4YY

The publication of this translation has been made possible
through the financial support of SODEC Quebec.

SODEC
Québec ✚✚ ✚✚

For sales and distribution, please contact *info@orendabooks.co.uk*

Contents

To my parents, Claude et Colette.
I love you.

'Some folks show up here to show off. Big talkers, y'know, who like to strut their stuff and blow their own horn. Tourists, that's how we call 'em.'

Bass, from Bonaventure

FISHING GROUNDS

Alberto (1974)

The moment O'Neil Poirier glanced out of his porthole and saw the hull of the sailboat moored alongside, he figured the day was off to a very bad start. From the Magdalen Islands, was Poirier. His personality too, and his two deckhands. They had motored into Mont-Louis two days prior to stock up on their way to Anticosti Island, where the cod and the herring were waiting. Wanting to leave at dawn, they had hit the sack early the night before, and hadn't heard the sailboat dock beside them. The hum of their generator must have covered the sound of the neighbouring crew's footsteps.

O'Neil Poirier barked at his men to get up and clambered out on deck, intent on making a bit of racket to show these fair-weather sailors they were far from welcome. When a man gets up at half past three in the morning for a hard day's work in the frigid waters of the Saint Lawrence Estuary, he does not want to have to shift a boat out of his way, especially not one that's full of sleeping tourists who'll grumble about being woken up early and fret about fishermen not retying their mooring lines properly.

Poirier sniffed around outside. Talk about nerve. The owner of the sailboat had had the gall to hook his power directly to the fishing boat instead of running the cable across to the wharf! The fisherman yanked the plug out of the socket, leaned over the monohull and rapped firmly on the deck.

'Out of there, you heathen! I've got a bone to pick with you!'

That was when he heard the sound of a woman groaning from below deck, a long, harrowing wail. Poirier felt the hairs on the back of his neck stand on end, since these were sounds unlike anything the fisherman had ever heard. But O'Neil Poirier, who had tackled seventy-five-knot winds off the coast of Anticosti before, wasn't afraid of a thing. He grabbed the long knife he used for gutting cod and jumped aboard the sailboat just as another scream sounded out, more breathless than the first. Poirier yanked the hatch open and scrambled down the five steps in a split second.

'Hey, give it a rest!' he growled.

No response. It was hot and humid inside the cabin. All he could hear in the darkness was heavy breathing and something moving, but not in any controlled sort of way. It was such a mess down there, it took Poirier a while to ascertain what was happening. Still on his guard, he slowly approached the berth where she lay. When he saw what was going on, he acted without hesitation and plunged in headfirst with the kind of determination he had always been known for. He slit the umbilical cord with his own knife, bathed the baby in warm water and tossed the placenta to the fish.

Then he mopped the young mother's brow and placed the carefully swaddled newborn in her arms, before wrapping them both in a warm blanket and leaving the sloop without a sound.

That day, the men aboard the *Alberto* ever so gently moved the sailboat belonging to the woman who had been forced to emergency dock alongside them. They double-checked that her mooring lines were tight and plugged her power cord into the outlet on the wharf themselves. They were a little late setting out to sea and looked over their shoulders for a long, long time.

Bearings (2007)

Cyrille said the sea was like a patchwork quilt. Fragments of waves joined together by strands of sunlight. He said the sea would swallow the stories of the world and digest them at its leisure in its cobalt belly before regurgitating only distorted reflections. He said the events of the last few weeks would sink into the darkness of memory.

Before, I used to think of myself as white and translucent. Flawless. An empty glass. Even my doctor thought I looked pale. Too pale.

'You don't have much colour in your cheeks.'

'This is my natural skin tone.'

'How do you feel?'

'Well, I've maxed out my quota of bad days and I've stopped adding up the hours.'

'Adding up the hours?'

'Yes. For a while, when I woke up, I would count how many hours I had to live through before I could go back to sleep again. I stopped two months ago. I think it must mean something.'

'It means a lot, actually. Are you seeing a psychologist?'

'No, I don't think that's really my cup of tea. That's what my friends are for. I don't want to have to pay just to have a chat.'

He took off his rectangular glasses, put them down on the desk. Over the years, this man had given me my vaccines and saved me from measles, appendicitis and countless colds, bouts of the flu and other tissue-box ailments. He had known me for so long that he was entitled to his opinion about me.

'Why do I get the impression, Catherine, that you're not doing so well?'

'I'm OK, doc. It's just … It's like I've lost the manual for having fun. For getting excited about anything. I feel empty. Transparent.'

'Do you ever feel like the world is turning without you? Like you've got off the train and are standing by the side of the tracks and watching the party from a soundproof box?'

'Well, I'm nowhere right now. I'm not at the party and I'm not watching from the sidelines. I'm just a pane of glass, doc. No feelings, nothing.'

'How old are you?'

'Thirty-three, but there are days when I'm way older than that.'

'You need to take care of yourself, Catherine. You're a pretty girl, you're in good health—'

'Sometimes my heart feels, well, tight. I get all dizzy and everything goes black. I end up flat out on the floor, waiting for the hand of death to move out of the way so I can get up again.'

'That's your blood pressure dropping. Does this happen to you often?'

'No, but I worry it might happen more. It's weighing on my mind.'

'Well, next time it happens you can try lying down on the floor with your legs up against a wall. That'll make you feel better.'

'And what do I do about the rest?'

'The rest?'

'Yes – the horror stories on the TV news, the death of my mother, plants that don't flower in the winter, the crappy weather, comedians who just aren't funny, ads you can't fast-forward, films that shoot themselves in the foot, housework that doesn't get done, the dust of our days, bedsheets with creases in them, and reheated leftovers that stick to the bottom of the pan – what am I supposed to do with all that?'

He sighed. He must be sick and tired of troublemakers like me who don't know what to do with their lives and waste the miracles he prescribes. What good are antibiotics to a man with a bad cold who ends up hanging himself the very next week?

'How long has your mother been dead now, Catherine?'

'Fifteen months.'

I had told myself that, when my parents died, I would leave. I had been sailing around lakes for years, and I had set my sails to the wind everywhere along the west side of Montreal proper, yet it was the sea I saw in my dreams. I wanted to see how the Gaspé Peninsula opened the way to the river, to take refuge in the Baie-des-Chaleurs and scream into the Atlantic. I had every reason to leave. Recently I had even received a letter, mailed from Key West, summoning me to a small fishing village in the Gaspé. I knew that, to get to the bottom of my story, I would have to start there. But I lacked the courage, and racked up the seasons in layers of grey on the bookshelves of my oh-so-Zen condo. What good would come of wanting? Dreaming? Loving? I didn't know anymore. In spite of myself, I felt an uncertain freedom as I stood watching the sidewalks, cracks threading their way beneath the feet of the passers-by. I was a landlocked sailor, stranded in dry dock without a sail. With lead for ballast.

'You need to take your mind off things, Catherine.'

'Take my mind off things? This is all real, doc! Other people out there have hopes and dreams. Me, I … I'm alive, but I don't see what I should get so excited about.'

'You're an idealist. You wish life were exciting. But excitement is a youthful ideal. Truth is, life is just one day after the next. You only have two options. You can lose hope, or you can learn. It's time for you to learn, Catherine.'

'To learn that everything's just blah?'

'To learn what beauty lies in every day, just waiting to be discovered.'

'Ah.'

Behind him, dust floated on the soft light filtering through the vertical blinds. The same light that had, over the stubborn years, yellowed the old Latin diplomas hanging in their frames.

'Summer's coming. Why don't you go on a trip somewhere?'

'A trip? You think swanning off to Morocco for a spot of sex tourism's going to spice up my life?'

'No. I'm just suggesting something a bit more exotic.'

'Exotic is a ploy, doc. A temporary diversion for people who take snapshots and make a scrapbook out of their lives.'

'You're stubborn and complacent, and irony isn't doing you any favours here.'

'I'm sorry. It's true, I do enjoy driving. It gives me a sense of freedom. But it's a waste of fuel and it's bad for the environment. So I go around in circles and always end up right back where I started.'

He stood up, white coat and all, to show me the door.

'You used to go sailing with your father, didn't you?'

'Yes, but you know what they say: Leaving is like cheating – Or something like that.'

'So cheat away to your heart's content, Catherine. Shed your skin, leave all your thoughts behind. And try not to come back too soon.'

I went home and read the letter from Key West again. Where the heck was Caplan? I looked it up on the map. Then I took care of business, packed my bags and hit the road. Like the doctor ordered. Let's see, I said to myself.

And see, I did.

Today, the swell rolls like a watery carpet, lapping against the hull of the sailboat, flickering in the slivers cast by the rising sun. The wind fills the sails as the horizon glows red, dawn washing the sea with colour and transforming this story into a scarlet fresco. The sky turns blue, with just enough of a hint of pink to pave the way for the sun. One last time, I turn my light-flooded pupils towards the rugged coastline of the Baie-des-Chaleurs, which, already far behind, fades into the stubborn mist of sunrise.

I lean overboard. In the broken mirror of the water's surface, I am splinters of stained glass, a tarnished mosaic, a dysfunctional memory out of sync, a jumbled assortment of images pieced together by a watery goldsmith. I open my hands and let the spool of my memories reel out onto the swell, one last time unto the waves.

Dredgers and trawlers

'Well, let me tell you, *mam'zelle,* that hotel and bar over by Caplan beach – burned to the ground, it did!'

He opened the dishwasher too early, allowing a scalding cloud of steam to escape. He slammed it shut again and turned to me. Leaning over the counter, he tried to catch a glimpse of the letter from Key West I had reopened to remind myself what it said, but I pulled it away.

'And let me tell you, quite the fire it was and all! The whole village came out for a ganders in the middle of the night. Folks even came up from Saint-Siméon and Bonaventure to see! I made the most of it and opened up the bistro. It didn't let up for two days! The flames were licking all up the walls, and bed springs were popping all over the place. Had the firemen running around in circles, it did! You should've seen the ashes all over the beach! And let me tell you, it all went up in smoke! The hotel, the bar, even the slot machines! You're not too disappointed, I hope?'

I smiled. If I'd driven for ten hours to feed the slots at the Caplan beach hotel, then yes, I probably would have been disappointed.

'Over there, see? It was just the other side of the church – a bit further west. But now there's nothing left of it. Must've been about two months ago, I'd say. Everyone knows what happened. I can't believe you didn't hear about it – it made the front page in the *Bay Echo.* They even did a special feature about it, with colour pages and everything! They say it was probably arson, and the insurance won't pay up. Cases like this, they're always looking to point the finger. But let me tell you, it's funny they told you to go sleep there, you know…'

I checked the date. The letter had been mailed from Key West two months ago. I put it back in my bag. I had nothing to hide, but nothing to say either. He cleared away my leftover pizza, tossed it into the bin and took a step to the side, not entirely satisfied.

'Let me tell you just one thing, the best place to stay is at Guylaine's, right here, just across the way. You'll be a lot more comfortable there than up at the hotel that burned down!'

Keeping his distance this time, he opened the dishwasher again, which was still rumbling away. He picked up a red-chequered tea towel and started flapping the steam away like a matador struggling to tame a mad bull. Then, brimming with local pride, with the tip of his chin he pointed out a big house to the east of the bistro, nestled against the cliffside, looking out to sea in quiet contemplation. A charming *auberge* that promised a warm welcome.

'It's the finest one around! Quiet too. Guylaine doesn't have kids or a husband. And further down, over there, that's the fishermen's wharf and the Café du Havre is right alongside. If it's fishermen you want to meet, you should go there for breakfast mid-morning, when they come back in. Guylaine will be out for her walk right now, but she's sure to stop by later. She always comes in to say hello.'

He visibly softened. Without thinking, he picked up a scalding glass, juggled with it then flung it onto the counter like a curse. He gazed out towards the *auberge* again, then turned to me with a sigh. 'How about a coffee while you're waiting?'

I've never really liked those bed and breakfasts where you're expected to make chit-chat, tell people who you are, where you're from, where you're going and how long you're staying, and listen to the owners spouting on about their country-home renovations. But it sounded like I might as well forget about finding another hotel around here, and I'd never been one for camping, so Guylaine's was beginning to look like my only option.

He cleared my plate and empty glass away and placed a mug on the counter in front of me before charging back for more, index finger pointed questioningly at my bag. 'If you're looking for someone around here, I can probably help.'

I hesitated. Swivelled my chair around to face the other end of the bistro. As I recall, the sea was the only thing on my mind right then. The thick smell of it. The breakwater darkening into shadow, ready to slip beneath the heavy blanket of night. With no lights out here, how much could you see along this coast?

'Let me tell you just one thing, though, I know plenty of folk around here.'

I still didn't have the words to talk about her. She had always been unpronounceable; but now, all of a sudden, I had to casually drop this woman's name into conversation. Should I roll it seven times on the tip of my tongue, swish it around my mouth like a vintage wine or crush it with my molars to soften it?

'Spit it out, then. Who are you looking for?'

I figured I'd have to get used to the name, for a while anyway. Put on a brave face and add it to my vocabulary at least, if not my family tree. So for the first time, contemplating the sea, I said it. I took a deep breath in and let it all out.

'Marie Garant. Do you know her?'

He recoiled. All the sparkle in his face fizzled out, as if I'd blown out a candle. Suddenly on his guard, he looked at me suspiciously.

'She a friend of yours?'

'No. I don't actually know her.'

He picked up the glass again and started rubbing the heck out of it.

'Phew! You had me worried there. Because let me tell you, that Marie Garant, she's no woman to get close to. Especially not you, if you're a tourist that is. I wouldn't go around shouting about her if you want to make any friends around here.'

'Excuse me?'

'But you're not from around here, so you weren't to know, of course.'

'No, I wasn't.'

'Is she the reason you're here?'

'Er … No.' It was barely a lie. 'I'm on holiday.'

'Ah! So you *are* a tourist! Well then, welcome! I'm Renaud. Renaud Boissonneau, dean of students at the high school and businessman with business aplenty!'

'Er, pleased to meet you.'

'Let me tell you, we'll take good care of you. How did you like the pizza? Most of the tourists haven't arrived yet – this place is usually full of them. That's right, it's always packed here. People think it's nice and rustic. Did you see the decor? This place has history, let me tell you. Because you might not have noticed, but we're in the old rectory. That's why the church is right next door! The patio wraps all the way around, so anyone who wants to avert their eyes from the steeple while they're drinking their beer can go and look at the sea or the fisherman's wharf instead. Oh, and the curate lives upstairs. Which means, let me tell you, that when you've had a couple of drinks and you're ready to confess your sins, you can just go right on up!'

Having successfully tamed the dishwasher, he was now noisily unloading some mercifully unbreakable plates.

'I do pretty much everything around here, I do. How about that decor? … See. I was the one who did it all. Let me tell you, I brought up everything I could find in the basement. See how original it is? There's wagon wheels up on the ceiling with oil lamps hanging from them, clogs, little wooden birdhouses, tools, saws, cables and rope, and I hung some old oilskins in the corner. Do you need a rain jacket? I suppose it's been a nice day today. But it has rained a lot the last little while, don't you think?'

'I hadn't noticed.'

'Ah, a city girl!'

As if the distance gave him permission to confide in me, he leaned in to whisper something. 'And let me tell you, I do all the decor, wait tables and wash the dishes, but you'll never guess what – soon I'm going to be cook's helper as well! At fifty-three! Never too old to be young again, *mam'zelle*!'

He straightened up and slammed the dishwasher shut again.

'Everything you see over there, it's all from our place. That globe, them old cameras, the marine charts, the grandfather clock, the two-handed saw, the horseshoes. Do we say horseshoes or horse's shoes? Let me tell you, I reckon you can say either. Oh, and them bottles, the clay pots, them mismatched mugs, even the recipe books! So tell me, which way did you come? Through the valley or round the point?'

'Er, through the valley.'

'Good on you, not going out of your way for nothing!'

He rubbed the counter like he was trying to make his rag all dizzy.

'Out of my way for nothing?'

'The point! Percé, the Northern Gannets, Bonaventure Island … talk about going out of your way for nothing, *mam'zelle*! Think you want to go there?'

'I don't know. I haven't made any plans yet.'

'Because we just got some tourist brochures in today! I haven't read through them yet, but … Ah! If it isn't the fair Guylaine herself!'

All at once, he flung the rag away into the sink as if he had dirt on his hands.

Guylaine Leblanc, to look at her, must have been at least sixty-five. With salt-and-pepper hair pulled up into a loose bun, she had about her that air of goodness that grandmothers in American family movies exude. She laughed tenderly with a twinkle in her eye for Renaud, who was clearly putty in her hands.

'Have you met our new tourist, Guylaine? What was your name again?'

'Catherine.'

'Catherine what?'

'Day. Catherine Day.'

'Catherine Day wants to stay at yours; you have a room for her, don't you?'

Renaud kissed Guylaine on both cheeks and then she walked me over to her sewing shop, Le Point de Couture, on the south side of Highway 132, where she sold clothes and did alterations. The *auberge* was at the rear of the shop, well away from any road noise. The vast ground floor was decorated in the same fashion as Renaud's bistro with a surprisingly comforting hodgepodge of antiques and easy chairs, and there was a deep veranda overlooking the shore. Guylaine had three rooms for tourists upstairs; she must have slept somewhere at the top of the staircase that led to the attic. She gave me a room facing the sea – her favourite, she said – all decked out in white and blue, with driftwood trim and a hand-stitched quilt on the bed. It was a very nice room.

My first Gaspesian morning unfolded beneath a motionless yellow sun. I went downstairs to join the others staying at the *auberge* for breakfast.

'...well, my four kids had flown the nest, you know, and my second husband had just passed away, so of course I had a rough time of it when my doctor told me they'd have to cut off my boob ... I really didn't know what would become of me...'

I poured myself a coffee. A young couple – tourists – cooed at each other at one table, while an older lady chattered on and on at Guylaine, shadowing her every footstep.

'...because there's no point pretending, you know. I'm sixty-six years old, and I'm not getting any younger. Plus, with only one boob, what kind of man is going to want anything to do with me? I've always lived my life for my kids, you know...'

Our landlady was whisking the pancake batter with the kind of laid-back yet attentive air that makes people feel like you're listening to them and gives chatterboxes carte blanche to pour their hearts out even more than usual.

'...so this is the first time I've ever gone away, because I've never travelled, I've never done anything, really. I don't even know what I like to eat! Do you have a favourite meal you like to eat? Well, I don't! See what I mean?'

I downed the rest of my coffee and took off for the Café du Havre.

That's where I would have breakfast almost every morning from then on. It's a pretty spot, basking on the quayside, with its nautical decor and its servers calmly, yet efficiently, breezing around. The hubbub inside bounces off the walls, drifts out the window and seeps its way back in through the side door. It's the kind of place you know you're going to lose yourself in a little, cut yourself some slack from all those daily imperatives to be oh-so polite, oh-so on time and oh-so beyond reproach throughout the never-ending loop of days. A time zone unto itself.

'Christ in a chalice! What did I tell you? Look at them Indians coming back in on the ebb again!'

He was a strong man, gripping his coffee mug with every muscle in that big body of his as he waited for his breakfast. Long hair tied back over his neck and a red bandana on his head. Jeans, work boots and grey sweaters they were wearing, him and his deckhand. They had just returned from fishing pretty much empty-handed. I had been sipping my second coffee when their boat came in. Tails between their legs like that, I figured the lobsters must have given them the cold shoulder. The waitress breezed over with her red hair, green eyes and youthful smile. She set their plates of scrambled eggs down on the children's drawings that adorned the table top. The men looked up and thanked her. She walked away.

'Well look at that, will you! Christ in a chalice, they're only going to get stuck again! That's the first boat coming through … Jeez … are they going to make it?'

The café basked in an almost-too-bright light as splinters of sun danced in the east on the falling tide.

'Talk about cutting it fine! And the other one's nowhere near back yet!'

I love men. Their presence. Their sheer manliness. It pains me sometimes to see how generously and tenderly some of them love their wives.

'Christ in a chalice, they've got a nerve, that lot! Suppose they can afford to, with their boats paid for by the government and all!'

'N-n-not really, th-th-they pull their weight too—'

'If you say so … You on holiday, then?'

The fisherman turned towards me so suddenly, he caught me off-guard. I'd been staring at him, and I must have crossed the line into effrontery without realising it. Those oh-so-blue eyes of his were so quick to bore into me, I lost my balance and had to hang onto the table to stay on my feet.

'Yes.'

'Not much happening, eh?'

'Er … No.'

'Well, things do happen, but not like in the city. Things at sea. In the summer, the men live off the season … the good weather, you know.'

Tanned, boxy hands.

'And in the winter?'

'In the winter? They live on hope. Fishing's a hell of a game. See, there's just four boats here. Mine, Cyrille's and them Indian boats. One of theirs is still out. They're always late, that lot.'

'Where are they from?'

'From the reserve. Gesgapegiag. They put their boats in here because their fishing spot's not far away. You know, if the government came and dredged the channel, there'd be a lot more boats! Christ in a chalice, they don't though, they just let it all go! Put a nice wharf in here and just watch the fishermen and tourists come rolling in. And it'd be a hell of a lot better for business at the café too!'

'Why do the Indigenous fishermen come in so late?'

'That's the way they are. They go to bed late, they get up late then they miss the tide! You take your life into your own hands, coming in here at low tide. But what do you want me to say? They never time the tide right. Always the same story. They bring the boat into the harbour mouth, one of them goes up front to guide the captain through the channel, but it's too shallow. So the captain gives it some throttle to get over the sandbar, but they end up high and dry. Hey, what did I say? The second one's on its way in! Christ in a chalice! They're going to get stuck!'

'Aren't you going to help them?'

'Ah! If you want to get your feet wet, mademoiselle, be my guest. But that water's too cold for me. They'll figure it out.'

'They're u-u-used to it,' the other fisherman chimed in.

'If not, they'll just have to wait till the tide comes back in. Or they'll tow her in. What did I say? By the skin of their teeth every time! That Jérémie's not even breaking a sweat.'

Standing at the bow of the second boat was a tall, strapping giant of a young man who looked like he was carved out of solid wood, like an old-fashioned mast. He was casually holding a lasso of mooring rope in his left hand.

'What's your name, then?'

Early sixties. At least. If not older.

'Catherine Day.'

'I'm Vital Bujold. My boat's *Ma Belle*. This here's Victor Ferlatte, my deckhand. You on holiday for a while then, Catherine?'

'I don't know.'

'You going to visit Percé?'

'I'm not sure I feel like doing the tourist thing, but I'm worried I might find the time a bit long—'

The men burst out laughing, as if I'd just slipped down a step in high heels.

'Christ in a chalice, that's all there bloody is in the Gaspé – long time!'

'Is it really that boring?'

'Boring, no. It's just different. The Gaspé is the kind of place where time stands still and things never change. If you're going to stick around in Caplan, you're going to have to learn how to sit still!'

He pushed his plate away slowly, knife and fork together, napkin on the side, and leaned his forearms on the table. The waitress breezed over, refilled their coffees, cleared the rest and walked away. Victor stared out at the Indigenous fishermen, apparently without seeing them. The giant jumped onto the wharf, tied his moorings and started chatting and joking with the crew of the neighbouring boat. Suddenly, the hubbub of the café seeped away into the cracks between the floorboards, and I felt something wash over me.

'Funny bunch, them tourists. They come here on holiday and spend half their time looking at their watches and yelling at the wait-ress when it takes more than ten minutes to get served…'

'W-w-when it rains, they get mad at us l-l-locals, like it's our f-f-fault!'

'Tourists pass right through here. They phone up, book a room, roll in at the end of the day, visit the church, look for agates on the beach, have dinner at the bistro, and then they go to bed. Then the next day, they get up, have their breakfast and rush right back off again. What's all the hurry?'

Victor shook his head in sympathy for all the tourists just passing through.

'Christ in a chalice! Can you wrap your head around that, Victor?'

Vital hammered his gaze into mine again like an iron bar. 'If you're looking for adventure, you'd be better off in Disneyland. There's nothing to write home about here. Nothing but the sea. We're living at a standstill. We've even stopped dreaming. Sometimes all we want is for time to stop catching up with us. Most tourists just can't wrap their heads around that, so they move on.'

'W-w-we wouldn't hold it against you if you wanted to l-l-leave.'

'And what if I stay?'

'You got time to lose?'

'I've got nothing to gain or lose.'

'Well stay a while before you go, then. Hang around. On the wharf, at the beach. You'll see.'

I had my eye on the tall, Indigenous fisherman.

'What's going to happen, then?'

'Christ in a chalice! Nothing! That's what I've been trying to tell you. When you look out to sea, you don't need anything else to happen!'

'Y-y-you could pick up some agates. L-l-lots of them to find along the shore.'

'Okay, then, that's what I'll do. Nothing, I mean.'

The men stood up. 'Right, we're off to sell our lobster. We'll leave you to it with the natives. You can even go over and talk to him, if you like.'

Maybe I blushed. He leaned in towards me for a moment. 'Him over there – Jérémie – you wouldn't believe how strong he is, Christ in a chalice! Strong folk, them Indians, I'll give them that. Right then, love ... see you around!'

They walked out. I kept on looking at the tall, Indigenous fisherman. Jérémie.

Nothing's going to happen, I thought.

Later that day, down from the sky came a frigid, spitting drizzle that would have soaked you to the skin with an October-like chill. I curled up in an armchair at the *auberge* and opened a coffee-table book about sailing that was lying around. Bad idea. Soon I was up to my eyes in the blues and sinking fast.

The sun was just starting to dry it all up again at the end of the afternoon when I headed over to Renaud's.

I found him polishing kitchen implements. Three big, new butcher's knives.

'So, you want to go to Percé, then?'

'Not necessarily. I was just wondering what you thought about the place.'

'Ah, you're getting itchy feet, I see!'

'I know. I'm on holiday and I have to learn how to do nothing, but it's harder than it looks.'

He placed the blades down lovingly on a wooden chopping board, which also looked new.

'Well let me tell you, you're going to need the guide! Have you seen the Gaspésie tourist guide they printed?'

'No.'

'They sent me a whole stack just the other day. If you're thinking of hitting the road, you have to let me show you!'

He reached over and plucked one from the rack, opening it and leafing through the pages in front of me.

'Will you have a look at that! See all those lovely colour pictures? Let me tell you something, tourists normally take the circle route, you know. But you have to come around the north side, though! See how they've thought it all out? You start off along the coast, "Visit the Reford Gardens, see the famous salmon run and six-wedding house in Matane", it says, then after that you're into the Haute-Gaspésie. Let me tell you something, I don't know if they're any higher up than the rest of us, but in any case, here's what it says: "You'll be amazed by the wind farm in Cap-Chat and won't want to miss the Parc national de la Gaspésie or the La Martre Lighthouse Museum." Then you move on to the point, "and its colourful villages and shops, the Northern Gannets of Bonaventure Island, Percé and the Rock, and Forillon National Park." And last but not least? Ah! Ah! The Baie-des-Chaleurs, "where the whole family can relax and enjoy a swim in the sea!" Then, after all that, let me tell you, you get back in your car and drive up through the valley to get back to Montreal as fast as you can along with everyone else and their uncle to make sure you don't miss the Labour Day Weekend traffic jam, and you get home absolutely whacked after driving three thousand kilometres – just in time to do your laundry and start back at work the next day!'

He slammed the guide shut, rolled it up and waved it over his head like an evangelist shaking a satanic flyer.

'Let me tell you something, sounds like a dream holiday, right? Well, it isn't! Listen here, *mam'zelle* Catherine, you can hop in your car right now and play the tourist all the way from southwest to northeast, but what good will it do you, eh? None at all! Everywhere else, the villages are poor, the motels are cheap and nasty, the restaurants are drab and the sea's freezing cold! Everything the shops sell is tourist tack! Nothing but knock-offs, mugs that say "Percé" and shot glasses with pictures of the Rock on them, Canada *tuques*, lamps made of shells and number plates that say, "My wife loves your hot rod!" A load of old codswallop, if you ask me! And let me tell you, you'd be sleeping in a pigsty! Show up any time after five and the guy on the hotel front desk will try and tell you you're lucky to be able to spend the night at his sister-in-law's who rents out a stupid little room with a view of the back yard, for silly money! Is that what you want, eh?'

'What? No.'

'No!'

There was a clang as he pitched the tourist anti-bible straight into the gaping-wide waste bin.

'And that's not all, if you go up towards the point you're only going to have to follow the guide backwards, and that'd be one heck of a pain, especially being on holiday and all! If there's a road well travelled, it's a heck of a lot easier to just follow it! And you, *mam'zelle* Catherine, you don't even need to go all that way around because you're already here! Feeling bored already, are you? It's just because you haven't settled in yet!'

'Ah—'

'Let me tell you just one thing, *mam'zelle* Catherine, them tourists, they bring too much of themselves on holiday, they do. When you take off, you have to leave yourself at home, you know!'

'Ah—'

'Listen, it's all very well for you to go on up to the point, but let me tell you, you're a heck of a lot better staying here with us. At Guylaine's!'

Having finished his little spiel, he went off to fetch a bag from the kitchen. From the bag he delicately extracted a new apron, which he proudly unfolded and carefully put on. Emblazoned across the chest in embroidery was his latest title, 'cook's helper'. Pulling on a silly little hat, he placed his clean knives down on the new chopping board.

'Renaud…?'

'Yes, *mam'zelle* Catherine, what can I do for such a lovely, lovely customer as yourself?'

'Vital ... Do you know Vital, the fisherman?'

'Ah! Well, let me tell you, you're in love, aren't you? Your heart melted into a puddle when he serenaded you with his famous "Christ in a chalice!" didn't it? And now you're going to want to polish your shoes and get married, eh? Guylaine! You'll have to make her a wedding dress! Our tourist's getting married!'

Guylaine had barely set foot in the door when the barrage hit.

'Oh, really?! Who to?'

'Let me tell you, to Vital!'

'To Christ in a chalice? He's already married, Catherine.'

I was flailing like a lobster in a pot of holy water.

'No, that's not it! I met Vital down at the café and he told me about the—'

'About Cyrille Bernard, eh!' Renaud interrupted.

'Cyrille Bernard? Who's he?'

'Cyrille, he's single, you know...' Guylaine chimed in.

'I'll give Vital a call tonight so he can introduce you! Are you going to the café tomorrow? Because let me tell you something, *mam'zelle* Catherine, when your soul's all adrift, it's because your heart's not tied down! And you know what, you can count on us lot to find you your someone to love!'

'Renaud's just pulling your leg, Catherine, but he's right. Cyrille, he'll take your mind off things.'

'Oh, you'll see, you won't be wanting to go to off to Percé or on any of those other flights of fancy!'

Okay, then. I might as well say it right off the bat. When I found myself swept up in the glorious love story every fairy tale I read as a child guaranteed would happen to me and every other girl, I didn't know how to handle it.

I never talked about it. Never. I'm not naturally gifted when it comes to matters of the heart and it was hard for me to admit to my betrayal. Nine years of living together, and I sent it all up in smoke in a single night. One misguided spark was all it took for me to reduce our relationship to ashes.

So shame had left me afraid to take a seat again at the strip-poker table of love, and I prudishly buttoned the collar of past romance all the way up to the lump in my throat. Out of fear, hopelessness or avoidance, I tooted the single horn, proudly proclaiming 'I'm a free woman!' to all and sundry and swallowing my lonesome nights with reheated pasta and chick flicks starring disgracefully romantic actors. Truth was, I didn't quite know what to make of that awkward loneliness, and silently I dreamed of testing the waters. My heart was a burned-out shell. I doubted love could relight my fire, yet I secretly lived in hope.

The previous day, seeing the carefree strength of Tall, Indigenous Jérémie had made an impression on me, arousing my curiosity. Obviously, then, I was keen to meet the other fisherman. And so that morning, when I was still barely awake, I leaned out the window of my room to look down at the wharf. No sign of the boat belonging to the curiously named Cyrille Bernard. Faster than lightning, I cleaned myself up, made myself up, dolled myself up. I opted for my prettiest summer dress, the one with the plunging neckline, and slipped on my high heels. In hindsight, it did seem strange to put on make-up and high heels to go and meet a man who'd just got back from fishing, but I never could strike quite the right chord with femininity.

Anyway, I was sitting at the café well before the fishermen came in, my feet all trussed up in heels, my hair tucked behind my ear, my summer dress bearing nary a wrinkle. A gentle, warm breeze was blowing, ruffling skirts, drawing the sea air in through the window and turning my cheeks all rosy.

The boats made their appearance late in the morning. By then I had drunk so much caffeine, my clammy hands were shaking. They made their approach, moored up at the wharf. I leaned back casually in my chair and crossed my legs. The fishermen jumped out onto the dock.

I honestly don't know what could have led me to imagine Cyrille Bernard was a handsome, strapping young man. Really, I have no idea. Vital, Victor, Renaud and Guylaine, they had all warned me not to harbour any expectations about the Gaspé, so why the hell had I dolled myself up like this? Because, let's face it, Cyrille was nothing special to look at. Age had thinned his hair, stretched his ears out of proportion and wreaked havoc with the spacing of his teeth, and scars streaked his face. So, in spite of all his kindness, it took a while to get used to his physical appearance.

In a split second, I realised my only option was to make a swift exit. I left money on the table, grabbed my bag and made a beeline for the door, but they had come over so quickly, on their way in they were blocking my escape route. And Vital took care of the rest.

When he caught sight of me, he turned casually to Cyrille and pointed at me in the way you would a thirty-cent trinket on a cheap souvenir stand. 'That's her!'

The old sea dog lifted his gaze and looked down at me, like a ship's captain sizing up a rookie sailor. I forced a smile.

You can never know the sea.

He looked me up and down, down and up, as I, my handbag, my skimpy dress, my bejewelled décolleté and my heels melted into a puddle of shame on the doormat.

'That's her, the girl who wanted to meet you.'

'I … I've finished my breakfast … I was just leaving … Can we do this another time?'

'Christ in a chalice, Cyrille, you never were a ladies' man, were you?'

Laughter rained down on me as, embarrassed by all that I was, I squirmed my way towards a door firmly obstructed by a Cyrille who was clearly not about to step aside. Vital, Victor and the other fisherman carried on to a table, but Cyrille Bernard stood there, unmoving

like a stubborn hockey goalie. I felt a pang of anxiety, I had to admit.
Panic, almost.

The water and the salt.

'Heee … Calm yourself. If you run off on me, I won't have enough
breath to catch you, will I?'

His every whistling in-breath was laboured.

'Excuse me … I … I have things to do—'

'Tourists never have anything to do. Heee … What's your
name?'

'Catherine.'

'Catherine what?'

'Day. Catherine Day.'

'Heee … Look at me, then, Catherine Day.'

I lifted my gaze and his blue eyes saw right through me in a flash.

*The unfathomable depth, the unpredictable nature, the backwash,
the tides.*

He took a step backwards.

Yet…

'Heee … Where are you from?'

'Montreal.'

'Why do you want to see me? Heee … Hoping I'll take you on a
boat ride? I don't like taking tourists out fishing.'

*When the hull turns seaward, when the long, ephemeral waves hoist
me to the top of the world and carry me home in their whispering cradle,
when the wind wisps into the genoa and fills the mainsail, only then do
my cares drift and fade away. I trim the sails, take the helm, and the
horizon is all mine.*

'No, no, it's not that. I … I'm on holiday, I've got nothing to do
and Renaud said that you might—'

'That I might what?'

'I don't know … Take my mind off things … tell me all about the
sea, teach me.'

He started to chuckle – mocking, insulting me.

'If you want to learn about the sea, you're going to have to stop running, love. Heee … That's the very first thing I can tell you. Find a rocking chair, sit on a porch looking out at the waves … heee … and rock. That's all. Just relax and you'll be halfway there. Heee…'

That's where I am happy, amidst the terrifying, tumultuous splendour of the open sea.

He moved aside and I was able to slip away. Though, strangely enough, I no longer felt the urge to escape. Slowly, I walked back up to the *auberge*. I slipped off my heels to walk barefoot over the seaweed-streaked pebbles. Against the tide, out at sea, the Indigenous fishermen were pulling their lobster traps up from the horizon.

The first tourists were starting to flock to the beach, but the sea was still too chilly for many to dare take the plunge. Sitting on the sand, I hung around aimlessly.

When the tide retreats, an anchor takes hold in my throat. With every wave that passes it pulls a little more, choking me. As the tide races, I feel the pain right here, in my chest. An echo, swallowing the outlines of words, gnawing at whispers. The loss.

Half past twelve. In the sun, brave children dared to venture into the sea's chilly folds. Perfect girls shivered in colourful bikinis, stealing glances at semi-tanned, frisbee-throwing boys.

The sea shakes these turbulent pictures of mine around in its heavy backwash as the headless hallelujahs of my castaways sway from the ends of my dangling arms. And I am powerless.

I got up quickly. Too quickly. In a daze, I stumbled over to the water's edge to stretch my legs. Throwing stones into the sea, I smiled through my teeth at passing children. Standing barefoot on the shore, I grabbed fistfuls of rocks.

'Started picking up agates then, have you love? Heee…'

The whistle of his breathing sounded like tanned-leather bellows. It could only be Cyrille. I lifted my gaze.

'Show me.'

I opened my hand. Half a dozen red, green, white stones. 'I keep finding pretty little rocks, all marbled and streaked, but no agates.'

'Heee … I've never understood why people spend their time hunting for agates. Trying their patience, I suppose.'

I curled my fingers back over my palm. 'They're semi-precious stones, apparently.'

'I don't know if they're precious or not, but those ones aren't half lucky to be in your hand. Heee…'

I opened my hand again for a look.

'For what it's worth, there's a great big agate right next to your left foot.'

I picked it up.

He started walking, and I followed him. I was happy he'd come to find me.

'Changed out of that fancy dress, have you? Didn't get to see that for very long, did I?'

'Some things have to be earned, you know!'

'Renaud told Vital you wanted to meet me. Heee … Want to come fishing, do you?'

'No. It was Renaud's idea. He said you'd take my mind off things with your stories.'

'Heee … You must be bored out of your tree!'

'I've been feeling a bit off ever since I got here. I'm not sure I like all this. Whenever I spend a long time by the sea, I get this uneasy feeling … I don't know … like there's something in my heart trying to break loose.'

'That's normal.'

'Normal?'

'You come here on holiday, you're feeling happy and healthy, and you think the sea's going to do you good. Heee … But that's not true. She's a harsh one, is the sea, and you've got to have a thick skin to look her in the eye. She'll set your memories all in a spin, like a washing machine.'

'I don't have that many memories to spin around, though.'

'Doesn't matter. The sea, she'll make some up for you. Heee …
In the meantime, my chalet's just over there. Come on, let's smoke a
joint on the deck and count the waves coming in. Heee…'

I gently placed my rocks down on the front steps of the chalet, like
little treasures I might forget to pick up when I left. The blinding sun
splintered the water into fluid shards.

'Pretty, isn't it?'

'Makes you want to dive right in!'

'Heee … You won't catch me doing that. I can't stand going in
the drink!'

'What? You're a fisherman and you don't swim?'

'There's not a fisherman round here that knows how to swim! It
sounds strange, but that's just the way it is.'

'But I thought you loved the sea—'

'I love the sea, not the water! I can't stand the blooming water.
There's far too much rubbish down there for me to take a dip!
Heee…'

'Turns you off, does it?!'

'Doesn't stop me thinking it's pretty though, does it? Heee … Like
a mosaic, isn't it?'

'You're quite the poet, Cyrille Bernard!'

'No, I just smoke too much pot!'

I burst out laughing. He rolled the joint, sparked up; time was
suspended over the sea.

Two waves.

'This one's padded out with seaweed and sea salt, love. Heee …
Smoke this and you'll be floating, even on land … Heee … And you
can go for miles!'

What could I say?

'Out here, back in the love and peace years, you should have seen
all the drug trafficking. Heee … Some of the things that went on!
There was one dealer, once, who was so scared customs would catch
him he pitched all his barrels into the drink. Imagine when we saw
them wash up on the shore! Heee … I've still got three empty barrels

in my cellar. And you know what? Thirty years later, it still smells like Mary-Jane from the southern climes! Saves you a packet in plane tickets. Heee … Stick your head in there and you'll be in Jamaica before you know it!'

He passed me the joint and the day lightened up. Three waves.

'You're single, then?' he asked.

'Yes.'

'Heee … How come?'

'No reason. That's just the way it is.'

'Not spooning with some lucky man, then?'

'What?'

'Normally when you're twenty, you fling yourself into love and then you fall into the routine. Heee … Your *I* turns into *we* in a little love nest under the eaves, and soon there's more kids under your roof than you know what to do with, then you spoon yourselves to sleep. Not a spooner then, are you?'

'No.'

'Why not?'

Three, four, five waves.

'I did try, but…'

'But?'

'Hard to say. You find yourself a job, a house, a better half, make a cosy little nest for yourself, but then you hit your thirties. You start to freak out and wonder where the hell you're going and what the whole point of it all is. You take one look at your other half and you think he's boring as hell, so you can't imagine yourself pushing out a whole bunch of mini hims. And everything you found handsome and funny about him has turned fat and stupid.'

'You're not fat, though.'

Three waves.

'One night, I cheated on him. We hadn't made love in months. I know I shouldn't say that, it's not a failure. I don't do failure. The next morning, at nine o'clock, he left me. Without a word. Packed his bags in ten minutes flat and never looked back.'

'Heee … What a shit!'

'What?'

'Managed to give you one hell of a guilt trip, didn't he? To hold onto a woman, you've got to act like a man. If not, she'll go looking elsewhere. That's normal.'

Six waves.

'Heee … Sinking a ship doesn't make you a fair-weather sailor, love.'

'Are you married, Cyrille?'

'No. Heee … But that's never stopped me holding a woman in my heart!'

'I never suggested otherwise!'

'You thought otherwise, though!'

'You're not a spooner either, then?'

'Heee … No.'

'Why not? A fair-weather sailor, are you?'

He shrugged his bony shoulders and squinted out to sea, resting his weathered hands on the arms of his rocking chair. He cast his gaze afar. 'Sometimes, love, you don't get enough chances to tell a woman you love her.'

One wave.

'She married my brother.'

I laughed so hard, I nearly exploded.

'I'm sorry, Cyrille.'

He smiled sweetly and ran his huge mop of a hand through my hair. The sun was shining softly, not bothering a soul, as the east wind rolled a whitecapped swell on the rising tide. Cyrille let the waves go by, taking it easy.

'I never married, love … Heee … And I'm realising what I've missed out on the most is having a house to come home to and a wife standing at the stove. A wife to warm the plates, the kitchen and my bed. Think that's funny, do you? Heee … She would have gone to the hairdresser's every Friday morning. She would have planted flowers around the front steps.'

'She'd have forever been on your back to take out the rubbish!'

'And I'd have taken it out as well.'

Two waves.

'Heee … I would have liked to have a wife to protect, love. I would have churned up the grass with a tiller and made her a nice vegetable garden. She would have planted tomatoes.'

'Tomatoes?'

'And lettuce too – the kind with the frilly leaves – carrots, strawberries and blueberries. Heee … If I'd had a wife, I'd have had blueberries.'

'Why blueberries?'

'I've always dreamed of having my own blueberries.'

'Plant some, then!'

'Heee … Takes a long time, does growing blueberries. One year you prepare the soil, then the next year you plant your bushes, and it's only in the third year that you get to pick your blueberries.'

'Just plant some! You'll have your blueberries in three years' time.'

Five waves. Perhaps six.

'Heee … Still a bit strange, don't you think, for a pretty girl like you to waste her time waiting for an old man like me.'

I stayed up late that night, cocooned in a patchwork quilt, lying on a sun lounger on the veranda at the *auberge*. Young sweethearts walked hand in hand along the beach, laughing, whispering sweet nothings to each other, oblivious of the world around them. Lovers preparing to draw their bedroom curtains. On waking the next morning, the young woman would plant a kiss on her man's warm shoulder. Entrenched beneath the wrinkled sheets, he would slowly breathe in the uncertainty of the day. Against the wharf, the boats were moored in peace. The image of Jérémie and his strapping physique crossed my mind. It must be reassuring, I thought, to moor up against something solid. I turned my gaze out to sea.

It's stronger than we are. We step aboard and cast the world away because we harbour the infinite within and the horizon is our only answer.

'In truth, fishing never made any French-Canadians rich.'

'Catherine, have you met our Father, the curate? Heee ... He's no fisherman, but we don't hold it against him. He grew up on Fourth Lane.'

Father Leblanc pulled up a chair. He served two parishes, I soon learned – the church and the bistro. The four of us – Vital, Victor, Cyrille and I – were already at the table.

'It's true, here in the bay, fishermen have never lived the rich life! Heee ... My dad, he did it all, you know. He worked for the English, he had a *Gaspésienne*—'

'Right, a-a-a-and he ended up getting r-r-r-royally screwed over!'

'Do you know what the *Gaspésiennes* were, love? Heee ... Great big boats the federal government supplied to the fishermen. They leased them boats so they'd buy them down the line, you see, but fishing only raked in peanuts, so as soon as the government caught on, they took their boats away! No compensation, nothing. Two years of fishing down the drain! Heee...'

'1960, that was when they pulled the plug. They lost everything. The *Gaspésiennes* ended up rotting in museum car parks.'

The red-haired waitress offloaded the eggs, poured the coffee, smiled and walked away. The men, plaid shirts, jeans, work boots and all, planted ravenous forks into their omelettes.

'But fishing pays better today, doesn't it?'

'Heee ... It pays for paying's sake, but the sea's empty!'

'Climate change?'

'Y-y-y-you know, there are plenty of theories, b-b-b-but that can't help.'

'It's all the clam dredgers' fault! Heee ... They tear up the seabed.

Marine deforestation, they call it. That's why the sea's empty. Heee … They've torn it all up!'

Father Leblanc picked up the conversation. 'Global warming, dredging, government meddling … Those are the fisherman's three evils!'

The plates were soon emptied.

'And don't get me started on the kind of crab fishing they make us do now … heee … They're telling us to throw the females back in the water and only keep the males. That's all well and good, but when there are no males left, the females aren't going to make baby crabs all on their own, are they? Heee… And even then, the wharves are in a hell of a state. Have you seen the wharf?'

'W-w-w-we've got so much to complain about, w-w-w-we're going to have to g-g-g-go on unemployment this winter!'

'Heee … We can't work all year long and complain as well, can we, love?'

Gradually, I was starting to feel at home, like these were my people. 'So that's why you fish, to have something to complain about?'

'We fish because we're fishermen. Heee … I've done this all my life! I'm not going to start mowing lawns now, am I?'

'In truth, telling old fishing tales is much more exciting than a day mowing lawns, isn't it, Cyrille?'

'Well, Father Leblanc, I'm not expecting much more out of the summer. Heee … The age I'm at, if I didn't have any memories, I'd just be a poor old man.'

'Christ in a chalice! Memories or tall tales, Cyrille?'

The old fisherman shrugged his shoulders. The red-haired waitress swept by, carried off the plates.

'We're fishermen and we tell tales about the past. Heee … if we can't stretch out our fish a bit, we might as well die of boredom and keep our gobs shut forever!'

Victor nodded approvingly. One last swig of coffee. Cyrille glanced at his watch and gathered his net, his fish and his memory, ready to leave. Vital looked unhappy.

'Don't you tell fishing stories, Vital?'

I said it as light-heartedly as an early-summer day goes by. To my great surprise, he whirled right around. We had just stood up to leave, and now he was so close to me I could sense the cracks forming in his tough shell.

'No. Not about fishing or anything else. Christ in a chalice, I just shoulder my daily burden, that's what I do. I don't want to tell any stories.'

I raised my head and his eyes pinned me to the door frame.

'And I don't want to hear none from anyone else, either.'

For a second I thought he was onto me, so I left some money on the table and made a quick exit. Outside, the conversation had taken another tack and I momentarily forgot about the incident. The curate started off towards the rectory, then turned around questioningly.

'Are you going to pull up your traps tomorrow?' he asked.

'S-s-s-suppose we'll have to.'

Vital sidled over too, visibly softened by the sea air and silky murmur of the shore.

'Tomorrow or the day after.'

'The fishing's all finished?' I asked.

'I-i-i-in three weeks' time, there's going to be the c-c-c-crab. G-g-g-good ones to eat.'

'Heee … That's another kind of trap.'

'And what are you going to do in the meantime?'

'Christ in a chalice, nothing!'

We burst out laughing. It struck me how handsome a man he was. Feet planted firmly, knees holding strong beneath his worn jeans, he stood anchored to the ground, roots stretching down to the earth's core.

With a wave of his hand, Father Leblanc bid us farewell and went on his way.

Cyrille turned to me again. 'Heee … You know, love, if you've nothing to do and you want to learn about the beauty of the sunrise over the sea, you can come aboard. Heee … Tomorrow, we're going to start bringing up the traps. We're going to set off a bit later than usual, Gérard and me. There's room for you if you like.'

'I thought you never took tourists on board, Cyrille.'

'Heee … Never.'

'Why me, then?'

'It's not the same, I'm the one inviting you!'

'I'm not sure—'

'Cyrille is r-r-r-right. If you w-w-w-want to get to know the sea, you should go aboard. His boat's really s-s-s-stable.'

'Only thing is you might get a bit wet, but it's nothing to be scared of. Heee … And I'm going to be there too!'

The group went their separate ways towards their pickup trucks. I followed Cyrille.

'I'd like to go to sea, but—'

'Heee … Tomorrow, we're going to pull up a third of the traps, so we're going to set off about half past five. Just show up with your boots and your woolly hat, and we'll get you aboard. Heee…'

He climbed into his truck, started the engine.

'Let me think about it, alright?'

'Half past five, on the wharf.'

A quick wave, a little cloud of dust, and there I was, alone on the shore.

'Let me tell you, *mam'zelle* Catherine, you having yourself a nice holiday, then?'

The head whatever of the bistro stood peeling carrots, sporting his classy cook's helper apron and a silly hat with a hairnet.

'That's right, Renaud. Cyrille's even invited me to go fishing with him tomorrow.'

'Good idea! *What* a good idea! You going to go?'

Peeler in hand, he whacked the carrots so hard, the orange shavings spurted everywhere like a volcano erupting.

'I haven't made up my mind yet.'

'Go. You should do it before the season's over! And let me tell you, you should count yourself lucky to be invited aboard by Cyrille Bernard, because he's not one to have tourists on board! Once in a blue moon he invites people aboard, he does. You're going to love it – the boat, the swell, the lobsters … and the sunrise! The sunrise here's much, much prettier than over there in Bonaventure!'

'You sound keen, Renaud! Want to come? I can ask Cyrille if you like.'

He raised the murder weapon and started waving it around excitably. 'Oh, no, *mam'zelle* Catherine, not me!'

'Why not?'

A piece of carrot landed on his silly hat. He carried on oblivious, concentrating.

'Oh, no, I don't want to go! Let me tell you one thing, it's far too dangerous! Out here people end up drowning left, right and centre. You set off fishing all in a good mood, then the wind picks up and you get seasick, the boat starts rocking about and you don't know where to hold on, then it all goes belly up! Glug, glug, glug and you're drowning! There's even statistics about it, if you want to know how many. You wouldn't believe it, but there are more folks who die drowning than on the roads! And when folks who've drowned wash up, they're not a pretty sight, let me tell you. All puffed up and bluer than blue, they are.'

Disgusted, he threw the peeler into the sink, pitched the carrots into a pot, splashing water all over the worktop, then hurried off with the pot to the kitchen, before reappearing again and continuing.

'Every year there's people who die, *mam'zelle* Catherine! Tourists, fishermen, you name it, they all drown. And they come from all over. Mostly New Brunswick, but Percé as well … It's the currents that swirl the bodies about in the bay. Once we even had twins from Maria wash up. Twins! They had the same parents! And let me tell you, that's no laughing matter. I know, because in my family we're not fishermen, none of us are, but I lost two brothers in a canoe.'

Grabbing a cloth, he set about cleaning his chopping board. He scrubbed it so energetically, with both hands, it looked like he was giving it a cardiac massage.

'In a canoe?'

'It was a long time ago. Let me tell you, my mum made me go home to feed the chickens, otherwise I'd have been out there with them. We used to go off hunting for partridge along the coast, with pellet guns. But because of the chickens, my brothers set off without me. Then the squall blew in and drowned them. Thirty feet from shore in eight feet of water. You can't believe it, can you, *mam'zelle* Catherine?'

Two impatient customers gesticulated from the other end of the bistro. They had been waiting a while.

'That's so sad. I'm sorry.'

'Let me tell you just one thing. In my family, we've had more than our fair share of tragic deaths, you know. It's all because of a great-great-great-uncle who married his daughter off to a cousin and never paid for the dispensation. Do you know what a dispensation was, *mam'zelle* Catherine? It was a paper that gave you the right to marry your cousin. And he should have paid up for it. The folk in the village came over twice to kick up a fuss, and let me tell you, the third time, when he still wouldn't pay up, they made a scarecrow of him stuffed full of straw and threw him off the railway bridge, you know where? Just up here, where old whatshisname with the limp died a couple of years ago.'

Clearly getting worked up now, the customers gesticulated again.

'So let me tell you just one thing, we've had violent deaths in every generation since. And when my dad was run over by his tractor, I got fed up, so off I went to fetch the priest and we did an exorcism.' He tapped his right index finger on the counter like a judge making a point.

'What did you exorcise?'

'The house. Our place. But not by Father Leblanc here, mind you. Let me tell you, we went off to fetch a blessed priest.'

'A blessed priest?'

'The priest in Bonaventure, he's had the blessing and he knows what he's doing. Any folk in the village who wanted to come, they came over and, let me tell you, they were praying all over the place! After that, we went around the house three times with the pot of Easter Water, and the priest had me pour Easter Water on the rose bush in the corner that our great-great-great-grandmother planted. And you know what? The rose bush died – dried right up it did, two weeks later! We'd been exorcised! Now there's nobody dying anymore in my family!'

He whipped off his silly hat, took off and lovingly folded his cook's helper apron and hurried away to take the impatient customers' order.

I found myself alone for a few minutes, the silence weighing on my shoulders.

He returned.

'Have you ever thought of moving away, Renaud?'

'Where to, *mam'zelle* Catherine?

'I don't know ... Away from the sea.'

'Away from the sea? You can't be serious, *mam'zelle* Catherine! The sea is our home. It's not because there've been a few drownings that I'm going to move away. And let me tell you, drowning's not that unusual. So that's no reason not to go!'

He grabbed a couple of beers from the fridge, some glasses, a tray.

'Go where?'

'Fishing, with Cyrille! As a tourist, you need to know what the sea and drowning are all about! But you won't catch me out there, that's for sure. It's an experience, though. And you have to do these tourist experiences, don't you? So let me tell you just one thing, it's a good idea to go off with Cyrille. Go on! With him, there's no danger, his family's already paid their dues!'

'What do you mean, his family's already paid their dues?'

Slowly and methodically, he opened the bottles of beer. 'Cyrille, he lost two brothers as well. And their bodies were never found.

Dead people from round here, it's funny, but I reckon they drift out
to sea. It's the currents that do it. Will you have another beer?'

'Cyrille lost two brothers?'

'Don't look at me like that, *mam'zelle* Catherine. People have
drowned in every family. In mine, in Cyrille's…'

'And what about Vital's?'

He averted his eyes without giving me an answer, then carried the
beers off to the table in the back before reappearing in front of me.

'Let me tell you, the boys are going to bring up their traps then,
are they?'

'Cyrille's starting to pull them up tomorrow, yes. He's doing it in
three trips.'

'It's better that way, not as draining for his health, you know. And
it's one heck of a good idea for you to go, *mam'zelle* Catherine!'

'I'm going to think about it.'

He dutifully donned his silly hat and cook's helper apron, smoothing it down with the flats of his hands, as I placed some money on
the counter.

'Right. I'll be off then, Renaud.'

'Already?'

'Yes. I'm going for a walk on the beach.'

'Come back for supper, if you like! Let me tell you, there's going
to be fish with little carrots grated by hand!'

I missed seeing the Indigenous fishermen come in. I went down to
the wharf too late, coming on for the evening. I sat beside the fishing
boats. They were dozing there empty, gently rocking to the rhythm
of the waves, snoring against the wharf. They barely raised an eyelid
when I arrived. They didn't care. Sighing, they slipped back into
slumber, like fat, lazy cats sinking into the great blue cushion of the
water. I read their names and cast my gaze towards the horizon.

Across the breakwater, the bay slipped into her gown of scarlet sequins, like a cheap old lady of the night. The main event of the evening was in full swing. Up on the cliff, the setting sun illuminated the windows of the houses looking westward. She was out there. Somewhere. The woman who had given birth to me was probably enjoying the same show I was being treated to.

I had been here a few days and the effect of the sea was starting to set in. I wanted to be from here too. From the swirling depths of my blood to the crests of the waves, the tides flowed through my body and the twinkle in my eye was surely a flake of salt.

There, on the battered old wharf at Ruisseau-Leblanc, where the river flowed into the sea, I thought it was probably high time I let the bitterness and resentment ebb away. So, I made up my mind to go along with Cyrille and ask him whether he knew her. I took a deep breath in through the darkness.

Meeting Marie Garant.

The thought of it calmed me. I must have spent a good hour imagining that meeting, stretching my hands beyond my comfort zone to bring this woman out of the purgatory to which I had banished her, trying to fit her photo back into the frame of my virgin memory.

They willed Pilar to me and off I went.

Later, when asked what I'd done with my evening, I would have a hard time answering anything, other than that I had revived from the forgotten – like a lost tin lamp you stumble across in the attic and rub back to a shine so you can relight the wick – the woman who had given birth to me. And that I had been happy.

They willed Pilar to me and the sea was my oyster.

I went back to Guylaine's early, said a quick hello, and went up to bed. For the first time in a long time, I was looking forward to something. Looking forward to the morning. Looking forward to going to sea, on a fishing boat with Cyrille, to entering the seascape and meeting Marie Garant.

They willed Pilar to me. In spite of the dues we must pay to the sea, we will set sail – you, me and all of our own.

'Heee … Hello there, love! You came!'

'Course I did!'

'We're not setting off straight away, though.'

'How come?' What's up?'

'It's Vital. Heee … You like your fishing stories, don't you? Well, you're in for quite the tale!'

'I don't understand.'

'Apparently he's caught a body in his nets … Heee … He said so on his marine radio.'

The dues we must pay to the sea.

'Who is it – the body?'

'Not one of us lot, we're all here! Nah, I'm just kidding, love, we don't know yet. If Vital didn't say, it can't be someone he knows. Must be a tourist from New Brunswick who went kayaking and got lost. Or a swimming champ who got caught out by the tide. Heee … It's always something like that.'

Cyrille's deckhand, Gérard, was leaning against the side of the pickup truck. There were two unfamiliar boats moored up at the wharf. Further along, a man was struggling to speak into a radio.

'Who are all these folks?'

'Guys from New Richmond. They've come down for a look. With something like this going on, the lobster can wait for an hour or two, eh? Heee … Dead bodies, they drift in circles around the bay, you know, so chances are it's someone from up their way … And that's Robichaud, the coroner. I don't talk to him. He rubs me up the wrong way.'

He seemed friendly enough to me, though. He even winked a distracted hello to me, hollowing a formidable dimple below his left eye. Cyrille rolled himself a joint, even though it was barely six in the morning. Coroner Robichaud turned a blind eye. A few men were gathered casually around the truck where Cyrille was blustering on.

'In any case, heee … I want them to bury me upright – I want to be standing up. Not stuffed, mind you, but facing out to sea.'

'Dream on, Cyrille, any taxidermist around here would only tell you to get stuffed anyway!'

'On my land, with my eyes open. That's what I told my sister. Heee … I said to her, "When I die, I want you to bury me upright, wrapped in the sheet from my death bed, in front of the chalet." I want to be able to see the sea long after I die so I can make sure the lobster traps are filling up in May and check the mackerel are biting in August.'

'Not one to miss a day's fishing, are you, Cyrille?'

'No, sir! Heee … I want to see the autumn high tides salt the wharf. And the sunrise. I don't want to miss a thing!'

He took a drag. The men chuckled, taking it easy.

There was no hurry.

Through the smoke from the joint emerged the outline of the salt-and-pepper hair that was gradually deserting that wrinkled forehead of his, which harboured a deep scar from long ago. He had a hard time breathing in, but he never stopped talking.

'Cyrille,' I said, 'I don't mean to be difficult, but I don't think you're allowed to be buried anywhere other than the cemetery.'

'That's what my sister thinks, too. Whims like that – that's what she calls it, a whim! – get on her nerves. Heee … I've no time for the cemetery, love. Too many people in there for me! It's not that they're a nuisance or anything, they're a calmer bunch than plenty of living people I know! But that's just the point … heee … there's just no life to the place!'

'Why don't you get yourself cremated, Cyrille? Then your sister can scatter your ashes at sea.'

'Don't be so daft, love! Heee … I've never liked the heat.'

Everybody laughed, except for Gérard, Cyrille's deckhand, as silent as the shore after the rain. He barely said a word anymore, not since he sold his fishing quota. He thought he was onto a good thing, taking the two hundred thousand dollars, but two years away from early retirement, he'd had to cast the net out again and join Cyrille's crew.

'That reminds me, last month I saw some will-o'-the-wisps … You ever seen a will-o'-the-wisp, love?'

'No.'

Fingers pointed and chins jutted as Vital's boat suddenly emerged as a faint blemish on the horizon.

'They're not hard to see. You just have to go to a cemetery where they bury people. Heee … Not too dead a place, though! A real cemetery where there's a bit of life. Best to go in the spring, especially if lots of folk have passed away over the winter. Heee … Are we supposed to say passed away or passed over? You must know that, love, don't you?'

'You can say either, Cyrille.'

'Heee … Anyway, in the spring, the big freezer's full to bursting and at some point, when the ground thaws, they decide to start burying the bodies. That's when the will-o'-the-wisps come out to play. So, in the nights that follow, you cross your fingers the moon won't be too full … heee … and you keep your eyes peeled. As the dead bodies thaw, it's like they start to sigh from the bottom of their lungs, and then the gases catch fire, I think, when they come to the surface. Heee … They come up from the ground and when the wind sweeps them away, up that little mound they go and off into the woods, up by Fourth Lane. Heee…'

The boat shifted into focus as it drew nearer. Cyrille still had an audience, but everyone was now looking out to sea.

'Anyway, my place is right next to the cemetery, and I see them all, every year. I don't want to be buried with that lot. Heee … Honestly, why would I want to be buried with a bunch of old farts I don't know from Adam who are going to spend the rest of their days huffing and puffing at me behind my back?'

Cyrille fell silent. The boat entered the marina, came alongside and moored at the wharf. Vital looked incensed and Victor looked like he had his heart in his boots. Downcast, he barely acknowledged anyone on the wharf and avoided Cyrille's gaze. Beneath a tarp on the flat bottom of the big fishing boat, in between the bins and buckets, lay a body.

The coroner stepped aboard.

'Heee … Robichaud's the doctor as well. He's the one who's going to certify the death.'

The fishermen lifted the tarp. From the wharf, you could only vaguely see the body, tangled in a great green net patched with yellow-and-pink thread.

'They're going to have to bring it ashore all swaddled up like that…'

The coroner addressed the crowd with the official air of an actor stepping into character. 'We're supposed to wait for an investigator from the Sûreté du Québec, but nobody's free this morning down at the SQ. So, we ought to get some men together to help carry the body in the net up to the Langevin brothers' funeral home.'

'On foot?'

'The Langevin brothers are out fishing. They won't be back for another two or three hours. I've got the key to the mortuary. We ought to take the body up to their fridge. Cyrille, you ought to back your truck up here.'

Cyrille flinched at the sound of his name. 'Heee … Why me?'

'Because your cargo bed's empty.'

'Well, that's just charming, isn't it! Just minding my own business and I end up carting off the bloody body. Brings bad luck, that does! Heee … People's cars weren't made to cart death around, you know!'

'Christ in a chalice, boats weren't made for that either, but I still brought the body back here!'

'Cyrille has a point – cars aren't meant to carry bodies,' Gérard said.

'Gérard, would you carry it in your van?' the coroner asked.

'My van's due in for a service.'

'Listen, Cyrille, we need you right now. We're not exactly going to wait for the body to rot in the sun, are we? We ought to take it up to the Langevins'. No two ways about it.'

The old fisherman shook his head like he was trying to make room for the idea. He hesitated for a moment, then reluctantly gave in.

'Right, you ought to back down the boat ramp, but leave a good ten feet free so we've got room to manoeuvre. Anybody who can help, you ought to get yourselves between the boat and the truck and help pull the net up.'

Cyrille backed the truck up as the fishermen gathered around. Decked out in plaid hunting shirts and old, salt-washed jeans, these burly men of the sea, their faces furrowed by the stubborn blustering of the wind, eyes narrowed to nothing but slits from squinting into the sun and scanning the surface for buoys in the dawn light, their beards black and their caps pulled down tight, fell over themselves to get to Vital's boat and lift the body out.

Closing in on the smell of death, they stopped their jostling and a thick silence descended on them. Cyrille leaned against the truck bed, sulking a little. The men grabbed the edge of the net and started pulling clumsily, haphazardly.

'Don't pull too hard on the net! We don't want to mess up the body!'

Coroner Robichaud seemed all tangled up himself. No one really knew how to go about this. Someone must have made a sudden movement, because the head moved. The coroner flinched.

'Go easy! Go easy with Marie Garant!'

'WHAT? Heee … That's Marie Garant? Heee…'

Everyone stopped in their tracks. Cyrille barrelled right into the boat, shoving the fishermen aside, and fell to his knees before the dead woman, clearly devastated. I don't really know how, but I found myself perched on one of the concrete blocks that littered the wharf.

'Marie … Heee … Marie Garant…'

Carefully, he lifted the cold body to his, rocking it slowly and gently like an ocean swell.

If you're reading this, I've drunk the sea. Tell Cyrille my time has come. Now I've drunk the sea as well.

The men in their stained gloves and fishing boots turned away and swallowed the horizon. Such a deep silence washed over me, my ears were buzzing. As if life had just given me a slap in the face. As he kneeled over the dead woman, Cyrille's whistling breath stabbed at the air, his thin body reeling from the blow. The rogue wave that knocks an old fisherman overboard.

The coroner had his back to the scene. He was playing the part of an official, trying to maintain an air of dignity, but he was sucking in deep breaths of air like any layman suppressing the urge to throw up. Vital looked at Cyrille in either anger or shame, then he went off to the front of the boat and didn't come back.

Victor stepped forward. He made the sign of the cross before the dead woman and bent down to place a hand on Cyrille's shoulder and whisper something in his ear. Cyrille nodded, still clutching the dead woman to his chest. Vital's deckhand straightened up and turned to face the wharf.

'L-l-l-let's do a Hail Mary.'

The men made the sign of the cross as the stutterer undertook the prayer.

'H-h-h-hail Mary, f-f-f-full of grace, the Lord is with thee; b-b-b-blessed is the fruit of thy womb, J-J-J-Jesus.'

'Holy Mary, Mother of God, pray for us sinners, now and at the hour of our death. Amen.'

Slowly, they approached. Gently, they lifted the body out of Cyrille's hands. He then got back on his feet, soaked to the skin with her. He stood there watching them for a moment, unmoving, in a daze. Then he stepped off the boat and went over to his truck. On his way past, he gave me the look of a man all washed up with no place left to drown his sorrows. That look seeped its way right to the back of my eyes, and I knew it would stay with me as the very image of anguish.

In silence, the fishermen delicately laid Marie Garant's body down in the bed of the pickup truck. Cyrille rolled up his parka and slipped it under her head so she could rest in comfort. The net was too long and dragged on the ground, but no one dared to drape it back over the body, which was tangled up enough already.

That was how the strange funeral procession for Marie Garant left the wharf. The coroner drove ahead, while the pickup driven by a despondent Cyrille, carrying a delicate elderly woman with tangled white hair, followed behind. Marie Garant. The woman Cyrille had loved. The tangled net around the dead woman's bluish body spilled over the back of the truck bed. Four men, out of respect, gathered the edges of the net and formed the end of the unusual funeral train.

I only stood up again much later, when the Indigenous fishermen rolled up. They parked their trucks off to the side and slowly made their way over to the wharf as the clean-up operation aboard Vital's boat drew near an end. Tall, Indigenous Jérémie smiled at me. I felt so sick, I had to turn away from the sea.

Traps and nets

He had always hated working in the summertime. In summer, the bodies decomposed more quickly, the odours encroached aggressively on the air and the putrefaction was just astonishing. When the sun softened the tarmac and aqueous vapours blurred the outlines of things, when the sweat beaded in the corner of your eyelids and your shirt stuck to your skin, you could only imagine what dead flesh must be enduring. There was no way finding a body in winter could be called engrossing. In summer, though, it was just gross.

The season made tensions run high too. Degrees of impatience rose in line with the heat. People killed more in the summer, that was no secret. Murders of passion, family feuds, road rage ... Summer idleness could unleash the rampant murderer in the most unassuming of holidaymakers.

Not to mention the interrogations, the badly air-conditioned interview rooms and the hum of the fluorescent strips casting their weak, grey light. When you came up for air, you teetered a few steps in the blinding sunlight before you found your feet again.

No, being a detective was a job for the winter. Since the day he arrived in Quebec, Joaquin Moralès had been sure of it. This year, for the first time, he had managed to book a whole month of holiday time. And he had earned it – he had worked hard, done all the shitty jobs, put in long hours, and worked his way up the ranks. Did that mean he was now living a life of leisure? Yes and no. This was the calm before the storm.

And it wouldn't really be a holiday, anyway, because he'd be busy. He and his wife were moving out to the Gaspé coast, the Baie-des-Chaleurs. As a sculptor, she needed space, she said. The kids had flown the nest, he had secured a transfer and now they were off. Or at least, he was.

Sarah had asked him to go five days ahead of her, to scout things out, clean up their new place and be there when the furniture arrived. He couldn't really see the need, but she had insisted. She told him it would do him good, at this midpoint in his life, to be alone for a few days and take stock of things.

Women say that when they're going through The Change. They say they want to go on a retreat, or to some all-inclusive resort in the sun with the girls, to Find Themselves. All that stuff just got on his nerves. He didn't hunt, he didn't fish, and don't get him started about getting away from it all on a bloody meditation retreat! And as for her idea of him taking a trip back to Mexico, the place had changed so much since he left! Every time he'd gone back in the last few years, things had gone pear-shaped. He'd been robbed by bandits in Mexico City, lost his way in the touristy streets of Cancun and had kids in his old neighbourhood answer him in English. No, Joaquin Moralès wasn't looking to put down any more roots than he already had, but neither did he want to be apart from his wife.

He wouldn't deny, though, that his fifties had given him a tap on the shoulder. And while he wouldn't come to any conclusions about whether or not the male menopause existed anywhere other than in self-help books, he did find himself feeling ever so slightly down once in a while. But to go from that to Finding Himself? Just because he might be feeling a bit down, it didn't mean he'd lost his way!

Oh, well. Sarah had insisted, so he said yes. He often said yes to her. It was easier that way.

He left about three in the morning. He couldn't sleep, and since he was going to hit the road anyway, he might as well enjoy the sunrise over the river as he drove. Five days alone at the seaside. He was going to miss his wife, for sure. He would do some cleaning while he was waiting for her. He might even make the most of the time to do his own thing. Go for a run before dawn, watch the fisher-men, leave his dirty socks around the living room, watch boring films full of ads on TV, eat barbecue-flavoured potato chips, sit on a patio sipping third-rate tequila and look at the pretty tourists in bikinis. Why not? Press pause on life and watch the world go by. Oh, to put his feet up and be left in peace for once. Thank you and goodnight.

The very thought of it brought a smile to his face. Car and trailer loaded to the brim, he found himself whistling as he neared the end of the long drive, like a man who could see himself there already and who realised he was looking forward to getting there after all.

That's the way it was.

It must have been around noon when Joaquin Moralès turned towards the lighthouse by the Île-aux-Pirates. In the driveway of his new home a woman stood waiting for him. Early fifties with a sarcastic air about her, and dark braids with the occasional streak of white neatly tied up and falling behind her broad shoulders, Marlène Forest patiently watched him pull in. It was only the second time Moralès had seen his new boss.

He got out of the car. 'Is this my welcoming committee?'

She raised an eyebrow. 'Hi there, Sergeant Moralès. Enjoy the drive?'

'Yes.'

As she shook his hand, Moralès felt his time to himself crumbling to sand.

'You know, there are some people who would do anything to keep all their cases to themselves. Not me. I've got plenty of work to share around. And at the moment, I have to say, we're a bit overloaded. On top of the usual deaths and the summer surge, we're working on a big drugs case with a special task force. The task force was supposed to take some of the weight off our shoulders, but you know how it is, they're always under our feet. So we're happy to have you here.'

This didn't bode well.

'Who told you I was arriving today?'

'Your wife. We called her around ten this morning. Did you turn your phone off?'

'I'm on holiday at the moment—'

'The Gaspé's no place to take a holiday, Sergeant Moralès. Especially not in the summer. You were the one who put in for this transfer and I'm happy to be the first to congratulate you on it.'

'Thank you.'

'Are you hungry?'

'It can wait.'

'In any case, you don't have a say in the matter. We have to go see the body right away if we want to send it off for the autopsy this afternoon.'

'Sorry?'

'The autopsy lab's in Montreal. It's a long way away, but we always get the results quickly. You'll see.'

'Listen, madame Forest—'

She breezed over to the car and opened the door. 'Lieutenant. I think it's best we take my car, since yours is bursting at the seams. I'll make sure you don't get home too late.'

'I've been driving for hours, and I have to get my house set up…'

She turned to face him. 'For your wife? That's very romantic, sergeant, but we have a dead body on our hands and your wallpaper can wait. Don't worry, you'll get your holiday. But some other time. Right now, I need you on a routine investigation. Probably won't be a major case, but I've nobody else left.'

'I'd imagine—'

'Imagine as little as possible, sergeant. Be content with the facts.'

She got into the driver's seat and slammed the door. After a moment, Moralès joined her. Marlène Forest drove away. He had one last look back at the house – how could he not? – before he turned his eyes to the road.

'Have you seen the body?'

'No. It's been a crazy morning, and when I found out you were arriving I thought I might as well wait for you.'

She drove without any hurry.

'Wait for me?'

'Caplan's a small village, sergeant. I know the guy who found the body, and he's not one to joke around. Last night there was a break-in up on Fourth Lane and it was his sledgehammer they used to smash the door in. So he's already had a grilling from a young rookie who tends to come on a bit strong. He must be a nervous wreck. Apparently, he rubbed her up the wrong way too, though, if you know what I mean.' Marlène Forest smirked at her catty remark. 'Anyway, I didn't think there was much point subjecting him to three interviews in the same day, you see?'

'Is he the one responsible for the break-in?'

'No, not by the looks of it. He's a decent guy who lends out his tools and now it's bitten him in the behind. Vital does have a temper, but we should cut him some slack. He snagged a body in his nets at dawn, then, when he moored up at the wharf, he found out his tools had been used in a break-in. All that will get a man all worked up, don't you think? Just goes to show, even though we're a long way from the big city, there's still trouble. We just brew our own.'

'Where are we going, then?'

'The SQ station is down in Bonaventure, but we're headed to the Langevin brothers' funeral home in Caplan. Vital found the body early in the morning and the fishermen took it there for safe-keeping until it could be sent off to the autopsy lab.'

'Why didn't they leave it at the crime scene?'

'The crime scene?' She flashed him another mocking smile. 'Look to your left.'

They were driving westbound on Highway 132.

'They caught the body in a net. That's the crime scene, Sergeant Moralès. The sea.'

'Marie Garant.' He repeated the name to himself.

Men tend to dominate the summer drowning statistics. Ambitious swimmers, keen kayakers, drunk fishermen. He had been expecting this to be a case of carelessness and to have to palm some red-eyed, weepy tourist off on the duty psychologist.

Marie Garant, though. A woman. Sixty years old, thin and blue, tangled in a fine-mesh fishing net, her white hair streaked with salt, her skin washed pale by the sea. Marie Garant. When Langevin the undertaker, albeit delicately, zipped open the stiff body bag, Coroner Robichaud seemed oddly quick to slow the proceedings down. 'Go easy with Marie Garant!'

Moralès pulled on a pair of gloves, then hesitated. Should he touch her? It was the same thing every time: How do you touch a dead body? Especially a woman. He harboured a certain sense of modesty around a woman's corpse. Alive, she might refuse. *Don't turn up my collar, no, don't read the label on my clothes, don't lift up my head, don't hold my hand, I won't let you.* Dead, she no longer had the option to refuse. Dead women were disarmed, and Moralès found that embarrassing. You wouldn't stand for just anyone undressing your mother's abandoned body, would you? In a gentle gesture, Moralès smoothed Marie Garant's hair back into place where it was sticking out of the net. Should he uncover her face? He didn't dare. Best leave it to the autopsy team to free her from the cumbersome netting that had wrapped around her, mummy-like.

So he looked at her. That was all. Thin lips, eyelids closed, arms crossed over her chest. As if she figured dying meant she had to lie sweetly, like a child being rocked to sleep. A plain blue blouse with the buttons popped off, probably when the body snagged on the net. Well-tailored clothes. Cotton trousers, also blue. Bare feet. Had she been wearing shoes, and did they come off in the water? Sandals maybe? What about glasses? No jewellery. No earrings, bracelets, rings or necklaces, unless the fishermen had robbed her. Soft wrinkles furrowed her temples, but there was no air of fragility about her. Rather, she gave the impression of solidity, despite her femininity and her age. Calm strength in her shoulders. Confidence. And something else. He looked at her again, more closely this time. What? Something was niggling at the detective. And suddenly, he understood. This woman was happy. He took a step backwards. It made him uneasy, how peaceful and certain she was of her happiness. No one was that happy, it was impossible. In life or in death.

Langevin the embalmer zipped the bag closed over Marie Garant's body. Marlène Forest was still outside, petting the Langevins' big Nordic dog as it lazily kept watch from the edge of the porch. Moralès realised she was palming the investigation off on him, only too happy to be free of a case people in her village were tangled up in.

The men barely said a word on their way out. Moralès wanted to go and see the fishing boat, but Vital was waiting at the station to be interviewed, so Marlène insisted on taking him and the coroner to Bonaventure.

She was still the one driving. The coroner was telling the story. He spoke slowly, with a lump in his throat, as if Marie Garant were still right before his eyes.

'It was Vital Bujold and his deckhand, of the *Ma Belle*, who fished her out. About quarter past five. They pulled up their net and there she was, among the plaice and the starfish. They put her body in the boat and covered her up with a tarp, so they didn't have to look at her, or so the sun wouldn't eat away at her, I don't know. You ought to understand, they brought her back to the marina like that. Vital must be going on sixty-eight. The other man on board was Victor Ferlatte. About the same age, give or take. They've been fishing together for years.'

The coroner turned to Moralès, looked him up and down. Could *he* be trusted? Robichaud wondered. Marlène had insisted on handing over the investigation to him. Probably because she knew what a minefield of controversy the Marie Garant business would be around here. Still, it bothered him to see a stranger poking his nose into their affairs. Mexican, as well … He'd be keeping an eye on him, because trouble and strife was easy to come by in a little village like this.

Robichaud continued: 'It's most likely an accident, although I don't have a choice but to investigate. You'll see, it'll soon be sorted.'

Sitting next to the coroner in the back seat, Joaquin was sizing him up too. An old man ordering an investigation into a death that didn't even appear to be suspicious; it smelled of a tragic love story to him.

The coroner sighed. 'Where do you want to start?'

'Did she live in Caplan?'

Moralès barely had an accent, Robichaud was surprised to hear.

'Yes and no. You ought to understand she travelled a lot. By sailboat. She had a house on the cliff, but she'd been gone for two years. She was probably coming back from somewhere warm down south when it happened. Her sailboat hasn't turned up yet, but it won't be long before it does.'

'She sailed solo?'

'Yes. You ought to understand, sergeant, that Marie Garant was no ordinary woman. When she was five years old, she was already sailing with her parents. First her father died, then her mother. When she was twenty, she went off to sea alone. Everyone was against it, but there was no stopping her.

'She stayed away for a long time. Four years, maybe five. You ought to understand, she lived dangerously. They were the good old days. With a Canadian passport and a solid sailboat, you could have had a tidy little business going, if you know what I mean. No doubt she was onto a good thing down there. We don't know much about her, about Marie Garant, deep down. Then again, when you think about it, you don't really know much about your own family, do you? Or even about yourself.

'Anyway, she came back. Such a beautiful woman. She had these colourful dresses and she would drink rum and laugh with abandon. You ought to understand that wasn't the kind of thing you saw a lot of around here. She got married and wound up a widow soon enough though. After that, she started kicking up all sorts of fuss. I thought she'd gone mad. Maybe she was already. Maybe we all are a little bit, when life rips our heart out.'

'What kind of fuss?'

'She would go out to bars, kick things, swear, spit on the ground … that kind of fuss.'

'Spit on the ground?'

'You ought to understand, she wasn't exactly good news, if you know what I mean. She spent her life sailing the southern seas and coming back again. We never knew if she was coming or going.'

'So, nobody knew Marie Garant was back in the Gaspé?'

'I ought to say nobody knew. At least to my knowledge.'

'I'll need to see her medical records, her will—'

'I'll get you her medical records, I was her GP. She was sick, but she kept it in check with good medication. I'll give you the details. And I'll ask the notary about the will. He's a friend, so he'll dig it out quickly.'

'And a list of people who knew her, loved her, hated her—'

'She didn't really live among the rest of us. She must have come back out of nostalgia. Nostalgia's a big thing around here.'

'Can we find out which boats were at sea that night?'

'There's no marine traffic control.'

'And what about the weather conditions in the last three days?'

'Yes, Marlène can pull that up for you.'

'We'd better find the sailboat. Is there a lighthouse keeper, a marina or coast-guard station around here?'

'The coast guard is in Rivière-au-Renard.'

'We need to see whether she sent out a distress call.'

'Marlène can take care of that, can't you, Marlène?'

'Yes, coroner.'

'If you'll sign the search warrant for me, I'll pay a visit to her house.'

They arrived at the station. The coroner looked up and Marlène discreetly made her exit.

'You ought to understand, sergeant, there's not much of the ordinary in this village. You've only just arrived, so you couldn't know. I ordered an investigation because I couldn't do things any other way. Someone dies, you have to give reasons, and I'm old enough to know you can't get away with sending any old paperwork to the authorities. If it were up to just me, though, I wouldn't have ordered anything. It can happen, an old woman dying at sea. Especially if she's living on her sailboat. She was on her way back from warmer climes and we hadn't seen her for months, so her house was sitting empty. So it's the sailboat we ought to find. But to do that, we ought to find out where she anchored when she came back to the area. And that's anybody's guess because Marie Garant always was a stubborn and elusive woman.

'Around here, you ought to understand, the sea puts food on people's plates, but every family pays their dues to the water. Drownings are frequent. A fisherman, a careless child ... Every time, there has to be an inquest. And what do we find? It was an accident, a bit of clumsiness or a stroke of bad luck. That's what life's like by the water. That said, we couldn't live without the sea. You see, I was born with the sea in my backyard. I played in it all the time in my youth. When I was away studying in the city I missed it so much I came back. And I've not managed to leave the village again – not ever.

'You ought to understand, the sea's all of this. She's the wave that drags you away from shore and then carries you home. A whirlpool of indecisiveness, hypnotising, holding you captive. Until the day she chooses you. I suppose that's what passion is ... a groundswell that sweeps you up and carries you further out than you thought, then washes you up on the hard sand like an old fool.'

He closed his eyes – as if to picture Marie Garant once more on the blank screen of his eyelids.

'You'll have your piece of paper tomorrow. Tomorrow. Today, I'm old and I'm tired. I don't feel like having just anyone go into Marie Garant's house any old how.'

'Sorry?'

A vague hand gesture, wiping clean the slate of the past. 'Langevin's taking her body to Montreal for the autopsy. Start by questioning Vital Bujold. He's been waiting for hours. Then you can go and unpack your suitcases in your new home. You can go into Marie Garant's house tomorrow.'

Taken aback, Moralès wondered whether he should react. Insist on going to visit the house straight away. Show he knew how to lead an investigation. Impose his own pace on these Gaspesian clocks. But he hesitated. And by the time he was done hesitating, it was already too late.

'You know, sergeant ... Is it sergeant or detective? Christ in a chalice, what an idiot I am, but it's been a long day! And it's been slim pickings, this season. Christ in a chalice, talk about slim pickings! You're not from round here, are you, so you couldn't know. And now we're fishing bodies up in our bait nets!'

Vital Bujold had barely had time to get home and take a breather after his disastrous fishing trip when he was called in to the Bonaventure police station to undergo his second interview of the day. He didn't appear nervous, though, he just seemed exasperated and would clearly rather have been somewhere else. But he was managing to restrain himself. Moralès sat down across from the man. Being anywhere else was obviously a holidaymaker's luxury.

'Would you like to tell me how it happened?'

'There's not much I can say. I went out fishing about quarter past four. I always set off before everyone else, especially them Indians! You won't have seen, will you? They only set off at six o'clock! Not that we have anything against that Native bunch, but they've never had the knack with timing the tide right!'

'And then?'

The fisherman sighed. A good fifteen years older than Moralès, he was taller and stronger too, sculpted from thick clay, with a seaward look in his eye. Moralès suddenly envied him. That stature, the strength of a man who knows where he's at.

'I started pulling up my traps. Three lobsters this morning. Not even big ones, either! Christ in a chalice! Any less and we'll be paying out of our own pockets to go fishing! Then, when I got to my net

… I only cast one net. For bait, you know. Sometimes I catch a few plaice or a water hen I can sell along with my lobster. When there's some around.'

With his chair pushed a long way back from the table, he made simple, honest gestures as he spoke.

'And as he was pulling in the buoy to haul in the net, Victor shouted, "We've caught a big one here, you should feel it pulling!" Well, he didn't shout it quite like that, he stuttered it, but it's all the same. So anyway, I went over to give him a hand and make sure nothing got broken, and Victor said he could see something strange. He stuttered when he said that too. He stutters all the time, when he says anything. When he was young, he fell into a well. Ever since then, he's stuttered every sentence. I knew him before his accident, but I've got used to it. I'm a patient man. I wait for him to finish, because I don't like it when other people finish his sentences for him.'

'Carry on, please.'

Moralès caught the fisherman raising an eyebrow. He knew there was no point ruffling the man's feathers, but this wasn't a good day for anyone.

'Christ in a chalice, there's not much to say! We saw it was a body soon enough, so we hauled it aboard. We didn't see who it was right away because we pulled it up feet first. We took care to pull it up with our bare hands, mind you, even though that's nobody's idea of fun. Christ in a chalice! I don't know how you police do it! Or the undertakers either. Just goes to show, we're all made for different jobs.'

'If you say so.'

Another eyebrow raised, perhaps in contempt.

'So anyway, we pulled it up on deck and put a tarp over it. In the morning, the birds circle around us a lot; they like it when we throw them our fish scraps. We didn't want the seagulls to start pecking away at the corpse's face.'

'And then?'

'Well, after that I put a call in to the coast guard. They're all the way up in Rivière-au-Renard, so they don't get down here much. Usually they send the coroner out; he's got a boat and he likes to put his volunteer-police hat on. Must suit them, I reckon, because it's always him they call. Wasn't much to do this time; they told us to come back to shore, even though we weren't done pulling up the traps. So that's what we did. In any case, we couldn't have done any work with that thing on board. We were careful, even though she was a nut job.'

'A nut job?'

The fisherman had let the words slip. He'd been more candid than he wanted to be. Too late.

'That's one way to put it. A woman who was always sailing off abroad. She would leave, and people thought she was never coming back, then – *bam!* – her boat would just reappear overnight!'

'Did it bother you that she would go off travelling? Or that she came back?'

'Where are you from, then?'

Moralès was used to this. 'Just outside Montreal. Longueuil.'

Vital Bujold nodded. 'I'm not saying people are crazy just because they travel to other countries. I'm saying she was crazy because she had a strange way of behaving. She would get off her sailboat and start kicking kelp around. Kelp, for crying out loud! Who in their right mind kicks kelp? Nobody! Christ in a chalice, you'd have to be a bloody nut job to do that kind of rubbish!'

'You didn't like Marie Garant—'

'It wasn't just me. She wasn't well liked, Marie Garant. But that was no reason to want to see her dead! I don't want you thinking things like that. All I did was fish her out. Not much point wishing her dead, not at her age. And at my age, Christ in a chalice, we've all learned killing's not the answer. We know death's going to come all by itself. Let's not make a song and dance about all this, eh? An old woman who fell off her sailboat and drowned won't be much of an investigation for you. As for the rest, it's dead and buried.'

'What's dead and buried?'

'Nothing.'

'Tell me anyway.'

'Tell you what?'

Vital leaned forward in his chair and laid his hands flat on the table as if he were about to get up and leave. Something was ticking him off. But what? Joaquin Moralès racked his brains. What could be getting on the man's nerves? If Vital were to lose his rag, he might just say something important. Or maybe not. He didn't look like the kind who was easily influenced.

The fisherman looked at Moralès, pulled himself together and put his hands back in his lap.

'Well, you know, detective, things were different back in the day. Fishing, for one – it's not what it used to be. Before, the bay was full of fish and, believe me, the fishermen used to pull in a hell of a catch! In the spring we'd land five, six piles of herring, each ten or twelve feet high. We'd fill up carts and spread them all over the fields as fertiliser for the spuds. Now they're spreading smelt instead. Not that it changes the taste or anything, but just to say there's no herring left! No more cod either!'

A wily one, this fisherman. Wriggling his way around the question.

'What's this got to do with the dead woman?'

'Well … Just to say that everything's changed. The sea's empty now. An empty shell. Christ in a chalice, even the water's in short supply! Back in the day, there used to be way more water in the bay! And drownings … there are enough drownings to make anyone lose their mind. Sometimes we wonder how so many accidents could happen. I always thought there was no way the sea could just keep swallowing up so many people, but the proof's always there in the inquests. Natural drownings, accidents—'

'What happened with Marie Garant?'

'You have to understand, sergeant, things were different in the past. Take the tides, for one. Before, the tides were bigger; in the spring and the autumn, there'd be the king tides. The old folk used to say the sea was heavy. The water was different, the waves were thick and full of salt. They'd leave a mark on the wharf. Speaking of which, that wharf was supposed to have been built straight, but the engineer ended up dying after the first hundred feet. Drowned, he did. So they hooked it around, and look what it did. The entrance keeps filling up with sand because there's a kind of whirlpool that forms there—'

'You're not telling me anything about Marie Garant's death!'

'I'm doing nothing but that, detective. It's just that I'm casting the net far and wide – I'm not one for the finer details. When I was young, my mother always told me I bit off more than I could chew. It's the same with the sea; her eyes are bigger than her belly. She can't possibly be that hungry. And she can't be guilty of everything. She died of grief, did my mother. If she'd seen that, this morning … Christ in a chalice! Just goes to show, you never know what the sea's going to pitch into our nets.'

Moralès didn't know what to say.

'Well, anyway … If you don't have any more questions, I'm off to get my boat ready for tomorrow.'

It had not been a good day. And Moralès didn't know it yet, but the Gaspé was far from done putting him through the wringer. Not to mention Sarah – how come she wasn't returning his calls?

Shortly after the interview, Marlène Forest gave Moralès a lift home. It was only when he got to the door that he realised he'd left the keys to his new place back in Longueuil. He tried calling Sarah to see if she knew whether there was a spare set somewhere, but she didn't answer. Neither the home phone, nor her mobile. Moralès winced. No, it wasn't because things were going badly with Sarah. It was just that … How could he put it?

Thirty years earlier, Joaquin Moralès had met the girl who would become the love of his life. As a young rookie in the Mexico City police, he would patrol the streets at night while studying to be a detective at the Instituto para la Seguridad y la Democracia by day. At the tender age of twenty-two, he whistled at girls in miniskirts, spent his holidays on the beach in Cancún and dreamed he would have a gaggle of sun-kissed children, running naked through the crystal-clear water of the Caribbean. As a face of 1970s law enforcement in a country that had become a veritable warehouse for drugs of all sorts that were sold across North America, he had the dream of justice and the spirit of a superhero. Hailing from an upstanding family brimming with integrity and good intentions, Joaquin Moralès was born to rescue widows and orphans from their dirty rags and clad them in the finery they deserved. His forehead shimmering with virtue, and honesty and decency flourishing in his buttonhole, he had designs on punishing cruelty, patching the potholed road to justice and becoming the idolised, albeit discreet, architect of his own modern odyssey.

One June evening, while Mexico City was sleeping soundly under his watchful eye, the young police officer happened upon a young woman as he was patrolling the area around Benito Juárez International Airport. Visibly upset, she was trying desperately to make herself understood by passers-by – though they clearly understood her predicament more than they did the French she was speaking.

Patrolman Moralès parked his cruiser and approached the pretty, tearful young girl. He had heard so many sordid stories of pretty *gringa* tourists yearning for adventure that, in spite of himself, he found her most desirable. At the tender age of eighteen, her eyes moist with desperation and her peasant skirt all wrinkled, Sarah Blanchard was the very image of an orphan in distress crying out to the poetic soul – and body – of a budding superhero.

With a puffed-up chest, looking as confident as he was benevolent, Joaquin Moralès made his way over to the young lady. What could possibly be the matter? Relying on eloquent sign language and her questionable English, she got him to understand that she needed to make an overseas phone call, but she had no idea how to go about it, since Mexican telephones filled her ears with too much inexplicable Spanish gibberish for her to decipher.

In fact, Sarah Blanchard had managed to land herself in the kind of predicament only her spirited youth could explain, if not justify. The only daughter of a respectable suburban couple, she had decided in the aftermath of a heated squabble with her mummy dearest to rebel and live like an aspiring Bohemian enveloped in the smoky illusions of peace and love. Running away from the family home, like the proverbial schoolgirl desperate for adventure and convinced that travel broadened the mind, she had boarded the first flight to Mexico, where, she later assured him, an enthusiastic pen pal who had bombarded her with love letters was waiting to take her into his arms. The young man had given her directions from the airport to his bachelor pad, but Sarah Blanchard, as much of a novice at running away as she was in matters of the heart, had mixed up the airports and purchased a flight to Mexico City instead of Cancún. So near and yet so far.

It was only when she landed and set foot in the pestilent maelstrom of that suffocating city that she realised her mistake and broke down in desperation. How foolish her dreams of freedom and travel had been! What kind of stupid drug had she snorted to fly off on such a whim? What was she doing here? Overcome by anxiety and panic, she wanted to buy a ticket straight home. She hurried to the ticket desk, but, alas, misfortune seldom comes alone, and she found herself short on money. Trembling in distress, tears streaming down her face, she left the airport and walked down the street on autopilot. Having now lost all her youthful pride, she made a beeline for the nearest phone booth, which was where, twenty minutes and countless tissues later, the future Sergeant Moralès came to her rescue.

And so it was thanks to Good Samaritan Moralès that Sarah Blanchard managed to get through to her mother and to find a clean, safe and nondescript boarding house where she could spend the three days it would take for the money to arrive from her parents that would enable her to buy her ticket home.

In the meantime, did the young patrolman Moralès cross the line of duty and seduce the young runaway? Certainly not! Rather, it was the other way around. Sarah Blanchard, mortified at her lack of grace before such a handsome, young, tanned and muscled Mexican police officer – she who usually breezed around in such a liberated way, smoking cigarettes in the street and wearing see-through blouses *sans* bashfulness or brassiere – now wanted to show the woman beneath her girl-from-the-suburbs veil. What's more, she had pilfered a trio of condoms from the bedside table of a friend's father and had stashed them in her handbag, on the off chance. The second evening, when patrolman Moralès came to pick the nubile Québécoise up from her prim and proper rented room to take her out for dinner in town, he couldn't help but notice the three little packets she had set out on display by way of – so she thought – subtle invitation. Not being the type to allow any obstacle to deter him from carrying out his duty to serve the honest citizen to the utmost satisfaction, Moralès ended up bursting all three past-their-sell-by-date condoms over the course of the unbridled night of love that followed their spicy Mexican meal.

And so it was that in those times of sexual liberation, Sarah Blanchard lost her decidedly passé, nonsensical, cumbersome virginity at the same time as she lost her aspirations to travel. So it also was that she flew home and discovered she was pregnant, and that her mother contacted the Instituto para la Seguridad y la Democracia to report the young policeman, who, being as upstanding as he was proud, handed out cigars, packed his bags and that Christmas hopped on a plane to Quebec to wed the knocked-up *demoiselle*.

So it was eventually that Joaquin Moralès became a Canadian citizen, learned to detest the grey of November, the frostbite of February and the sweet, pervasive reek of maple sugar shacks in the spring, and, learned, occasionally, to curse in some decidedly local language. He also learned to speak an almost accentless French and became first a fine policeman and then a brilliant detective. He even came to be praised, at times, for his hawk-like patience and observational skills – his ability to circle his prey and then crack the toughest of the tough.

But above all else, Joaquin Moralès had been in love with Sarah Blanchard. Passionately. No sooner had he landed in Quebec than the delight of both becoming a father and being reunited with his pretty, tearful, pale-skinned princess had enveloped him like a cloak of hotly spiced colours that made him shine so brilliantly, Sarah Blanchard, yielding to his Hispanic charm as much as his chivalrous graces, had for years reciprocated his undying love.

That was that.

Two children and thirty years of marriage later, Joaquin Moralès's head was butting against the uncertainties of his fifties. Was it normal, sometimes, to feel down, to have hesitations and … doubts?

Why wasn't Sarah answering the phone? She had insisted he leave five days ahead of her. Now he was wondering whether he could smell a rat. He shook his head. The distance, the fatigue from driving, his boss's irony and the pointless interview were muddling his thoughts. It was nothing to worry about, he told himself. She would call back later.

He climbed back into his car, still loaded to the brim with luggage, and drove off to Vital Bujold's boat. He clambered aboard and sniffed around, but found nothing. What was Vital hiding? The fisherman was trying to wriggle his way out of something, but Moralès suspected he wouldn't wring the truth out of him anytime soon. Marlène Forest must have been laughing all the way home at the fact she'd managed to palm the dead body off on him.

Finally, as night fell over the wharf, he remembered how hungry he was. Seeing the light of the bistro, he returned to his car and made for the only place still open in the village.

'Ah, well, let me tell you, it's not that I don't want to be accommodating, but the kitchen's closed at this time of night.'

'Just some toast, or some cheese … Don't you have anything at all?'

Renaud looked him up and down. 'Let me tell you, are you a tourist? Where are you staying?'

'I bought the Vigneault house. Over by the Île-aux-Pirates.'

'Ah! So you're the police inspector?'

'Sergeant Moralès, yes.'

'Well, let me tell you, where are you from, then? Mexico? Punta Cana?'

'Just outside Montreal. Longueuil.'

'Ah. Well, I wouldn't have thought so.'

At the bar, a man in a priest's collar turned his head slowly towards Moralès.

'Well, let me tell you, it's not every day we have a new inspector from Longueuil here with us in Caplan. So let me tell you, I can reheat you a pizza, if you like. There was a mix-up with an order, and we still have one in the fridge. Now, why don't you take a seat at the bar and we'll have a chat.'

Joaquin didn't reply. He checked his text messages. No news from Sarah. The detective in him should have been jumping at this chance to hear all the village gossip, but tonight he was in no mood for such a windfall. Not tonight.

'Yes, please, to the pizza. But I think I'll sit over by the window, thank you.'

'Ah—'

The silence was deafening.

'Right you are, then! Sit wherever you please!'

Moralès ordered a beer and went over to the window as Renaud pulled on a silly hat and cook's helper apron and proceeded to bang the hell out of the kitchen counter as if he were personally hammering a particularly vicious chunk of pepperoni to death.

Find the sailboat. Search the house. Check the will. Wait for the autopsy results. Should be an open-and-shut case. So what was bothering Moralès all of a sudden? Marlène? Vital Bujold? Watching his holiday spiral down the drain? … Sarah?

'Are you working on Marie Garant's death, then?'

Joaquin Moralès nearly had a heart attack. Sneaking up on him like a spy from an old B-movie, Renaud spat this out as he set the beer down on the table.

'Yes.'

Renaud glanced around, then bent down to whisper in Moralès's ear.

'I can tell you plenty of things, inspector, because I know everything that goes on around here.'

'Ah, yes. Very well. Thank you.'

You found someone like this in every investigation; Moralès had had the bad luck to stumble across him tonight. Talk about a rough day.

'Let me tell you, I'm not going to waste your time.'

'Were you a friend of Marie Garant?'

'No!'

'An enemy?'

'Shhh! Not here!'

Moralès looked around the room. Besides the half-drunk man of the cloth sitting at the bar, the bistro was empty.

'Why not?'

'Let me tell you, I have plenty of things to say to you, Police Inspector Moralès, but only at the station, in a proper interview room.'

'You want me to take you in for questioning?'

'Well, that depends.'

'Depends on what?'

'On whether you want the true truth.'

'Fine. Tomorrow afternoon?'

'Let me tell you, I can't tomorrow, because a bistro like this gets busy, busy, busy, believe me, and I work long days … I do want to answer your questions, mind you, but it can't interfere with my schedule … How about the day after tomorrow?'

'Fine. Two o'clock, then.'

'Morning would be better, before we open.'

'Naturally. Half past nine.'

'Right. Let me tell you, are you going to haul me in?'

'No, just come into the station, please.'

'And are you going to leave me your card, in case I have any urgent information?'

'You can call the station and leave a message.'

'And what if you're not there?'

'Isn't that the smell of my pizza burning?'

Renaud hurried off.

Moralès turned to the window, which, in the opacity of the night, had morphed into a mirror. The table appeared longer, the place settings multiplied, the beer found company and Moralès found himself face to face with his twin. He hated that. Staring himself in the face and wondering what he was doing there, in the antechamber of nowhere, waiting for a phone call and a burnt pizza.

Outside, a sliver of moonlight opened a crack in the sea and the glass was once again transparent. A female silhouette walked slowly into the shard of light scratching the water's surface with its giant nail. Moralès watched as she walked up towards the *auberge*, hesitated, then turned towards the beach.

'Let me tell you, that's mademoiselle Day.'

'Ah.'

Renaud placed the pizza on the table. The blackened edges had clearly been scraped away with a knife.

'She's a tourist who's staying at Guylaine's, the seamstress's place.'

'Renaud?'

At the bar, the man with the priest's collar was summoning the bistro owner.

'And let me tell you something, I just have one thing to say—'

'Renaud!'

'It's that—'

'RENAUD!'

Our Father wanted another drink. Right now.

'I'll tell you in the interview.' As he walked away, the bistro owner winked knowingly at the exhausted policeman.

Moralès dug into his pizza, his eye on the solitary feminine figure, silhouetted like a Chinese shadow puppet on rice paper as she climbed slowly, delicately eastward. Until she disappeared out of sight.

Why wasn't Sarah returning his calls? For some months, it had been as if the threads of his life were slipping between his fingers, tangling around his ankles, catching his feet, and tripping him up. It crossed his mind he was just getting old and … how could he put it?

A cloud swallowed the crescent moon, leaving only the tired reflection of his own face in the window, which darkness had once again turned into a mirror. Joaquin Moralès took a look at himself. Fifty-two years old. The salt and pepper of time had streaked his hair like shooting stars. Some said it lent him a certain charm. He caught his own eye. *Old and … just a fool*, he thought.

Then he lowered his gaze.

2

CHARTED WATERS

Alberto (1974)

When O'Neil Poirier returned from Anticosti seven days later, the sailboat was still moored at the wharf, right where he and his men had left it, silent, unmoving, its hatches battened down.

The fisherman tied up the *Alberto* and went to see the guy in the fish warehouse, to ask him…

Ah, yes, there had been a woman with a baby in the sailboat. But she'd had things to do in the city, apparently, and so one of the delivery drivers had taken them on board his fish truck – her and the bairn – must have been two or three days ago. Was that Tuesday or Wednesday? Poor driver, stuck with a woman and a newborn, what a hassle! But she paid well, apparently. And the driver had just got married – didn't have a lot of money – so it suited him. Know who I'm talking about, O'Neil? Daraîche, the tall, gruff one who never says a word? Well, he was the one who went off with the girl and the baby. When are they coming back? He came back yesterday. Took a while in town, 'cos there was a problem with the truck. Transmission was worn, apparently. Could have had an accident. Can you imagine, with a newborn? Would have been a hassle! Her? Nobody knows when she's coming back. Daraîche told her his schedule and she said she'd contact him, apparently.

Anyway, the guy in the fish warehouse added, the boss reckons the sailboat is in the way, so they're on about moving it, taking it down to the end of the wharf. The cargo ships from the Schefferville mine make a big wake, O'Neil Poirier said, so that might bash the sailboat up against the wharf. Sink it, even. The guy in the fish place shrugged – all they cared about there was offloading the fish without any hassle, and the sailboat was in the way. Poirier said he was the one who moored it there, and that his men would take care of it.

And so that's what they did. They emptied the *Alberto* of her catch and tied the sloop alongside without breaking a thing. Then they towed it slowly to the middle of the bay to free up the wharf and the boat ramp, and keep it clear of the cargo-ship channel. They took the sailboat to the lobster-fishing area. If the small fishing boats could pass through there, it'd be deep enough for the sailboat too. They dropped the sloop's anchor off to the side, then used the *Alberto* to pull the chain tight, to make sure the sailboat wouldn't drift free. And that night, since it was warm out, Poirier slept out on deck, just in case. Two days later, when the men set off again, the sloop was still in the same spot. They added an extra anchor to *Pilar* (Poirier made a mental note of the sailboat's name, just in case) – one they had aboard the *Alberto* that would hold fast in rough weather. They also attached a float to the warp, so that, if the woman came back and wanted to set sail in their absence (which O'Neil feared might happen), she could just cast off and his crew could recover the anchor using the float.

But as it turned out, the *Alberto* had the time to sail the seas and fish almost all summer long, and then sold her season's catch before the young mother returned to her sailboat and O'Neil finally got the chance to talk to her.

Charted waters (2007)

Cyrille said that all truths were ever-flowing and elusive. Those who went to sea knew that anything atop the waves was forever breaking up and reforming. Differently. He said that the wind, the current and the ocean swell were insatiable; that you could never be too careful, even on a glassy sea. What was true in the here and now would make a liar of you not ten minutes later. He said the only reason we exist was the ever-shifting lie that is life.

Until then, I had accepted, in spite of myself, that happenstance would lead me to my destiny and that the incomprehensible would cross my path. But down on the wharf, seeing Cyrille on his knees before Marie Garant's body, tangled up in the net, I didn't have the heart for Victor's Hail Mary.

I ummed and ahed for a while before I made up my mind, then, during the dark hour when the wolves come out to play, I rang the bell at Father Leblanc's door. Encased in a questionable fixture, a feeble bulb attracted a cheery bunch of summer flies, who revelled in its yellowish halo. One of them buzzed fretfully, trapped inside the globe. I waited. I had gathered he often enjoyed a tipple down at the bistro. It didn't bother me that I might be bothering him. I was looking for somebody to enlighten me and, being a man of God, he should have some answers. Etched into the pane of frosted glass was a dove flying towards a triangle of light. I rang again.

Father Leblanc eventually opened up, looked at me somewhat disbelievingly and wedged himself up against the door frame. The wine on his breath preceded the man himself by a good few feet. Unsteady on his legs, he leaned on the door handle, which did a valiant job of keeping him upright.

'I'm sorry to bother you, Father, but I need to speak to someone.'

'In truth, I'm not in a condition to be someone at the moment, mademoiselle Day.'

'Garant. My name is Catherine Garant. Marie Garant was my mother.'

He scratched the back of his neck. 'Are you here to pray or to gossip?'

We both stood there, hands against the door frame, me trying to talk my way in, him attempting to shoo me away.

'I shouldn't have told that white lie about my name. I hope you'll forgive me. I … I'm going through a rough patch. I came out here to the Gaspé to meet my mother, but … she's dead. I … I don't have any answers and I … I feel alone.'

'What do you want me to do about it?'

'I don't know … Ask me in? You did take a vow—'

'The only vow I took, mademoiselle Garant, was to be able to enjoy my drink in peace and quiet before I go to bed!'

'You're drunk.'

'In truth, it happens. Even to alcoholics. But you're not going to hold seeking a remedy for misery against me, are you – is that why you're knocking at my door in the middle of the night?'

I hesitated for a second, just long enough to lose my patience. Then I climbed right back onto my high horse.

'Well actually I am, Father! Your drink can wait until tomorrow! Because I've been paying my tithes all my life to a church I've never set foot in, and the one night that I come asking for help, you're not going to leave me out in the cold! The rest of the year, you can knock back as much as you please, but tonight, it's out of the question for a man of God to hide behind his wine bar of an altar and deny me—'

'Deny you what, my dear child?'

'An explanation! I came to the Gaspé to meet my mother, my father, a lover – someone! Someone who has answers! But no one's here and I'm left empty-handed. And now even you don't want to talk to me!'

He let go of the groaning handle and took five steps backward to sit down on the staircase. He sighed. Heavy feet had taken their toll on the stairs. There were finger marks along the handrail and the grooves in the wood suggested cats had used it to claw their way upstairs. The walls were painted that tired pale shade decorators call off-white. If you ask me, it's a drab, dirty white. A miserable white. Father Leblanc's black clothes blended in with the whole setting: wrinkled trousers with a worn-out belt; shabby shirt with an unsavoury priest's collar.

'Catherine, you're knocking on the wrong door.'

'Renaud told me a priest had blessed his house and that ever since then…'

He wiped a wrinkled hand across his balding forehead and his expression turned into one of compassion. *At last*, I thought.

'Is that what you want, a miracle? In truth, you show up here at silly o'clock with your little white lies, as sorry as a winter sea, and you want me to bless you to help you sleep tight?! Yet who, my poor child, sleeps peacefully these days? Who? Name one person who can get a good night's sleep!'

'I don't understand.'

He stood up, evidently ushering me back to the other side of the glass door.

'That's the mystery of faith: we don't understand, but we keep on living anyway!'

'You can't fool me with your mysteries.'

'Fool you? Go back home, Catherine Day, daughter of Marie Garant. The mystery is real, but you may sleep in peace now: in the name of the Father, the Son and the Holy Spirit, you are saved!'

'Hallelujah?'

'Stop searching and appreciate that life is something we're lucky to have! Love a man, bear a child, or follow in your mother's footsteps and take off somewhere, but just do it without me!'

He pushed me towards the door more firmly than I would have thought he was capable of. Retreating, despite my resolve, I played my final card.

'My mother has just died and that's the best you can come up with?'

'Yes.'

'So, tell me about my father! Who was he?'

'I won't lie to you, Catherine – you no longer have a mother and the only father you'll find here is God. And now, *this* father has nothing more to say!'

'That's not fair!'

'Goodnight to you!'

He closed the door, and I was left bathing in the yellowish halo of the dirty lamp. The fly was still there, bashing into the sizzling bulb in its futile attempts to escape the fishbowl.

Yves Carle barely slept anymore, not since a certain woman had toyed with his heart. He was a moocher. Fifteen years it had been going on, and Thérèse said it was worse in the winter.

'It's intolerable!' she would say. 'And it can't be good for your health, either!'

He would just shrug his shoulders and throw his arms to the sky. 'You're fretting for nothing! After three bypasses, my heart's made of Teflon!' Then he'd give her that tender, almost timid, smile he knew she couldn't resist. 'You're not going to ask me for a divorce, then?' he would tease.

'Are you nuts?! We're way too old to get divorced! It'd be far too much trouble!'

And so, each night, at the darkest of hours, when the hands on the clock turned to the right, Yves Carle would wake up, stare at the ceiling, note Thérèse's nocturnal breathing and get out of bed to start his day.

As winter turned to spring, Yves would wait for the ice to melt, like a maple expects the sap. Through the fog of April, he would keep watch. Stationed on his deck, he would patiently await the opening of the waters – for when the summer would fill the sea with abandon. He was used to it after all these years. At last, when the Milky Way was showing him the course he should take, he would hoist his sails and return only once he saw the fishermen set out to sea.

Thérèse said that was no better than in winter, that she would wake in the early hours and worry something might happen to him. After all, she added, no matter how old they were, 'men could never let women sleep in peace!'

The night I knocked in vain at the Lord's door, Yves Carle went to sea. Struck with insomnia in the wee hours by the clock hands, he cast off his earthly ties and hoisted his curtain of a mainsail beneath the starry firmament. The moon was shining in its full glory and he knew what he was looking for.

He had heard about Marie Garant's body being found and that was all he could think about. Marie snagged in a net. And *Pilar*? Sunk? Yves Carle had been picturing the boat upside down, its sails underwater, rigged and heavy. And everything else: plates and plastic glasses floating in the upside-down hull; tools, maps and naviga-tion dividers floating in the drink, bashing up against the side walls; the floorboards peeling away ... *Pilar* sunk? But there hadn't been enough knots in the wind to even make the sailboat lean, and if the hull had been leaking, Marie would have called the coast guard. Unless she had fallen overboard and *Pilar* had carried on along her course without her skipper...

Yves Carle had latched on to that theory.

He had mapped out the possible courses on his nautical chart. Rumour had it she wasn't disfigured, which meant she hadn't been in the water for long. He had checked the tide table and the atlas of currents, gone to bed, so Thérèse wouldn't get her knickers in a twist, and waited for the time to set off.

The wind was blowing from the west that night, fifteen to seventeen knots. Yves made it to the Banc-des-Fous in less than three hours. The parish rivalry between the Bonaventure-Caplan and Paspébiac clans was common knowledge, so he wouldn't have been surprised if the Paspéya mariners had spotted the sailboat and turned a blind eye to it. But Yves Carle did wonder why the Caplan clan hadn't set the detective on the right course. It was as if nobody wanted the sailboat to be found … Too many memories, perhaps. Or they were afraid.

The mariner rounded the point at New Carlisle, hugging the cliffs. Something told him the sailboat would be there. Yet, when he set eyes on her, from afar, he still didn't want to believe it, hoping the nightmare was just a dream. The boom was swaying from side to side and the hatch cover was open. Yves tacked and circled around once, twice. Then he lowered the sails, dropped the anchor.

He bent down into the hatch and grabbed the VHF transmitter.

'Rivière-au-Renard coast guard, Rivière-au-Renard coast guard, Rivière-au-Renard coast guard, this is *Night Flight*, *Night Flight*, *Night Flight*. Acknowledge. Over.'

The coast guard responded right away. At that time of night, they were not likely to be inundated with calls.

'*Night Flight*, this is the Rivière-au-Renard coast guard. Go ahead. Over.'

'I've found an abandoned sailboat by the name of *Pilar*. The police in Bonaventure are probably looking for her because her owner was found drowned yesterday. Over.'

Suddenly Yves Carle felt old. Tired. The coast guard asked for his position, told him to stay at the scene and not to touch the sailboat. To wait.

Yves Carle pulled his phone out of his pocket and dialled his home number. His hand was shaking.

'Hello?'

She sounded sleepy, her voice full of concern.

'Thérèse? It's Yves.'

'Yves? Where are you? Has something happened?'

'Don't fret. I'm just calling to say … well … I still love you.'

Silence fell, like a pause in the course of the night. He closed his eyes.

'You found *Pilar*?'

'Yes.'

'It's painful for me too.'

He opened his eyes again.

'Yves?'

'Yes?'

'I—'

'I know, Thérèse. I know. Go back to sleep now.'

Somewhat reluctant to scramble a crew in the middle of the night to recover an abandoned sailboat, the coast guard in Rivière-au-Renard transferred the call to the Sûreté du Québec in Bonaventure, as the Marie Garant affair was in their hands anyway. Since the station only had two patrols working the night shift, and they were already out in the field, the dispatcher took the initiative and called the coroner, Robichaud, who was renowned for offering medical assistance to those at sea, and anyway, was always getting himself involved in police business.

That was why, a little later, Yves Carle saw the coroner's cabin cruiser draw near with only Robichaud's neighbour, a sport fishing guide on the Bonaventure River by the name of Marc Lapierre, for crew. Yves had never liked Lapierre. He was too skinny, his bones creaked and he avoided eye contact when he spoke to you.

'*Night Flight, Night Flight, Night Flight*, this is *Seas The Day, Seas The Day, Seas The Day*. Acknowledge. Over.'

Yves sighed and grabbed the VHF transmitter. '*Seas The Day*, this is *Night Flight*. Go ahead. Over.'

'Yves? Have you been near the boat? Over.'

'No, coroner. I've not moved from here. Over.'

'Perfect. We'll take care of it. But stay close. *Seas The Day*, over and out.'

'*Night Flight*, over and out.'

Yves Carle shrugged his shoulders. Perhaps he should make himself a coffee. The sun was rising effortlessly over the bay. The water was smooth, flattened by the wind as it dropped. He would have to go home under engine power. The coroner's cruiser was making a hell of a racket, reverberating raucously through the morning air. Sailboats generally detest that kind of powerboat. The animosity is well known. And reciprocal.

Yves Carle had vowed not to get involved any more than he already was, but seeing the coroner pull alongside *Pilar* and board the dead woman's sailboat, he instinctively grabbed the VHF transmitter.

'*Pilar*, *Pilar*, *Pilar*, this is *Night Flight*. Acknowledge! Over.'

'*Night Flight*, this is *Pilar*. Go ahead. Over.'

It sickened Yves Carle to hear a man's voice identifying *Pilar* – it made him want to spit on the deck.

'Listen, coroner, I'm not sure it's a good idea to clamber aboard Marie Garant's sailboat. We'd be better letting the police do their job. Over.'

'*Night Flight*, you ought to understand I'm taking this boat back for the investigation. And you're coming back with us because you're a witness in the case. *Pilar*, over and out.'

'*Night Flight*, over and out.'

Yves Carle slammed the VHF transmitter down in a rage, cursing Robichaud. Yves watched him tighten the mainsail's clew lines in order to stabilise the boom, start the engine and begin to skipper *Pilar* back to shore himself. The shameless so-and-so!

The old mariner wiped a slow hand across his forehead. What would they do with *Pilar*, now? Yves started the engine, raised anchor and followed them obediently back to Ruisseau-Leblanc. Lapierre, still aboard the cruiser, had gone on ahead, and there he was, waiting on the wharf beside a pickup truck.

Yves dropped anchor a good distance away. Witness he may be, but he would play along as little as possible. The coroner steered the sailboat towards the boat ramp, down which Lapierre was reversing a trailer he had found God knew where. And then they took *Pilar* ashore.

It takes one hell of a cool head to guide a sloop like that out of the water. Yves Carle looked away, suffering in silence, turning his back on the dawn. Even Thérèse, who hated sailing, would understand. He went down into the cabin and made his coffee.

Pilar was the boat that sailed away. Not every boat would travel far, but *Pilar* had sailed the Seven Seas. To sail away like that, you had to have suffered – to the point of jettisoning it all. Yves Carle was no stranger to that. If Thérèse had wanted to, he would have sailed away too. He'd have taken her with him. They would have sailed the crystal-clear waters, seen rocky islands and found an appetite for exotic fish. If Thérèse had liked sailing, it would've been … easier.

Yves came up into the cockpit, coffee in hand.

It was the time when the guillemots whistled over the water, skimming the calm surface, shaking the silence, waking the day.

He lifted his gaze. *Pilar*, on land, on a boat trailer. The sea was empty.

'*Night Flight, Night Flight, Night Flight*, this is *Seas The Day*. Acknowledge. Over.'

Yves Carle extended a weary hand. 'This is *Night Flight*. Go ahead. Over.'

'Yves, you ought to come ashore to speak with Detective Sergeant Moralès. Over.'

Over and effing out, he thought. One thing was for sure, Yves Carle was going to finish his coffee before he set foot on shore.

Moralès, for his sins, only woke around six, when a man as taciturn as he was monosyllabic knocked at his door before retreating to join two other comatose crime-scene technicians caffeinating their numb yawns in an unmarked van, on their way to dust *Pilar* for prints. The man had offered an apology and seemed put out that he'd had to do the dirty job of waking the detective up because the coroner hadn't been able to rouse Moralès on his mobile – or so he said.

Moralès vaguely thanked the technician, who shrugged before driving off. The phone hadn't woken Moralès because he had deliberately left it in his jacket pocket. He had come home late and had had to force a window to get into his own house. He had then emptied the car and trailer in the middle of the night, stacking boxes all over the place according to a decidedly male logic, before sinking into bed, exhausted, around the time Yves Carle went to sea. He had fallen asleep sulking about his wife's silence.

Cursing Marie Garant, the coroner and the trio of crime-scene technicians, Moralès showered, tripped over boxes, realised there was no coffee in the house and then hurried off to the sloop without eating breakfast. Driving down the hill to the Ruisseau-Leblanc wharf, he blinked in surprise. Someone had taken the sailboat out of the water. Why? A hull thirty feet long. He'd never seen anything like it. He was amazed by the size of the sailboat, how heavy it looked, how elegant it was.

He stepped out of his car and scanned his surroundings. The fishermen were nowhere to be seen, and the silhouette of another sailboat at anchor was rocking gently on the dawn swell.

Coroner Robichaud strode purposefully towards him like a man who had been up all night running the show.

'I ought to tell you, sergeant, I brought the boat in myself. The three crime-scene guys you met have lifted the prints and left you a box of things in the cockpit so you can see what they're planning to send to the lab. You ought to take care of bringing that down to the station.'

It occurred to Moralès that he was missing a second opportunity here to take the coroner down a peg – to remind him who was in charge of this investigation and how important it was not to spread unnecessary prints all over the place. But he kept his mouth shut. You don't make waves in a village you're just settling in to.

'I ought to tell you, they've gone for breakfast and they'll be waiting for you at Marie Garant's house. I've written the address for you here, on the search warrant you asked me for yesterday.'

The coroner handed an envelope to Moralès, who put it in his car.

'I ought to call the notary so he can pull out the will for you.'

'I can take care of that later, coroner—'

'No, no, he's a friend of mine. We're used to this kind of thing. I ought to introduce you to Yves Carle. He's the one who found *Pilar*. He knows sailboats, so he can go aboard with you and show you around.'

Moralès turned towards the newcomer. In his late sixties, he had the look of a man lost in nostalgia.

'Detective Sergeant Joaquin Moralès, from the Sûreté du Québec.'

Yves Carle's gentle nod made Moralès feel awkward and pompous, all suited up with his weighty title.

'Yves, you ought to tell the detective the boom wasn't secured.'

'The boom wasn't secured, sergeant.'

Seemingly satisfied, the coroner retreated to his car.

Alone with Yves Carle, Moralès once again found himself feeling like a fool without knowing why. 'You know your boats, then?' he asked.

'I suppose so.'

'Can you tell me about this one?'

'She's an Alberg 30. A great seafarer.'

'I'd like you to show me around her.'

The mariner nodded.

Moralès fetched a bag from his car. 'We'll have to put gloves and overshoes on so we don't contaminate the scene.'

Yves Carle acquiesced and they pulled on their plastic attire in silence and climbed aboard. A boxful of items bagged by the crime-scene technicians sat waiting in the cockpit. As for the rest, Moralès was clueless. This was the first sailboat he had been on, but with its cables, pulleys, electronic screens and giant compass, it was not as exciting as promised by the advertisements for holidays in the Caribbean.

'What's a boom?'

Yves Carle was standing on the bench seat on the port side. 'That's the horizontal part of the mast, right here, that supports the bottom of the mainsail.'

'The coroner said it wasn't secured—'

'When you loosen the mainsail sheets, behind you, it makes the ropes go slack and the boom can swing from side to side.'

'Ah.' He wasn't in a chatty mood. 'Could that knock you into the water?'

'Yes. With an unexpected change of direction, it could crack you on the head and knock you overboard.'

Still that same feeling of awkwardness at being with the mariner, who suddenly bent down for a closer look at some black marks on the deck.

Moralès pre-empted the question. 'That was the crime-scene team who did that. Those are fingerprint marks.'

Yves Carle nodded. The detective had made him put gloves on and slip plastic bags over his shoes, but *they* had sullied the sailboat, rifled through her and lifted Marie Garant's prints from the time-salted wood. And the other prints they found.

'Shall we go inside?'

'Yes, yes. Let's go.'

The man of the sea led the way down into the hull of the dead woman's sailboat, laying delicate, pale eyes on Marie Garant's card table, her galley kitchen, the skipper's berth in the forepeak. Detective Moralès stooped imposingly inside the cramped space just as Yves stopped in front of the berth with a look of surprise. He craned his neck, inspecting the bed, and raised an eyebrow.

'Have you seen something out of the ordinary?'

'No. Nothing out of the ordinary, sergeant.'

It was the same feeling he'd had the day before, with Bujold the fisherman. The old mariner was hiding something. It was annoying, but he had learned his lesson. These Gaspesians would only say what they wanted to.

Moralès scanned his surroundings. What was he looking for? A compass needle pointing right to the perp, a detail opening an avenue to a suspect or a snippet of evidence the crime-scene technicians had missed? No, as a matter of fact, and in spite of the move, the fatigue, the driving, the day-to-day annoyances, Moralès knew deep down that the accident theory was the most plausible one. Of course, they couldn't rule anything out, as any police training school in the world would tell you. Suicide, set-up – anything was possible. But what was the point in always spreading themselves so thinly in order to cover every vague possibility? In his youth, he would track down every lead. Now he had come to understand how much effort that was for so few results! Of course, an investigation that was out of the ordinary could occur, that was true, but usually...

Moralès took his time, while Yves Carle leaned against the stairs and waited. The thing was, Joaquin didn't approach a woman's space the same way he approached a man's. Feminine spaces were always brimming with life, with objects and memories. The sanctuaries of beautiful women harboured colourful fabrics, exotic photographs and fine china. It was amazing what beauty and comfort a woman could bestow on her inner sanctum, he thought. Man caves were generally more understated ... or messier. Moralès had noticed how some men's empty shells were simply an expression of absence, while others' places were somehow bursting at the seams, suggesting an imminent explosion. Their sufferings were latent and destructive: murder or suicide. Sometimes both at once. Moralès found men to be miserable. And violent. He would far rather investigate a woman's space.

This was a silent mystery. The interior of the sailboat was narrow, but comfortable. Shelves along the hull contained an abundance of essentials: plastic plates and bowls, nautical manuals, a first-aid kit. Everything was arranged in a practical order dictated by daily use. What about signs of femininity? Curiously, almost eagerly, Moralès searched for clues about her. Marie Garant. What did he know about women of the sea? Nothing.

He approached the forepeak; the door to the berth was open. A bed, a tiny closet on one side. He opened it: clothes. Simple things. Hints of colour, but nothing extravagant. Enough to be beautiful without laying it on too thick. A light fragrance of salty perfume, the female body; a white hair on the shoulder of a green blouse. Joaquin felt a lump in his throat as he closed the cupboard door. He missed the feminine touch. The tenderness, the intimate caresses, the wrinkled skirt he would lift as she unbuttoned his shirt, the moisture beading between her breasts – and other things too. The times she was afraid of the dark or frightened by a mouse, the times she worried about her make-up, the times she cried her heart out. Women didn't go in for that kind of thing these days. Femininity was no longer in vogue. They had become feminists, grown strong and independent. When they made love, they brought themselves to a climax. They wanted to be in control of everything. And Moralès felt useless. Old, and a fool.

The detective stepped back, turned around and looked at the skipper's berth. Empty. He opened the storage cupboards in the cabin. Cables, tools, a can of oil, some spare parts and instruction manuals in the drawers. Some unfamiliar objects, too: a compass, some dividers, a Cras navigation plotter, like the ones you see in black-and-white photos in sailing books, the use of which Moralès would have been hard pressed to explain. It was so indelicate, so unfeminine, that he almost felt for her – Marie Garant *sans homme*, alone atop the sea.

'Lift the cushions and you'll find the drinking water under the benches.'

Moralès turned to Yves Carle, almost surprised he was still there. 'Ah. Thank you.'

He lifted the cushions and opened the bins. Tins of food, canned goods and a water tank, yes. An idea crossed his mind and he went back to Marie Garant's cabin, lifted the mattress and opened the storage bin there: cloth bags. Still leaning against the stairs, Yves Carle didn't move an inch, as if he knew the immutable order of all marine objects.

'Spare sails. Probably a spinnaker. That's a complicated sail to rig, and since she was on her own and not getting any younger, she probably didn't use it very often.'

'Ah.'

Joaquin Moralès felt a shallow wave of disappointment wash over him. So few clues about her.

'The bilge pumps are under the floor.'

'Thank you. That'll do. The crime-scene techs have already done the rounds anyway. We can go.'

The men climbed back up into the cockpit.

'Is this a storage bin as well?' Joaquin opened the cockpit seat and raised a questioning eyebrow at Yves Carle.

'Fenders, mooring lines, tackle, life jackets, harness, hand pump, emergency tiller … it's all above board.'

Moralès closed the bin and looked at Yves Carle again. 'Where did you find the boat?'

'She was at anchor, over by Paspébiac.'

'What's out there?'

'A shoal. That's an underwater ridge, to you.'

'You're a sailor. Do you reckon there's a reason why Marie Garant anchored on that shoal? If she was on her way back from warmer climes, Paspébiac wasn't necessarily on her way, was it? So why go there instead of coming straight back?'

Yves Carle shrugged and stepped off the sailboat. Moralès handed him the box of objects from the boat, but the coroner hurried back over from his car to grab it. Somewhat encumbered though, he ended up putting it down on the ground. Robichaud was the first one to get a word in, of course, and Moralès knew he had to find a way to politely put him in his place.

'Yves found the boat over at the Banc-des-Fous. You ought to tell us what you were doing out there—'

'I was sailing, coroner. Everyone knows I sail mostly at night.'

'The Banc-des-Fous is an underwater ridge. A rendezvous for lovers, and for dealers. You ought to understand, sergeant, it's obvious what happened. Marie Garant anchored her sailboat there to take refuge from the storm. One false move, or a rogue wave came along, and the boom cracked her on the head and knocked her off balance. Then she fell overboard.'

Yves threw a wry smile, and it hit the coroner like a slap in the face. Yves couldn't help himself; he had to say something.

'You can think whatever you want, but no sailboat would ever anchor on a shoal in bad weather! It's too dangerous. Because of the swell, the keel might hit the rocks and break the hull. When the weather gets rough, a sailboat either has to be moored safely in the marina, or a ways out from the coast. Any sailor worth his salt knows that. You're investigating the death of a woman who knew how to sail, so try not to forget that.'

Yves Carle became quiet, bowing his head like a man who reckons he's said enough and people can put two and two together and figure out the rest. But the coroner wasn't going to give up that easily.

'You ought to understand, every sailor around here respected Marie Garant, but anyone can make a mistake. Now, sergeant, let's talk about the will. The notary can't open it without tracking down the heirs. He's given me the name of one, but he hasn't managed to reach her at home.'

Yves Carle's ears pricked up. *An heiress. A daughter!*

'He said we ought to phone her. That you might want to be the one to do it, sergeant.'

Yves slowly inched away. Deep down, it was none of his business and he wanted to get home. But then he suddenly heard something. He waved to Moralès.

'Excuse me, there's a phone ringing in your car.'

'*Merde!*'

Moralès dashed over to his car, grabbed his jacket, rummaged through the pockets, finally found the thing and picked up.

'Hello?'

'Let me tell you just one thing, inspector, this is Renaud Boissonneau here. And I'm waiting for you here at your station, for the interview.'

'Monsieur Boissonneau? Our meeting is tomorrow, not today!'

'Let me tell you, you're keeping a key witness waiting here.'

'A key witness? What are you on about?'

Rustling on the other end of the line.

'Sergeant Moralès? Lieutenant Forest here. You've been keeping a key witness waiting a good while already.'

For God's sake, that pain in the neck Renaud had put Marlène on his case! He must have been kicking up a real fuss down at the station.

'Lieutenant Forest, we've found the dead woman's sailboat and—'

'In the Gaspé, Sergeant Moralès, people matter more than things. And the crime-scene technicians said they left the scene more than an hour ago.'

Moralès turned around to see Robichaud telling Yves Carle he could go! Moralès waved at him, and slipped his way discreetly into the old mariner's path, covering the phone with his hand.

'Wait a second, monsieur Carle.'

'Excuse me, sergeant, but I have nothing more to say, and my wife is waiting for me.'

On the other end of the phone, Marlène Forest was growing impatient, to say the least. 'Are you listening to me, Moralès?'

The detective flinched. 'Yes, Lieutenant Forest.'

He looked on powerlessly as Robichaud dismissed Yves Carle, shooing him away with the back of his hand. The old mariner breezed off, forgetting to remove the plastic covers encasing his shoes.

'Here at the station, ten minutes from now. Is that clear?' She hung up.

Moralès began to check his phone, but the coroner interrupted him once more.

'I ought to tell you, when I spoke with Chiasson, the notary, I made a note of the heir's name and number – home and work – and you ought to…'

There were three messages from Sarah. Texts.

Robichaud held out a scrap of paper to Moralès. The detective grabbed it with one hand.

'Thank you. I'll call her later.'

'Why not straight away?'

Sarah's messages said that she needed some time. That she had some personal things to take care of. That she might have to delay her arrival. Moralès picked up the box of items bagged by the crime-scene crew. What did she mean, she 'needed some time'? He tossed the box into the boot of his car, the coroner lumbering after him.

'I ought to tell you, sergeant, I can be of use to you. You know, seeing as you're not familiar with the place.'

Joaquin Moralès slid in behind the wheel. His wife had 'some personal things to take care of'? What kind of 'personal things'? He waved to the coroner.

'Thank you for everything, monsieur Robichaud. I have to go, I have an interview to do.'

'An interview? Moralès, you're not going to involve the media in the investigation, are you? It's not like Montreal or Mexico around here, you know. We ought to talk about the implications—'

Moralès started the engine. What did she mean, 'delay' her arrival? Five days of alone time, wasn't that enough? Why did he get the feeling he was being taken for a ride in this whole moving farce?

The end of Robichaud's sentence fell on deaf ears as Moralès drove up the hill, away from the Ruisseau-Leblanc wharf.

Although yesterday, which seemed a long time ago now, he had dreamed of sipping a pale-pink drink beside the waves, the only thing Joaquin Moralès was praying for now, as he pulled up to the police station in Bonaventure, was a paper cup of hot coffee.

'Let me tell you, are you going to take me into a real interview room? Because it's a bit on the warm side in here. Have you got a room with one of those one-way mirrors in it? I swear to tell the whole truth, nothing but the truth, and ... how does the rest of it go, already?'

Following the directions he'd been given at the front desk, Moralès had found Renaud Boissonneau deep in conversation with Lieutenant Forest in an overheated kitchenette with south-facing windows that appeared to have been sealed since the beginning of time. *Now the tables were turned*, thought Moralès, seeing how Lieutenant Forest seemed to be enjoying playing hostess to the man who must have served her lunch every second day for the last twenty summers. The coffee pot was empty, of course.

'Lieutenant, could you show me where my office is, please?'

'Your office, Sergeant Moralès? Ah, yes, well, you see, you weren't supposed to be arriving so soon—'

Suddenly, the kitchenette door behind Moralès burst open.

Renaud Boissonneau immediately lost interest in the two of them, twisting away from Marlène and craning his neck towards the newcomer. 'Oh, well, well, well, look who we have here, if it isn't young Joannie! So, you're a policewoman now, are you? Let me tell you just one thing, you're a sight for sore eyes in your officer's outfit, aren't you!'

With a scowl, Marlène Forest turned to Moralès, whose pupils had dilated momentarily at the sight of the dazzling young recruit's inappropriately unbuttoned neckline.

'Moralès, isn't that your phone ringing?'

'What? Er ... ah, yes!'

Sulking, Marlène wandered off into the depths of the office while Moralès took three steps away to answer the phone.

'Hello?'

'Sergeant Moralès? It's the crime-scene team. We've been waiting for you at Marie Garant's house.'

'*Merde!* I forgot all about you.'

'What shall we do? Should we go inside?'

In the corner of the kitchenette, his back to Moralès, Renaud Boissonneau was in conversation with young Joannie, and seemed to be getting quite carried away.

'Er...' Moralès was still wondering why Robichaud had hesitated yesterday before granting him access to the house. Had the coroner been abusing his power out of sheer pig-headed secretiveness? Was it merely an old man's understandable weariness – or was it something else? It didn't sit right with Moralès, who was keen to see Marie Garant's house for himself before the crime-scene trio traipsed their way in there and wrecked the place.

'The clouds are rolling in and we're fed up of messing around,' the crime-scene tech said.

Boissonneau, the 'key witness' wasn't letting up with the young constable. It appeared he was trying to engage Joannie in a discussion about the bistro's turnover since the last wave of tourists rolled in.

'Er … no,' Moralès said at last.

'What do you mean, no?'

Moralès tiptoed carefully towards the emergency exit. 'Wait there for me,' he said.

The key witness still had his back turned. With a nimble step, Moralès snuck out of the emergency exit and found himself in the car park.

'I'll be there in five minutes.'

The detective found the crime-scene trio waiting in a white van outside Marie Garant's house.

They weren't exactly an enthusiastic bunch. The smell of cold coffee and stale doughnuts hung in the air. They had been waiting for Sergeant Moralès to get there and make up his mind whether or not they were to take prints inside Marie Garant's house. It was a horrible morning too. The heavens had opened and the rain was bucketing down, like a shower curtain enveloping their van. They could barely see the sea at the end of the jetty.

'They say we're in for another rainy summer.'

'You think so?'

'Yep.'

'I think I'll be booking my holidays in September next year.'

'Hmm.'

Finally, an aging Toyota turned into the driveway.

'That him, the new guy?'

'Looks like it.'

'Where's he from, then?'

'Montreal, I think.'

'Did you see him this morning, then?'

'Hmm.'

'What's he look like?'

'Like the rest of them.'

Moralès ducked out of his car and ran through the torrent over to the van. The passenger-side window slid down halfway.

'Got any coveralls I can use?'

'Give him a kit.'

They passed him a crime-scene clothing kit in a sealed bag through the van window.

'I'm going in for a look and I'll come back and get you.'

'As you like.'

Moralès galloped off through the rain to the porch, where he took off his soaking-wet jacket and pulled on the crime-scene suit.

They slid the van window closed.

'Won't find anything.'

'Let him get on with it.'

'Hmm.'

'Not from round here, though, is he?'

'Mexico, maybe.'

'No sign of an accent, though.'

Three sets of shoulders shrugged.

'When did he get here?'

'This week.'

Through the window, they could vaguely see the detective, who had managed to open the door and was entering the house.

'He's a keen one, eh?'

'Hmm.'

'He's just moved here.'

'On his own?'

'His wife's supposed to come and join him.'

'She won't come.'

'Hmm.'

Slowly but surely, beneath the irregular hammering of the deluge, the van windows fogged up.

'Whose place got broken into then, up on Fourth Lane?'

'Fourth Lane? That was Clément's.'

'What did they take?'

'Seems there was some cash in a safe.'

'Hmm.'

'They take the safe as well?'

'No. They took it outside and busted it open.'

'Hmm.'

'How'd they open it?'

'The police found a sledgehammer in the ditch.'

'That right?'

'Vital Bujold's sledgehammer.'

'Wasn't Vital who did it, was it?'

'Don't be daft. You know how Vital is. He lends his tools to folk. So that's that.'

'Hmm.'

'Jeez, though … Who'd he lend his sledgehammer to?'

'Dunno. He won't say. He said he'd tell the police, if they asked him.'

'And?'

'I heard the girl who interviewed him didn't ask.'

'Didn't she?'

'You know Vital. He said you should have seen the rack she was carrying.'

'Rack?'

'Dunno. Her gun, her badge, her baton. Stuff on her belt.'

'Must be that little blonde who questioned him. What's her name again?'

'Joannie.'

'Hmm.'

'Turn the engine, would you? Can't see a thing.'

'Put the heater on.'

The engine ticked over smoothly, and the rain slowed its cadence.

'Look, here's our detective. He's coming out. Hasn't found a thing.'

'What's he doing?'

'He's on the phone.'

'Hmm.'

'Open the window, let's have a look-see.'

They cracked the window open.

'What's he saying?'

'Arguing, he is.'

'Hmm.'

'Having words with his wife. She's got some "personal things" going on, by the sounds of it.'

'She's not coming.'

'Hmm.'

'Doesn't look happy.'

'Hmm.'

'Careful, he's coming over here.'

The rain let up just enough, giving Moralès a chance to rush over to the van.

'So?'

'Forget it. We're not going to find anything here.'

'Hmm.'

'Everything alright, sergeant?'

'Why?'

'No reason.'

'I suppose.'

'Right. Bye, then!'

They slid the window closed. Joaquin Moralès dashed off to his car.

'She's not coming,' they agreed.

And the van pulled out of the driveway.

He hated that. Talking to his wife on work time. Since he'd had a mobile, though, it had been inevitable. Most of his colleagues in the city were overjoyed to hear their beloved's voice in their ear whispering nothings no sweeter than 'Honey, you won't forget to stop in at the shop to pick up a loaf of bread and that DVD I've been wanting to rent, will you?' Moralès, though, was appalled by such habits. He thought it was insensitive to be talking about pints of milk and chick flicks while others in the vicinity were crying and screaming murder. When the gruesome underbelly of humanity was clamouring for your undivided attention, the frivolous things in life should just wait.

He parked in front of the notary's antiquated home, bounded impatiently the length of the overly long veranda and rang the doorbell.

Why had she texted him messages like that? Obviously, he'd had to call her back! But what had that achieved? Nothing – apart from a big fight, and him doing a shoddy job of examining Marie Garant's house. Detective Moralès was still seething when the notary, Chiasson, opened the door and led the way to his office.

He conceded it had been tactless of him to tell his wife it was out of the question for her to delay her arrival because of frivolous 'personal things', but who can be diplomatic when their nose is put out of joint?

And now here he was, facing an old, high-handed notary, who was sticking to his principles and refusing to disclose the will in the heir's absence.

'Monsieur Chiasson, as we speak one of my colleagues at the

Bonaventure police station is trying to track down Catherine Garant
through the use of her bank cards, but it might take a while.'

The notary shook his head firmly.

Sarah had said her husband never took any interest in her – that
he preferred dead women (her words were: 'You'd rather be with a
dead woman, Joaquin!'). After his scathing reply – that sometimes,
dead bodies were not as cold as his own wife, she had hung up on
him.

'You're too hot to trot, Sergeant Moralès, trying to trample all over
the Garant women's privacy by reading the mother's will without the
daughter's permission.'

'Monsieur Chiasson, if you prevent me from reading this will, I
will have to consider whether you are obstructing an active police
investigation.'

Chiasson the notary (and his three chins), to his credit, ruminated
in silence for what must have been a good minute before opening
the top drawer on his right, from which he pulled a sealed envelope.
He certainly took his time about it. Moralès was prepared to wait.

Marie Garant's will was brief. She had bequeathed all her assets
to her daughter, Catherine Garant. There was a letter along with
the will. Oh, how Moralès regretted calling Sarah back during work
hours! He motioned to the notary to open the letter.

Growling like a bear, the notary meticulously slit the envelope
open and read the missive in silence, his chins gradually wrinkling
into wide smiles of deep contentment.

'Why the smiles?' Joaquin Moralès was chomping at the bit.

'No reason. It's your investigation, after all.'

'What is it?'

With a hand as deft as it was pudgy, the notary proffered the letter
to the detective, who was currently more inclined to kill than keep
the peace. 'Nothing. It's just that…' the debonair old man accentu-
ated the gesture with an ironic chuckle '…this isn't a letter, it's a
poem.'

'I'd like to speak with mademoiselle Garant, please.'

'Are you a residential or commercial client?'

'Neither. I'm a police investigator and it's crucial that I speak with mademoiselle Garant.'

'One moment, please, I'll transfer you to monsieur Lapointe.'

Moralès frantically rocked back and forth in Marlène's chair, trying to keep his cool as he contended with the muzak on the line.

His so-called key witness had gone back to the bistro having denounced to Moralès's boss the despicable behaviour of the 'Mexican inspector from Montreal'. Lieutenant Forest had turned a blind eye to the affront, however, only too happy to see said key witness, infatuated as he was by that little blonde firecracker, being given the run-around by a colleague. She had even granted Moralès the temporary use of her office, promising him he could move into his own in a few days' time. The problem was, the retiree whose office Moralès was destined for was taking his time vacating the premises. He was hanging around, chatting in the hallway and emptying the coffee pot instead of gathering up his family photos. Marlène was reluctant to show the indolent dawdler the door, though. It was no secret how depressive retirees had a tendency to turn their guns on themselves, and Lieutenant Forest had no desire for drama on her watch. Moralès told her he understood the situation. None of this would have happened if he had been allowed to move in his own good time. They had made him start too soon, that much was clear, as was the fact that their gears were clogged with sand.

'Paul Lapointe.'

'Sergeant Joaquin Moralès, detective with the SQ in Bonaventure. I'm trying to track down a woman by the name of Catherine Garant. I was told she worked with your firm.'

'Worked is the operative word. Catherine is on leave right now.'

Typical. Moralès had always been suspicious of heirs.

'Will she be back soon?'

'I don't think she'll be coming back at all.'

'Why's that?'

On the other end of the line, the architect laid down his pencil. He was wearing a blue shirt with thin stripes. No tie, no jacket. His sleeves were unbuttoned and rolled up.

'Catherine left us following a series of bereavements. She gathered up her pencils and transferred her files to a colleague. If she ever returns to drawing, I suspect she'll be her own boss. At the moment, though, she's going through some difficult times.'

This reply rubbed Moralès up the wrong way. 'Difficult times'? Who doesn't go through 'difficult times'? Times were difficult for everyone at some point or another – dead people, killers, coworkers, you name it. And what about him? Wasn't he going through 'difficult times' too? It was no reason to bump off members of his family and vanish into thin air, though.

'Do you know where I can reach her?'

'Have you called her home number?'

'Obviously.'

'No idea, then.'

The interview had to go on, even though the detective wasn't in the right frame of mind: who did she keep company with, who were her friends, any enemies, how long had she worked there…?

'You said … er … she's been going through some, er, difficult times?'

'Going through what I think is called these days, a quarter-life crisis. Trying to find herself, you know women…'

Moralès sighed, a weary feeling suddenly washing over him. 'Not as well as I used to. You?'

'No, not that well either.'

'Are you married?'

'Marriage hasn't been in fashion for the last forty years, sergeant. Neither has living together. I've loved the same woman for nearly twenty years now, but love isn't the in thing these days. We're a modern couple. We each have our own condo.'

'Are you faithful?'

The architect spun in his chair to face the view of Mount Royal and the cross on the hillside.

'Faithful? What's that supposed to mean?'

'Did you have an affair with Catherine?'

'I wish I could say I had.'

'Is she a beautiful woman?'

'Yes.'

'Does she have any, er, particular friends? Lovers? A boyfriend?'

'I'm not quite sure why you're looking for Catherine, and perhaps what I'm about to tell you will have no bearing on your investigation…'

The light at the corner of Saint-Laurent Boulevard turned green.

'…But three and a half years ago, one of my employees lost her mother. Isabelle Arcand is her name. She's my secretary. She's young, barely twenty-five, but she's competent.'

'Pretty?'

'Very. Blonde, with curves in all the right places. Let's not get caught up in stereotypes, sergeant, but my clients are mostly men and they appreciate the sight of a beautiful woman when they walk into an office. It's only natural. That's not to say I'd hire a halfwit. Isabelle does her job well. But as I'm sure you know, if you have two young, beautiful women in the same office, they tend to bare their claws.'

Moralès recalled the catty smirk on Marlène's face when she told him how Vital had rubbed the new recruit up the wrong way.

'So, Catherine hated her?'

'It's not that they hated each other, they were just staking out their territory.'

'Was Catherine jealous because you had a relationship with Isabelle?'

'No.'

'I'm not sure I see what you're getting at, then.'

'When Isabelle lost her mother, she cluttered her place full of all the things she inherited – trinkets, china, photos, books, you know the kind of thing I mean. All the junk a mother can leave behind to weigh you down. Isabelle took it all. It's understandable, she's an only child and didn't want to see it all go to some random stranger. She filled her two-bedroom apartment to bursting.'

On the other side of the window, two nursery nurses were herding a procession of children in yellow bibs. On their way back from the park. The day was nearly done. Lapointe waited for them to pass before he continued.

'You know, sergeant, some say young people are looking for love, while others say it's freedom they're seeking. If you want my opinion, it's all a load of rubbish. They live a life of adventure, they travel, they party, but when they go home at the end of it all, young people just feel alone. Powerless. They'll never say so because they have too much pride, but most of all they just need comforting.'

Joaquin Moralès closed the door. There was a photo of a beige cat pinned to Marlène's bulletin board. His mind started to wander. What about him? Where were his own sons?

'Isabelle's behaviour I could understand. It was Catherine's reaction I couldn't fathom. When she lost her parents, believe it or not, she didn't keep a thing. In the space of a few weeks she sold it all: the house, the garden, the furniture and everything in between. Everything.'

And what about Sarah? Where was she? No, he shouldn't think about Sarah. Or the absent furniture, or the minefield of boxes, arguments and misunderstandings her arrival would bring.

'In a heartbeat it was as if she pulled herself up by the roots, and straightaway fell into the deepest depths. You know what it's like when you're walking down the corridor at the morgue – it's all grey, even the fluorescent lights are suffering, and you have to just keep putting one foot in front of the other in spite of yourself, because sometimes you just have to hit rock bottom. Isabelle went to Catherine's place to talk to her because we knew Catherine had nobody to turn to. No grandparents, uncles, brothers or sisters. Just that Zen, oh-so-Zen white condo of hers. But Catherine just showed her the door. The next week she handed in her resignation.'

Lapointe looked down at his mahogany desk. The letter had sat there for three days before he accepted it.

'I'm only telling you this, sergeant, so you know Catherine isn't on the run. Rather, she's on a quest for something, or perhaps she's taking a holiday. Surely it's only natural for her to want a breath of fresh air. What do you expect she would find here in Montreal? Overheated summer nights, a lifeless living room, burning-hot tarmac, faceless bars and bottles of white rum?'

Three cyclists zoomed by, crossing Saint-Laurent on a yellow light.

And Joaquin, what would he find, alone here in the Gaspé, where they hadn't exactly rolled out the red carpet for him?

'Thank you, monsieur Lapointe, that's all I wanted to know.'

'Sergeant Moralès?'

'Yes?'

'Catherine's no different from anyone else. So most of all, right now, she'll be looking for comfort somewhere.'

Wind drift

I sat in the rocking chair. A wooden chair, bleached white by the salty wind, that would beat time on the deck on a windy night.

In the distance, the indefinite outline of *Pilar* emerged through the thick humidity of the day, perched as she was in dry dock, like a dog with its tail between its legs. I still hadn't plucked up the courage to go down and see her. Was that how it would be for us? Thin, pale bodies drained of life by the sea, lying on the hard summer ground? Was that what we were destined to be – ships out of water?

The sky was clouding over with a promise of weary rain as the sea tumbled pebbles on the shore at my feet with the sound of broken glass and seagulls dropped hard crab carcasses on the rocks to crack them open. Grey and heavy, childless and abandoned by the sun, was the sea nothing but a sealed, silent grave rattling its coral bones?

'Teaching yourself to rock then, are you? Heee…'

'Yes.'

'You getting on alright?'

I didn't answer.

'Looks like you're going at it a bit rough.'

'I was waiting for you, Cyrille, but if you want to be alone, I'll leave you in peace.'

'No. Heee … Stay. Let's go inside the chalet, though. There's damp in the air. Heee … It's going to rain.'

'OK.'

'Want to bring the rocking chair inside?'

'Yes.'

We went inside. Cyrille handed me a wool blanket and I draped it around my shoulders like an old lady before sinking back into the wooden rocker.

'The sky's full of water. Heee…'

A fresh breeze was rattling the bug screens on the windows, seeping its way into the cracks in the chalet walls. Cyrille put the kettle on for tea, then he sat down at the table to crumble his hash into a paper. His movements were slow and deliberate. I found it calming. We weren't in a hurry. Nothing was going to happen, anyway.

It was daytime, but the chalet was bathed in half-light. Cyrille got up, poured the tea and lit two white candles, which he placed on the table. His breath, the rain, the spray of the waves. He sat back down facing the window. We smoked together.

'Was it her? Was she the woman you weren't spooning with?' I asked.

The raindrops began to fall with little delicacy, flattening on contact with the wooden veranda, the shore and the water's surface. The sea cowered like an animal being whipped by its master.

Cyrille stubbed out the joint in the ashtray and leaned against the back of his chair with a weary sigh. Those hands of his were useless. He drank one last swig of tea and put his mug down on the table, then he stood up and took the ashtray over to the sink to clean it. Cyrille was a thin man. He was swimming in the blue check shirt that was too heavy for the season. It billowed out at the waist where he had tucked it into his trousers. His leather belt had been cinched in a couple of notches. Judging by how the leather was worn, he had lost the weight recently. He put the ashtray back down on the counter. Mesmerised by the window, he walked over and pressed his forehead against the glass.

The water was streaming down the metal roof and into the gullies it had worn between two rows of weather-beaten, sandblasted chrysanthemums.

'That boat … heee … I spent my life waiting for it, you know.'

His whistling breath fogged up the window. From the chalet, all you could see was the top of the mast.

'Heee … Just up there, that's the corner of her deck.'

'Her deck?'

'The wooden house just this side of the Île-aux-Pirates, that's Marie Garant's house.'

He turned to look out to sea, its surface whitewashed by the rain.

'When she left, the first time … heee … I don't know if she was even twenty years old. She had no family left. Her father worked at the shipyard. He was from Brittany originally, and he used to draw boats. When he died, Marie must've been … heee … not much older than eleven or twelve. The English in New Richmond took her mother on as a cleaner, but that was just a ploy because, you know what? Heee … She knew how to draw boats too. Motorboats and sailboats. Her husband taught her everything he knew, and the English had her draw in secret … heee … so it didn't look like they'd hired a lady architect.'

A gentle wave unfurled through the fog.

'Heee … But she died as well, and I swear Marie Garant was still too young to lose her. Eighteen, maybe twenty, she was. She waded her way through the inheritance paperwork all winter, then when spring came, she decided to set sail on a whole different tack. That was in the May. The sun was quite the picture, but the wind didn't do her any favours. Heee … We were out fishing when she left. I saw her sailboat head out to sea, and I couldn't bring myself to wave her off. Don't ask me why. Maybe that's why I remember that day so well, because I never gave her a wave.'

His eyes came alive with iridescent images of the past, embellishing and beautifying his memories.

'Heee … I wasn't very old, love, but my eyes were ripe enough to recognise a beautiful woman when I saw one, believe me! And Marie Garant, she was a sailor to boot! You can't imagine what it was like for a fisherman's son to see such a pretty young lady hoisting sails with her eyes closed. Heee…'

Cyrille ambled back over to the table and pulled out a chair close to me, pointing it slightly outward so he could still see the sea. Tired

though he was, he kept his back straight as he sat down, resting his
hands on his knees like fragile, wrinkled autumn leaves.

'I thought she'd never come back. I reckon anyone who's waited
for a woman would think the same thing. Heee … But it's worse
when the one you love is away at sea.'

His voice was filled with sadness, but there was nothing I could
do for him, given how little I could do for myself.

'I'd be lying to you if I told you I spent five years waiting for her.
Heee … When you're young, you don't know how to be patient, and
you're in too much of a hurry in life, so you don't even realise you're
busy with other things. I just did what all the others were doing. I
learned to ride a bike on the church steps, I pinched liquorice from
old man Sicotte's shop, I kissed my cousins behind my dad's shed
and I reckon I must've gone to school as well to pass the time on
winter days … Heee … I was a teenager. My feet were too big for
my boots, and I thought life was something that would take years
to come about.'

Cyrille stood up. Indecisive, he turned his gaze first towards the
tip of the mast, then to the sink. He picked up the ashtray again from
the counter, placed it on the table, dug his hand in his pocket to fish
out his pot, and then sat back down.

'Heee … aren't you cold, love? You alright?'

'I'm alright.'

'I'm going to roll myself a medicinal one. Want some?'

'No, thanks. I've had enough.'

'My sister never says a word … heee … but she doesn't like me
smoking in the house.'

Like an old soothsayer, he bent over his herbs, rolled his magic
medicine and filled the chalet with the white smoke that reveals what
lies hidden behind closed doors.

'Marie Garant … did she come back, then?'

'Heee … you bet she did! She came back on Saint-Jean-Baptiste
Day, right on time for the national holiday!'

Back then, people would celebrate Saint-Jean-Baptiste Day down there, on the shore. All the girls would slip on their summer jackets and sit on the boats that were all dolled up and decked out for the occasion with bunting of every colour. The men would slip flasks into their jacket pockets and strut around boasting about the first catches of the season, ogling the budding summer beauties and giving them a little swig of moonshine when no one was looking.

There was a promenade of sorts, beside the fish cooler, where tables would be set up in the afternoon for the buffet. The women would make shellfish pâté and strawberry pies while the men stoked makeshift fires for the barbecue. The old curate would say Mass in a cassock that rustled in the wind, and those who were musicians would bring out their instruments. People would dance until late, right there on the wharf.

The day Marie came back, Cyrille said, the village was setting the stage for the Saint-Jean-Baptiste celebrations. Around mid-afternoon, the men were busy cracking open the first bottles of beer when the eldest of the Bernard brothers pointed to the southeast with his left index finger. 'Look, there's a sailboat coming in!' he called. As the sloop drew closer, binoculars were passed from one pair of hands to the next. Such an elegant hull gliding its way towards Caplan at a steady four knots. Could it be *Pilar*? Silence instilled itself in all the fishermen's hearts.

'It must've been four or five years since Marie Garant left, but none of us had forgotten about her. Heee … I say "us," love, because there were three of us boys at home, and all three of us loved only the one woman! Heee … We couldn't speak for the beating of our own hearts, you see!'

She took her time sailing in that afternoon. Around four o'clock, she lowered her mainsail and drew alongside the old wooden wharf flying a handkerchief of a sail from the forestay. It was her, alright. Marie Garant. The men were waiting to help her dock.

'And then … heee … she jumped out onto the wharf.'

The beauty the years had bestowed on Marie Garant, Cyrille was lost for words to describe. Everyone tiptoed over, taking two steps forward and one step back, bashful at having so little to show her for so much.

When Marie Garant came back, the summer she was twenty-three, and set foot on the Ruisseau-Leblanc wharf, the party stopped being about Saint-Jean and became about her homecoming. People said the wharf had been decked out and the bonfire lit just for her. The drink and the lobsters were all for her as well, they said. Even the curate's sermon waxed lyrical about prodigal children and sacrificial lambs, deconstructing Biblical words and infusing them with male enthusiasm; the Baptist's torn voice would have cried for forty days in the desert for her.

Listening to Cyrille, you would have thought the whole village danced to the heartbeat of Marie Garant that summer.

She had money. Where and how had she got her hands on it? Mystery or smuggler's secret, no one really gave a damn. She renovated, repainted and restored glory to the family home. And everyone was falling over themselves to help her.

The men traded their grubby sou'westers for fancy wide ties, even the fishermen. Even the most miserly of amorous suitors would discreetly leave a crab, cod or lobster at her door, sometimes a piece of fruit or two, with a kind note that their mother, sister or cousin had corrected in exchange for some favour that would keep their hands tied for nights on end.

That summer at the fishmonger's they sold lobsters with lace ribbons around the pincers, and the whole village watched its language. The women shortened their skirts a few coquettish fractions of an inch and cast off their loose cotton underwear in favour of skimpy lingerie and colourful corsets. If Cyrille were to be believed, Marie Garant's return had sent ripples of excitement through the village of Caplan, quivering many a thigh and rekindling moans behind parental bedroom doors that were fitted with new locks to keep the prying eyes of overexcited children at bay.

Even after stripping away the superlatives nostalgia tends to bestow upon old flames, it was clear from the sparkle in the fisherman's eye what a beautiful woman Marie Garant had been and how her laugh must have brought fond memories of youth, hope and accomplishment flooding back.

'Did you love her, Cyrille?'

'Heee ... How could I not have loved her?'

Watch over me, Cyrille.

The rain had saturated the air, but the candles gently burned away this humidity. He turned to me. Over my shoulder, the fogged-up window obscured the view of the grounded sailboat, but we knew she was there.

'Why didn't you marry her?'

'Heee ... It was my brother who married her, love. He's the one she chose.'

His brother? Cyrille was my uncle?

'How many children did they have?'

'None. Marie never had a child.'

I lowered my eyes. If he, the old fisherman who had been in love with her, didn't know I existed, who else would?

Cyrille ran a big, heavy hand over the wood of the table as if he were burnishing the patina of time. Then he shook his head and looked at his watch. We had lost track of the time, me more than him. Darkness was falling through the rain, sooner than anticipated, shrouding the chalet in a grey, November-like gloom.

'Heee ... I have to get home for supper, love. My sister will be waiting, and she preaches on at me if I'm late.'

I took a moment to compose myself.

'You live with your sister, Cyrille?'

'Yes. I sold my house last year. Heee ... It was getting to be too much work. My sister's always been a spinster, and she never moved out of our parents' house. Heee ... There's plenty of space for the both of us, and whenever we have cross words, I come down here to the chalet.'

'Want me to put the chair back outside?'

'No, no. Leave it there. Heee … Are you off to Guylaine's?'

'Yes.'

We stepped out onto the veranda. The rain was like a screen before our eyes.

'I think I'll pick up a ready meal at Sicotte's and heat it up at the *auberge*,' I said.

'Tasty stuff, that food at Sicotte's. Even my sister doesn't cook as well as that. Have you tasted their clam chowder? Heee … Try it, and you'll see!'

'OK.'

We walked to the end of the veranda and, just before he ducked through the curtain of rain, he turned to me.

'It's good to love someone, you know. You should try it yourself, love. Heee…'

'We'll see.'

'I might not have married her, heee … but loving Marie Garant, that was my whole life.'

The flow of the current

The next morning, as he was sitting, lopsided, in the cramped, overheated kitchenette at the Bonaventure police station, Joaquin Moralès heard some news that failed to surprise him in the slightest. Only yesterday, the heir had made a withdrawal from the cash machine in the village.

How come, in this village of twelve hundred souls – cemetery included – no one had thought to tell the detective about her? As the sun rose through the fog, the sky blew vast swathes of mist towards him. Surely somebody would have told him if she had a chalet in the area. Unless she was an unknown quantity.

What if she were here as a tourist?

Boissonneau! The interview ... What was the name that 'key witness' of his had mentioned, the big revelation he wanted to share? He would have remembered if her name had been Garant. Moralès grabbed his notebook, flipped back through the numbers he had scribbled down, dug in his pocket for his phone, realised he had left it in the car, dashed outside and bumped into Lieutenant Forest – 'Not running out on us again, are you, Sergeant Moralès?' – found his phone and perspired his way back into the sweltering kitchenette, where he dialled the number for the bistro.

'*Oui, allô?*'

'Monsieur Boissonneau, this is Sergeant Moralès.'

'Let me tell you, sounds like you're a bit out of breath!'

'I was wondering, monsieur Boissonneau – what was the name of the tourist you were telling me about the other night?'

'Ah, well, I'm not sure I know who you're talking about...'

'Of course you do, the girl you wanted me to interview you about.'

'Well, detective, let me tell you, you stood me up good and proper yesterday, getting me to come all the way to the police station for nothing. There I was, trying to find the interview room and the blooming interviewer only went and disappeared on me! So anyway, on the way home, I forgot what it was I wanted to talk to you about! Let me tell you, but I'll be darned if that road doesn't wipe your memory clean like a slate, I kid you not!'

This damned Boissonneau!

'Listen, Renaud, I'm sorry, but you know, in a police investiga-tion, we're often called away to emergencies. You're right, I shouldn't have left in such a hurry. But you have to admit, you weren't exactly in the worst of hands with young Joannie there.'

'I hope you're not suggesting anything…?'

'I'm suggesting nothing. But I do need to know, the woman you wanted to talk to me about, was her name Catherine Garant? Where did you tell me she was staying?'

'Catherine Garant? No, that doesn't ring a bell. And let me tell you, inspector, you know, over the phone … You never know, but someone might have bugged the line, and this is confidential infor-mation we're talking about…'

'That's impossible. I'm right here at the Bonaventure police station. In the kitchen.'

'Ah, but who can prove that? What's to say you're not being held hostage? Maybe me telling you things is putting your life in danger. Well, let me tell you, it's just too risky. You should have just done the interview with me yesterday.'

Sergeant Moralès was going around in circles here like a shark in a giant fishbowl.

'And what if I came to see you at the bistro?'

'Well, inspector, it's not that I wouldn't like that, but running a bistro is a lot of work, you know. So let me tell you, you're going to have to make an appointment.'

'Sorry?'

'Call me back, but not for twenty-four to forty-eight hours, OK? And let me tell you, good luck, alright!' He hung up.

Joaquin Moralès glanced at his watch. Morning had barely broken, and already he was literally boiling in the kitchenette. Marlène must have been in stitches somewhere. He flipped through his notebook again, dialled a number and was swiftly transferred to Paul Lapointe.

'This is Sergeant Moralès. We had a conversation about one of your employees, Catherine Garant.'

'Catherine, yes … I'm glad you called me back, sergeant.'

'Glad? Why?'

'Figure of speech.'

Moralès suspected as much. Who wanted to talk to him these days? Even his wife wasn't picking up the phone! Perhaps she was right. When you're an investigator, maybe you spend more time conversing with the dead than the living. The dead open up without any fuss, whereas the living protect their banal subterfuge to the death. People always had something to hide. That's why Moralès was always on his guard.

'I'd like you to tell me about Catherine Garant. About her parents. You said yesterday they were dead.'

'Yes.'

'Natural causes?'

'Her father was hit by a car and killed two years ago. And her mother died a few months later, of grief. I suppose the grief was natural, yes.'

'When you say her mother, you mean Marie Garant?'

'No, sergeant. I mean Madeleine Laporte.'

Finally, the tangled story was beginning to unravel. Moralès sat down and picked up a pencil.

'I'm not sure I understand.'

'Catherine Garant was adopted.'

'Adopted?'

'It wasn't a legal adoption. More of a guardianship.'

'Through social services?'

Paul Lapointe's secretary stepped discreetly into the office, but he motioned at her to leave, took a deep breath and leaned back in his chair.

'No. The mother arranged it herself. One day, there was a knock on the front door. Madeleine opened the door, and there was a young woman with a baby in her arms who wanted to talk to François. Madeleine's heart was in her mouth. She was infertile, you see, and her first thought was that her husband had gone and made a baby with another woman. You know how quickly women jump to conclusions.'

'Perhaps.'

'Are you married, monsieur Moralès?'

'Yes.'

'Clearly. And faithful?'

'Yes.'

'But your wife is giving you a hard time.'

What was Moralès supposed to say to that?

'You're not answering my question. She must be giving you a hard time, then.'

Moralès turned his chair towards the window. Across the street, the red doors of the Bonaventure church were open to let in the fresh sea air.

'Was he the father?'

'No. Turns out Madeleine had nothing to worry about. François knew Marie Garant from way back when they were kids in the Baie-des-Chaleurs. Marie Garant's mother used to work for his parents, from what I gather. It'd been more than ten years since they'd seen each other, because François' mother moved to Montreal.'

'And he's the one she wanted to look after her baby? *Him?*' Some days Moralès thought he'd seen it all.

'The two of them, yes. She didn't want to put the baby up for adoption. She said that if something happened to the parents, the baby would be sent off to God knows where and she'd lose sight of her. But to all intents and purposes, she handed her over to them for … forever.'

'Forever?'

'That's what she said.'

'And they agreed?'

'Yes. Like I said, Madeleine was infertile. They loved Catherine very much. Like their own daughter.'

'Did Catherine ever see her biological mother again?'

That struck the wrong chord with Paul Lapointe. He didn't like the term 'biological mother'. It made her sound like a birthing machine.

'Not that I know of.'

Moralès thought about his sons. How long had it been since he'd seen them? Two weeks? Boys were different, though. If he had a daughter, he'd want to know where she was, who she was seeing. Boys could be left to their own devices.

'And the father?'

'Which father?'

'Catherine's biological father? Did Marie Garant mention him at all?'

'Not to my knowledge. She had a certificate of baptism when she arrived, but the information was false.'

'False?'

'I'm telling you what I know, sergeant. Only Marie Garant could tell you more.'

'Marie Garant was found dead this week.'

'Ah. And you think Catherine—'

'I don't think anything, monsieur Lapointe. I'm investigating.'

'I see. Have you found Catherine?'

'Not yet.'

'You know, sergeant, if there's one thing that wouldn't surprise me, it's that she was in the Gaspé.'

'You think she'd come looking for her birth mother?'

'Her birth mother? No.'

'Her father?'

'Why would she want to see them?'

'To know who they really are.'

'Do we ever really know our own mothers, detective? Our parents, our children … our wife? Do we even know ourselves?'

'So, what else might have drawn her to the Gaspé?'

Lapointe looked down at his shoes. Stylish. Polished. 'Catherine is a strange woman, sergeant. She was good at her job, but…'

'But?'

'There's something inside her that's too big to be contained. Something insatiable. It's like she's been living life with blinkers on. I was kind of expecting that she'd just get up and leave one day.'

'Monsieur Lapointe?'

'Yes?'

'What was your friend's name – Catherine Garant's father?'

'His name was François Day. He was a great architect.'

Day. *Bingo!* That was the name Boissonneau had mentioned. Catherine Day. And she was staying above the sewing shop!

As I stroked my hand along the hull, my heart caught in my mouth. My mother's sailboat. *Pilar.* So this was how you were going to latch on to me? Without a ladder, there was no way to climb aboard.

I walked into the café and ate breakfast alone. Offshore, Vital was pulling up his traps. Cyrille was nowhere to be found. Even the red-haired waitress had the day off. I kicked back and relaxed for a good long while, waiting for the Indigenous fishermen to return from the sea.

The tide was falling dangerously low when they gunned it through the channel, and I couldn't help but smile. They drew alongside the wharf and docked. Their traps were piled high on deck. One of them backed up a pickup truck, and the show had begun.

The traps started to appear on the wharf, hefted by the strength of Tall, Indigenous Jérémie, who was unloading them all by hand with the kind of astonishing grace possessed by only the strongest of men. Two deckhands took care of the rest, lifting traps and loading them into the back of the truck. There must have been forty in all. Jérémie plucked them out like they were mere punnets of strawberries.

I paid for my breakfast and turned my eyes on him to extend this slovenly morning of mine. Jérémie. I watched him as he worked, enjoying the show of manly strength and opaque silence. When he was done, he pulled off his gloves, his boots, his overalls and the red bandana holding back his long hair. Then, he wiped his hands and waved to me.

I blushed all the way down my neck and meandered off for a walk along the shore.

Three agates. Real ones. I didn't pick them up, though. I took my time making my way back up to the *auberge*, making the walk from the beach as long as I could. Gentle waves were rolling in, and I reflected on how I didn't exist. That was all I could think about. Here I didn't exist, I was nobody and no one expected a thing from me.

But I was mistaken.

When I arrived at the *auberge*, a scene of pandemonium greeted me. All my things had been ruthlessly tossed outside into the parking area. A distraught Renaud was nervously standing guard beside the pile of feminine fabrics as if he thought they were under threat of attack. Father Leblanc was on his knees, picking up garments and clumsily trying to fold them and cram them into my suitcase. Further over, Guylaine was burning something in an old metal drum, cursing all the saints in Heaven.

'What's going on?' I asked.

Renaud was pacing up and down anxiously. 'Let me tell you, it's not like I'm enjoying this, *mam'zelle* Catherine, but really, you shouldn't have.'

I bent down to pick up my scattering of things. 'I shouldn't have what, Renaud?'

'You shouldn't have come asking for Marie Garant! Because let me tell you just one thing, the police don't think it's a laughing matter!'

I drew myself upright, stiff as a crowbar. 'Renaud, did you tell the police investigator I was looking for Marie Garant?'

He flushed red. 'Well … He wanted to interview me, but I told him I couldn't speak. And let me tell you, I didn't tell on you on purpose, but he was fishing – maybe for a suspect!'

'*What?* You said I was a suspect?'

Ashamed of himself, he looked all over the place, not daring to meet my eye. Like a child caught with his hand in the cookie jar.

'He put two and two together for the rest of it, *mam'zelle* Catherine, I swear!'

'You've put me in a hell of a sticky situation, Renaud!'

'Well let me tell you, you shouldn't have lied to us!'

'Lie? When did I lie to you?'

'Let me tell you, then. Your name, is it Catherine Day or Catherine Garant?'

The curate straightened up and, in a show of modesty, stepped aside so I could carry on picking up my clothes. I stuffed big armfuls of my things into my car.

'In truth, we didn't reveal a thing, Catherine. The investigator figured things out for himself and came over to Le Point de Couture to see if you were here. He must be looking for you at the Café du Havre right now. He's sure to come back. So take your things and go!'

'Go where?'

The curate was visibly dejected. Renaud too, but there was no consoling him.

'Let me tell you, though, at least *you* haven't lost anything.'

'Have you lost something, Renaud?'

'No, I haven't. But take a look at Guylaine over there. She's burning your sheets and your towels.'

My whole life was a mess stuffed into the back of a car, and they were incinerating my infested linen in a rusty oil drum.

'In truth, you should get out of here before he comes back!'

There were no two ways about it: things were going from bad to worse for Moralès. The Gaspesian hideaway that was supposed to be something of a semi-retirement love nest was beginning to look more and more like a far-flung bachelor pad.

While he had been on the phone with Paul Lapointe, a call had gone to voicemail: 'Joaquin, I need more time than I thought...'

What was that supposed to mean? What could a man say to that?

He had swung by Le Point de Couture and clearly ruffled Guylaine Leblanc's feathers by talking about Catherine Garant. Then he had gone down to the Café du Havre, only to be told the young woman had just left and was making her way back up to the *auberge*.

'I'm not coming out to join you. Not right now, anyway.'

Moralès felt discouraged. He had agreed to all of it, even the Gaspé, and now she was the one throwing in the towel! What are you supposed to do when your wife jettisons you like that? Try to win her back? He couldn't even remember how to seduce a woman. All that seemed so long ago now, floundering in a whirlwind of time, sleepless nights, suspects and investigations. These days, he spent his time running from one scream and one crime to another. His hands were full, but his arms were empty, his body out of action. At fifty-two years old, how does a man cope when he's lost his way and finds himself scrabbling for breadcrumbs like Hansel without his Gretel, dressed in lovelorn rags? How can you have mapped out your entire future yet still have the unexpected blow up in your face like a landmine?

'Do we even know ourselves?' Lapointe had said. It turned out the architect was right. Moralès could have told Lapointe how he no longer recognised himself, how he felt like an old fool and how Sarah's voice sounded like a stranger's in her cranky voicemail. 'I'm sending you the keys by express post.' The keys were coming. But not her. Where was she?

And what about Marie Garant? What could have driven her to sail so far away, and for all that time? What had she been running away from? What had drawn her daughter to the Gaspé? Good God! What was driving so many women away from their homes and loved ones?

Perhaps that was what Catherine Garant had come looking for: answers. Her adoptive parents had died, and she had given herself permission to come here and put together the pieces of her past. Because you can't always learn to live with unanswered questions. That was something Joaquin knew first-hand. He had become a detective for that very reason, to find answers. But how many cases went unsolved? And what about Sarah?

Moralès was so absorbed, he turned into the driveway of the *auberge* too fast and slammed on the brakes, smothering Renaud and the curate in a dense cloud of gravel dust. It happened so abruptly, the two men, who were stood chatting at the bottom of the steps, thought the detective was going to roll over like a Hollywood cop and pull a gun on them. Frightened to death, Renaud put his hands up as if he'd been caught butchering a corpse with his new kitchen knife.

'Where is she?'

'In truth, you're a bit tetchy now, aren't you?'

'I'm looking for Catherine Garant and I'm being given the run-around!'

'Catherine Garant?'

Buoyed by the curate's aplomb, Renaud awkwardly lowered his hands, trying to cleanse his sullied pride. 'Let me tell you, we've not met anybody by the name of Catherine Garant. No, not recently in any case…'

Moralès had to bite his tongue. Neither Renaud nor the curate were going to give him an easy ride.

'Where's Catherine *Day*, then?'

'Catherine Day … Ah! Let me tell you, you mean the tourist? Nice girl, eh, Father?'

'Polite, in truth.'

'Yes. That she is.'

'Where is she?'

'Let me tell you, I think she's gone.'

'Gone? What do you mean, gone?'

'That's right, she's gone. Let me tell you just one thing, seems you're down on your luck with women, inspector—'

'Detective! I'm a police investigator, not a food inspector!'

'If you're always that tetchy, there's no wonder women won't have anything to do with you!'

Moralès turned away and made to go into the *auberge*, but the two Caplan men quickly blocked the stairs. With their fancy footwork and the way they were jostling their knees, it looked like the three of them were dancing a jig in a pantomime.

'Monsieur Boissonneau, you are obstructing the course of a police investigation!'

'As God's representative and a respected person in this village, I can assure you, Detective Moralès, that I fail to see any way in which monsieur Boissonneau here is obstructing the investigation that's so frustrating you. In truth, one might even say you're obstructing yourself.'

'I'll find her with or without your help! Let me pass! I'm going to bring the crime-scene team in to take prints.'

'In truth, that would be pointless, detective.'

That spelled the end of the kerfuffle.

'Excuse me?'

'Mademoiselle Day was ill.'

'Let me tell you, infected, she was. Infected good and proper!'

'Infected by what?'

'In truth, we don't know. Women's ailments, you see ... But serious enough to warrant not only a hasty departure, but also a complete disinfection of the premises.'

'Let me tell you just one thing, there won't be any more of them germs left!'

'What? You're wiping away the prints of a woman suspected of murder?!'

'Murder?'

'Father, has there been a murder in the village? Who's been assassinated?'

'I don't see how, Renaud…'

Moralès tried one last dodge to get into the *auberge*, but Renaud and the curate stood firm, blocking the steps.

'Inspector, let me tell you, you don't really want to catch them germs, do you? You might get terribly ill—'

'What do you think you're doing? Threatening, intimidating me—'

'My, those are big words, indeed. In truth, above all, we want to protect Guylaine from *your* germs. She's in fragile health, you see, and you're far too worked up for her. We're protecting you too, in truth, because if you go in in such a clumsy, bull-headed way, you might end up finding that you have entered her premises without a warrant. Anyway, are you out here on probation, or is this a permanent posting?'

What could he do? Call the station? Who would come and back him up? Marlène? She'd laugh at him. The crime-scene trio? By the time he convinced those wet blankets to lend a hand, the whole place would be wiped clean.

Suddenly, Moralès decided he'd had enough. Enough of the move, the dodged questions, the fishing tales, the phone calls, the suspects and the Gaspé itself. Enough of Sarah. Enough was enough. As he turned to the sea, his anger turned to weariness and dejection. What had he been chasing? What had been eluding him all this time?

'Oh, my Lord!' Renaud snapped them all back to reality. 'Let me tell you, it's past eleven o'clock already! I should be opening the bistro!' He abandoned the *auberge* as if he were discarding an old dishcloth, and hurried off to the bistro in a fluster.

Father Leblanc took a step closer to Moralès. 'It's not all peace and quiet in the Gaspé, detective. In truth, things don't work the same way they do in the city. You'll get used to it. In the meantime, why don't we have a spot of lunch?'

And Joaquin Moralès acquiesced.

It was a humid midday, and in contrast to the previous day's nasty weather, it was too sunny now. The detective recalled, as they walked over to the bistro, how he hated working in the summertime. Without a word, the two men sat down on the church side of the room. The curate ordered two beers.

Why did you come here again, Joaquin? Wasn't it precisely for this? To let things go, to relax and unwind?

'In truth, I've been wondering, how do Montreal detectives go about tracking down a killer?'

Their ice-cold beers arrived, the bottles dripping beneath their veil of condensation.

'Well let me tell you, is it that different from out here in the country?'

'Renaud, bring us two seafood pizzas, would you? You aren't allergic to seafood are you, Sergeant Moralès?'

'No.'

'Well, this is something you have to taste.'

Taking umbrage, Renaud turned his back with a theatrical sweep of his tea towel, as if he were acting out a permanent dismissal.

'Why do you ask, Father?'

'In truth, it falls on me to preside over funeral ceremonies in this parish. It seems to me that usually the post-mortem report comes back around the same time as the body. Anyway, Marie Garant's body hasn't been returned to Caplan yet, which leads me to believe you're still waiting for the post-mortem report. What's more, you haven't had the time to conduct many extensive interviews, from what I gather—'

'Sounds like you missed your calling, Father. You should have been a detective!'

'I'm telling you all this, monsieur Moralès, because I find your persistent hounding of Guylaine Leblanc and Catherine Day entirely unreasonable. Either wait until you have a proper warrant to scare the living daylights out of them, or do as any smart detective would and leave the women of this village alone for a second instead of accusing them of Heaven knows what and chasing them like a mad dog.'

Moralès opened his mouth, but no words came out. The man had a point. What had made him so sure there had been a murder? Appearances alone seemed to suggest it was an accident. Had his anger towards Sarah made him veer off track? How many times had he reminded rookies not to let personal feelings get in the way of an investigation?

Renaud returned, dumping their pizzas on the table. 'Let me tell you, *bon appétit*, then!' Still sulking, he traipsed his way back behind the counter.

That was precisely the moment Robichaud the coroner chose to stride his way up the steps of the bistro – remarkably nimbly for a man of his weight – and breeze in the door with a spring in his step.

'Coroner Robichaud, do come and join us! Why don't I order us a cheeky glass of red?'

'Now that's an offer I ought not to refuse, Father!'

'Renaud!'

But the lunchtime rush had created quite the whirlwind, and the boss of the bistro, probably tangled up in his silly hat and cook's helper apron, took a moment to come over.

Coroner Robichaud greeted Moralès and pulled up a chair.

'In truth, monsieur Moralès and I were just discussing the investigation. Tell me honestly, what do you think, having brought back the sailboat and all?'

'I ought to tell you, Father, the only verdict we'll end up at is an accident. When I set foot on that boat, the first thing I saw was that the boom was slack, so—'

'Heee … So you're the detective who's come all the way from

Montreal to enlighten us about the circumstances of Marie Garant's death, then?'

Moralès, who hadn't said a word since the coroner arrived, quickly got to his feet and found himself face to face with a tall, gaunt fisherman, who had sidled over so quietly he'd escaped his attention.

'Yes.'

'Sergeant Moralès, I ought to introduce you to Cyrille Bernard, from Caplan.'

Cyrille couldn't give two hoots about the introductions, the curate or the coroner. His eyes were set on Moralès.

'I've been fishing here for years, and there's only one thing I have to say to you, detective. All that is nothing but a rotten pack of lies! Heee … Marie Garant would never have forgotten to secure the boom, and the sea had known her long enough to know better than to whack her on the head!'

'I ought to tell you, Cyrille, no fisherman's tales are going to change the logical course of a meticulous formal investigation.'

'Heee … And I ought to tell you, coroner, you can shove that bloody boom up your great fat arse!'

The sea was beating its shining carpet against the hard clay of the cliffs where the ghostly faces of the shipwrecked were imprinted. Dazzled by the clarity of the sun, goaded by the seagulls' cries and ousted from the *auberge* and my life in the city I might have been, but I wasn't going anywhere without knowing. Before I'd set out on my way to the Gaspé, the doc's orders had been to see things through, do better by myself – and pay attention to my own needs, so there was no way I was leaving here without answers. Where would I go, anyway?

The day before, Cyrille had pointed out the house on the cliff to me, so I didn't hesitate for a second. Peeling out of Guylaine's driveway, I turned right on the main road, right again on the island road, then right again where the gravel formed a T-junction and the road ran along the coast in either direction. Another five hundred metres beneath the canopy of spruce trees and there it was. A wooden house, wrapped on three sides by a veranda. Whiter than white.

Of all the scenarios my childhood fabricated, never did I imagine I would roll up to my mother's place as a fugitive. Out back, I found the window of the sunroom was missing a lock. I managed to open it and straddle my way over the sill and enter without permission.

Here I am *chez toi*, Marie Garant. Breaking in.

I walked around, touching everything, wandering like a stranger trying to make sense of the rooms in the house. No memories of mine were ingrained in the hardwood wainscoting. I had never run up those stairs, never raided the pantry, never fallen asleep atop a mountain of fur coats one Christmas Eve. My childhood memories were pristine, perfect, so why did it pain me to think I had never enjoyed any of the memories the house was conjuring up – memories that had never happened? It was strange to feel nostalgic about something I had never known. An impossible past. A past as dead as that pale woman washed up by the sea. So how come I missed it so fervently? My adoptive family had always been there to fulfil my every need.

In the living room, the walls were plastered with old marine charts. The Gaspé, the East Coast of the States, the Caribbean Sea. A hammock divided the room in two, suspended on the diagonal. In the dining room, there was another hammock, folded and hanging on a hook. Upstairs was the master bedroom. Dusty sailing books, warm clothes, a film of salty mist on the windows, nothing very personal.

The other, smaller, bedroom had been prepared for a child. The drawers harboured surprisingly trivial objects. Shells, pebbles gathered from the beach, fragments of salt-bleached wood. Placeless, dateless objects, now and forever drained of their memories. On the windowsill there were more rocks polished by the sea, more hunks of salty wood. And a rocking chair in the window. A chair that sat waiting, a chair that had been placed there by a man who smiled at a woman, who mustered all his tenderness to bring her here, sit her down, have a child with her perhaps, or want to at least.

I closed the doors upstairs. The hammock would be good enough for me too. I started down the stairs, and that's when I saw it. A photo on the landing. A woman in her forties and a young lady of seventeen or eighteen, in black and white, their backs to the sea. My grandmother and my mother aboard their sailboat, and my face reflected in the glass. Me, Catherine Garant, nose to nose with my own. Three generations of women looking at each other.

I stood for a long while in front of that photo. Outside, the sea was still battering the cliff.

Suddenly, I heard a vehicle approaching. I hurried over to the window to see Cyrille's pickup coming down the gravel driveway. He parked in the shade of the tall trees and moseyed over with a bag in his hand.

'Heee … I thought you might be getting hungry.'

'Aw, have you brought me something to eat, Cyrille?'

'Some bread, coffee, butter and eggs.'

'I'd better plug the fridge in.'

'And then, heee … put a pot of water on the stove, would you? I brought us two lobsters for lunch. You haven't had lunch yet, have you?'

I was lost for words.

'Nobody ever said they didn't eat well under your mother's roof, love!'

I spun around, and he stared at me so hard it hurt.

'How did you know I'd be here?' I asked him.

'I ran into Chiasson the notary. Heee … After that, I went looking for you. Renaud told me Guylaine kicked you out of the *auberge*. I figured you must be here.'

A long silence stretched between us, crisscrossed with so many waves, so many wonderings.

'Heee … let's eat these lobsters before they grow old.'

Cyrille led me into the kitchen. He showed me how to massage a crustacean's forehead before cooking it.

'It makes the meat more tender!' he said.

We ate in the kitchen, windows wide open to the bay below.

'He wants you to go and see him tomorrow. Heee…'

'Who?'

'The notary.'

'Why?'

'Stop wrestling with them pincers, would you! Heee … Here, take the knife and put the pointy end in right there, in the little triangle. Right, now go on, give it a little push and turn it a bit.'

A warm breeze swept into the kitchen, breathing life into the stagnant air.

'Just because you've inherited now, doesn't mean you can butcher a lobster!'

'What?'

'Heee … He told me you'd inherited.'

'Inherited what?'

'The house, love! What else do you want, a space shuttle? Heee … You've inherited a bit of land in the Gaspé.'

I didn't know what to say.

'What are you going to do with it?'

'Dunno.'

I cleared away what was left of the lobster shells and wiped the table down as Cyrille, ever diligent in his habits, rolled himself a joint. We went to sit outside.

'Where do you live?'

'Montreal.'

He chuckled to himself as he exhaled a smoky breath.

'What's so funny?'

'Nothing.' 'It's just that … heee … the Saint Lawrence in your neck of the woods, it's not really a river, it's more of a stream!'

'True.'

'What did your father do for a living?'

'He was an architect.'

He nodded his head, slowly.

'My parents were architects, Cyrille. Both of them.'

'Heee … how so, both of them?'

'Marie Garant left me with them when I was a baby, under their legal guardianship.'

'With the Days' son?'

'Yes. I figure my biological father's probably a man from around here, but I haven't seen any photos of him in the house…'

He took a long drag of the joint before he replied.

'They still alive, your Montreal parents?'

'No.'

'That's why you came, is it? Heee … Your parents died and you found out you were adopted, so you wanted to meet your mother?'

'Not adopted. It was a legal guardianship. And I didn't "find out" about it. I've always known.'

'So you came to meet your mother and she turned up dead. Heee … You must be disappointed.'

I shrugged. Anger and frustration surged through my blood like a dark tide. Yes, it was true. I did come out to the Gaspé to meet my mother, to talk to Marie Garant, and her death was depriving me of it all.

'Not disappointed, mad as hell!'

'No need to be, love. Heee … she was a good person, your mother was.'

'And my father? Who was he?'

He choked on his puff of Mary-Jane, coughed for a good spell and flicked the rest of the joint away. It fizzled out somewhere under the steps of the porch. He waited for two waves to go by, time enough for the sea to keep washing gently over the shore, erasing the memories in the sand.

'Heee … It's … complicated.'

'Why?' Did she sleep around?'

'Your mother wouldn't sleep with just anyone! Heee…'

'OK, so tell me what you know!'

'What did it say on your baptism certificate?'

'Alberto.'

'Heee … Alberto?'

'Was that your brother's name, Cyrille?'

'Does it look like I'm Italian, eh? Course that's not my brother! Heee…'

'Who is it, then?'

'I don't know, do I!'

'Listen, Cyrille … Renaud told me Marie Garant wasn't a popular character in the village. I saw the expression on Vital's face when he brought her body back, and now Guylaine's kicked me out. Sooner or later, somebody's going to have to tell me what happened, instead of making out she was all beauty, sweetness and roses, don't you think?'

Disheartened, he shook his head.

'Why won't you tell me?'

He stood up. 'Heee … I don't think today's a good day for me to be helping you.'

'Not a good day? For who? For you or for me?'

I watched him walk down the steps, stiff as a board, hurting from every drop of his love.

'Cyrille! I'm not leaving the Gaspé without knowing who my father was!'

He hesitated. 'Heee … How old are you, love?'

'Twenty-eight.'

He turned on his heels in anger, stormed off to his truck, got in, and reversed his way back to me. He lowered his window and pitched his parting words at me in anger.

'I can tell your father was an architect! Heee … If he'd been a fisherman, he'd have taught you to be a far better liar!'

He stomped on the accelerator and the truck shot off through the opening in the spruce trees, leaving me cloaked in a shroud of dust.

3

WHARVES AND MOORINGS

Alberto (1974)

Even before he entered the bay of Mont-Louis, he spotted the mast across the breakwater, noticed the sailboat had moved and began to fear the worst. Because, at thirty-three years old, O'Neil Poirier was starting to lose hope of snagging a woman like that in his nets.

It wasn't that he didn't love women – come on, he *was* a mariner! – no, he just didn't know how to talk to them. To sharpen his words, polish his sentences and sand his commas took some delicate tools. And slipping his hand around the fair curves of the female waist required a sculptor's flair – it was an artist's job and he, O'Neil Poirier, had only ever had the courage for painting with water and fishing knives. He was more comfortable shooting the breeze with the sea than with the fairer sex. But with her, it would be more … more natural, that much he was sure about. The woman on the sailboat was different from all the others. Young mothers weren't exactly few and far between, and some of them weren't too shabby either, no sir. But a woman like that, who could sail solo, whose waters broke at sea, whose umbilical cord he cut with the knife he used to gut cod, was a rare pearl indeed. He wouldn't be letting this one slip away, no sir.

No matter what fair-weather sailor might be the father of her child! He wanted babies of his own, did O'Neil Poirier. Seven, even – all bronzed and beautiful in the summer sun!

He would teach them how to fish, these children of the sea; how to darn the nets, dock the boat, keep the birds at bay.

As he approached the breakwater on this early-September day, the *Alberto* fisherman's heart seemed to float ahead on the swell. Yes, O'Neil Poirier was a man of courage, but he was a sensitive soul too. He had seen the woman on the sailboat was alone, but most of all, he had seen how beautiful she was.

Choosing your moorings (2007)

Cyrille said that sea days didn't tick by like other days, with hands rotating inside a watch casing. Sea days were measured in traps lowered and lifted, in calm mornings and heavy swells, in knots and unexpected fogs. They were stretched out by late departures, hopeful homecomings and severed mooring lines.

'Did Sergeant Moralès find you?'

'No.'

Notary Chiasson, a portly debonair man, nodded his three contented chins. To get to his office, I'd had to turn right, walk all the way along the wooden veranda, skirt the family home and knock at the door of a sunroom.

'He's a troublemaker, like all the rest. I abhor detectives. They want to read wills before the heirs, they ask such indiscreet questions. Digging for eels in the mud.'

He offered me a chair and sat down at his desk with unhurried pomp and circumstance.

'I don't think he has a warrant out for your arrest,' he said.

'Everyone says he's looking for me. If I don't go and see him, it'll look like I'm guilty and I'm trying to hide.'

'Facts are what point the finger at the guilty party, mademoiselle Garant, not appearances.'

He pulled a stack of papers from his desk and proceeded to plod his way through them, reading every meticulous, official word to me, as if to demonstrate he had enjoyed a classical Jesuit education.

I was to sign for my right to inherit left, right and centre, however his chins kept rippling with his excessive notarial blather.

'Count yourself lucky, because certain bequests come with somewhat questionable testamentary requirements, which is not the case here.'

I arched an ironic eyebrow.

'I must admit, it would not have been entirely inappropriate for Marie Garant to foist filial obligations on you.'

'True.'

'On the other hand, some heirs tend to entangle themselves in the most peculiar personal resolutions, purporting their mother or father would have wanted them to do this or do that. You don't have any of that to worry about either.'

'Right.'

Finally, he handed me the papers.

'Sign here, and here. Initial here and sign there. The investigation should be over soon. The boat will be yours to do what you want with once they've removed the seals.'

I signed it all and put down the pen.

'Monsieur Chiasson? Do you know where I can find my father?'

Taken aback, he opened his mouth, leaving all three chins dangling in midair.

'Excuse me?'

'Marie Garant was married to Cyrille Bernard's brother. Do you know where I can find him?'

'Have you spoken to Cyrille?'

'A little…'

Seemingly in an attempt to be reassuring, he stood, wobbled around the stacks of papers on his solid old desk and perched one pudgy buttock on a well-worn and obliging corner that was clearly accustomed to such use.

'Mademoiselle Garant … I doubt Lucien Bernard was your progenitor. Cyrille is a good friend of mine, and I would rather he tell you the story. Otherwise…' He picked up a piece of paper and wrote something. '…You could pay Yves Carle a visit, perhaps.'

'Yves Carle? Who's he?'

'You should, actually.'

'Why?'

He lowered his head in reflection and his chins rippled like an ocean swell. 'When he heard of your mother's death, Yves Carle went looking for her sailboat. He's the one who found it.'

'And?'

Frowning over the rim of his spectacles, he implied with his eyes that this should be blindingly obvious. 'Listen … I believe there is a law at sea that prescribes whomever finds an abandoned sailboat gets to keep it.'

'He wants to keep it?'

'Yves Carle is a great sailor. He loved Marie Garant too much, and he has far too much respect for *Pilar* to do such a thing.'

'He loved Marie Garant *too much*?'

'I spoke to him this morning. Go and see him. I've written his address here for you.'

He handed me the piece of paper, together with an envelope that was lying on his desk. An envelope with a broken seal and my name on it, written with a careful hand.

'I had to open it; the detective insisted I make a copy he could requisition. I'm sorry.'

I took the envelope, stood and slipped it into my bag.

'Thank you for everything, monsieur Chiasson.'

He escorted me to the door graciously and bid me farewell with a wink and a generous expression of triple-chinned bonhomie.

'You do look like your mother, mademoiselle Garant!'

'Is that a compliment?'

'She would have said the same thing.'

Empty-handed, but with a bag brimming with papers, I drifted my way back along the overly long veranda towards the sea.

I stopped by the chalet, but Cyrille wasn't there. I figured the old fisherman might not have wanted to answer my questions today anyway.

Tall, Indigenous Jérémie was strapping traps down in the bed of his truck. He was wearing big, bright-orange overalls. He looked me in the eyes. The afternoon was drawing to a close.

I hesitated, then I dug inside my bag and pulled out the paper from the notary. Yves Carle. How did he fit into this story of mine? I read the address and drove eastward.

The sailor lived in an old house with a sloping roof like Marie Garant's and a veranda overlooking the sea with gentle ease. I left the car at the top of the driveway, by the road, not wanting to impose by driving in under the trees.

To the right, near the shed, a woman in her sixties was repotting some indoor plants. She turned her red hat and gentle, friendly face towards me.

'Are you Marie Garant's daughter?'

'If you like.'

Carefully, she looked me up and down.

'Like it or not, you look too much like her to say any different.'

She removed a glove and extended a wrinkled hand. 'My condolences, mademoiselle.'

Slowly, I took her hand in mine. It was the first time anyone had offered me their condolences for Marie Garant's passing, and suddenly it dawned on me that her death was a concern of mine.

'Did you know her?'

'Oh, I'm not sure anybody really knew Marie Garant.'

'I would love it if someone told me about her.'

'Oh, don't worry, everyone will want to talk to you about her. But the less people know, the more they make up.'

She gave me a wink and pointed to the sea's edge with her potting trowel. 'Yves is down on the boat.'

Down at the end of the property, a solitary dock pointed out to sea.
I saw a sailboat moored alongside it. I made my way down to the
dock. The Yves in question was standing in the cockpit, working a
winch. White hair, blue eyes, broad hands. Concentrating hard on
a painstaking task.

For a moment, neither of us said a word. Having spent a lot of
time around boats, I knew it was a bad idea to bother a sailor while
he was working on his boat. Without lifting his gaze, he pitched
words towards me the way you'd dump a bag of dirty laundry on the
basement floor.

'*Pilar*, she's an Alberg 30. 1970. She's no spring chicken, but she's a
solid boat. Easy to sell on, especially as Marie Garant reconditioned
everything on board over the last few years. The Awlgrip paint on
the hull, the engine, sails, winches, electronics, none of it's more than
two or three years old.'

'Sell her? Why?'

He raised his head, looked me up and down. Cyrille had given me
the same treatment. I didn't budge.

'Are you a sailor, Catherine Garant?'

'I sailed when I was young. My father was François Day, from
New Richmond.'

His eyes wrinkled with interest. 'Henri's son? So you're Henri
Day's granddaughter by adoption?'

'By adoption, yes.'

There was no way any sailor in these parts couldn't have heard of
my grandfather. He was a naval architect and a heavy-weather sailor,
the kind who relished a big storm. One day, he went out to sea and
never returned. His wife took their son, François, to Montreal to
keep him away from the water.

'My father always had a sailboat. We used to sail Lake Champlain.
He sold it in the end.'

'You didn't buy it?'

No, I didn't. 'I should have, but the guy I was living with hated
sailing.'

'So, you want to take *Pilar* and put her on a lake?'

Neither yes nor no. 'I've never sailed on the sea. I'm not sure I'm cut out for it.'

He looked disappointed. 'Only you can be the judge of that.' He crouched down, almost poking his nose into the winch.

'Where can I go with a boat like that?'

He nodded to the east. 'Head that way and you can sail around the world if you like.'

I didn't really know what I was doing here. 'Thank you for bringing *Pilar* back for me.'

He shrugged. He wasn't leaving me much choice, but still I was hesitant to leave.

'And you, Yves Carle? Have you been around the world?'

'Why do you want to know?'

'The notary told me you liked to sail.'

He wound the mechanism. 'What does he know about that? He's the only man in the Gaspé who doesn't like fish!'

That made me smile. I started laughing. 'What's wrong with your winch?' I asked.

'Nothing. I'm just giving it a good greasing now to save an old man some elbow grease.' He looked up and gave me a gentle smile. Finally. These Gaspesians, you had to win them over one by one.

'We lived in Percé when I was young. My father had two old fishing boats. We used to ferry people over to Bonaventure Island, so I was a boatman for him. I bought my first sailboat when I was about thirty.'

'What kind of boat was it?'

'A Jeannot 25. Three years I kept her.' With his screwdriver he gestured vaguely at the cockpit, the mast, the deck. The whole boat. 'After that, I bought my Beneteau.'

'And what'll the next one be?'

'The next one? I'm sixty-eight years old. The next one's going to be a flying carpet.' He fiddled a bit more with the winch. 'A couple of years ago, I made the crossing over to the Magdalen Islands. I've never been any further.'

'Why not?'

He sighed, as if I wasn't catching on fast enough or life was too much to bear. 'I was twenty-two when I got married.'

The water was whispering between the pilings of the dock.

'Did you meet my wife on your way down here?'

'Yes.'

'She never did like sailing.'

Barely a ripple.

'I said to myself I'd leave anyway, when I retired, but two years before that they gave me a triple heart bypass.'

'And what about now?'

He looked at the winch, his hands useless.

'I would've had to have done it long ago, if I was to do it at all. I could have, though. I could've gone somewhere warm and fixed boat engines. If you're handy, you can go anywhere. I'd have needed a reason to make up my mind. Or a woman…'

'And now it's too late?'

He pretended to fiddle with the winch, but I could see he was done. 'Yes. There's an age for leaving, you know. If you don't go during the age of adventure, you're never going to go.'

A subtle swish, a gentle wave against the hull.

'If I'd gone, I'd have never come back. So I ended up staying.'

'Why? For your wife?'

He hesitated. 'Do you have children, Catherine?'

'No. Do you?'

He stared at me for a few seconds, fire in his eyes. Then he looked away. 'Two. And my eldest has a daughter. I'm a grandfather.'

Yves Carle finally let go of his winch and leaned against the companionway, turning his gaze southeast to where it could all have been possible.

'Her name is Camille. I was the one who gave her her first bicycle. I put a bell on there for her and Thérèse put some colourful streamers on the handlebar ends. When she comes here, she spends all night riding around the yard with her bell and her streamers. The last couple of years, she's been coming out on the boat with her dad and me. Last year, we took her out around Bonaventure Island. Takes three days from here.'

Every sentence he placed gently on the dock, one by one.

'She's eight years old, Camille. When she comes over, she leaves finger marks all over the place and it always takes a couple of hours for us to decide to wipe them off.'

He turned to me, the deep-blue water in his eyes spreading to my sky-blue irises. 'Our true moorings, Catherine, they're not made of nylon. And we can't cast them off.'

'That never stopped my mother from leaving.'

He lowered his eyes, trying to busy himself elsewhere. Remembering the winch, he closed it up. He put his tools away in a small box, wiped his hands and motioned for me to come aboard. 'Come on, let's have a little chat.'

I checked my soles, grabbed hold of the shroud and climbed aboard. I knew he was watching me and I didn't want to put a foot wrong with a rookie mistake like tripping on the lifeline or getting tangled in the genoa sheets.

I sat in the cockpit while he stowed the toolbox in the cabin, and that was where, from below deck and with his back to me, he opened my Pandora's Box.

'Do you know why Marie kept fixing up *Pilar* instead of buying a new sailboat?'

'No.'

'It was a lot of money to pour into an old sailboat. Do you have any inkling why she cared so much about that boat?'

'No…'

He turned back to look at me. 'Because she gave birth to you aboard.'

The water fell silent.

'How do you know that?'

He shrugged. 'It's not hard to figure out. Either she was here, or she was at sea. No one knew she was pregnant. She must have given birth to you in secret.'

He climbed back up to the cockpit and sat down across from me. A few ripples passed, without me counting them.

'Have you been aboard *Pilar*, Catherine?'

'Not yet.'

'She's an Alberg 30. Those boats have a skipper's cabin in the bow, but there's no berth in the stern. That means Marie was expecting a sailing companion and had *Pilar* fitted out especially.'

'Maybe she had a lover…'

'If you have a lover, you both sleep in the same bed, don't you? You build a separate berth for visitors. Or for your daughter.'

'But she never invited me!'

'No. And I've never had the courage to sail off into the sunset. But that doesn't mean I haven't dreamed of it every day of my life.'

The creases on the water were ironing themselves out.

'What are you going to do with *Pilar*?'

'I'm going to start by putting her back in the water.'

'Well, a car park's no place for a boat, that's for sure.' He stood up. 'Want a beer?'

'What time is it?'

'I asked you first.'

'OK, then.'

He disappeared below deck again and passed two cans up to me. 'I've got some old lines to coil. Mind if I do that while we chat?'

'No.'

He threw a tangle of ropes up to the cockpit as I opened the beers, then he came back up on deck. 'I changed everything yesterday. Halyards, painters, sheets, the lot. Might as well do it all at once.'

'Are you going to throw these ones away?'

'No. You can always find a use for old rope on a boat.'

We coiled his lines as we drank our beers.

'She really knew how to sail, did your mother. She went a long way with her *Pilar*, you know. She always went off wherever it was warm. I think she even went across to the Canaries. Whenever I saw

Marie hoisting her sails, I would sail out a little way with her to keep her company, then I'd sail back home again.'

He placed a coil on the deck and took a swig of his beer. 'You're disappointed. You came here looking for a grand sailor and all you found was a grandfather.'

'If I'd found a man like that somewhere else, Yves, the sea might not have called my name so much.'

'The sea's calling, then, is it?'

I was coiling a halyard in my left hand. 'I can't see any reason for me to stay.'

'The more you put it off, Catherine Garant, the less you're going to leave.'

'If I leave, Yves Carle, I won't be putting it off for long.'

He nodded.

'Do you know the route my mother used to take?'

'No. It must be in the memory of her GPS, but the detective took that away. He took the GPS, her logbook and her memories. His team put it all in a box and he chucked the box into the boot of his car like a case of empty beer bottles. A dead woman's things, can you imagine?'

'I'd rather not.'

'You're going to have to find your own way, then.'

'We'll see.'

We finished coiling the ropes. Yves Carle tied off the coils and stowed them in the rear bin. The blue-eyed sailor leaned down into the cabin, tossed the empty cans into the sink and stepped out onto the catwalk. I followed, ready to disembark.

'When do you get the sailboat back, then?'

'I don't know. I'll have to wait until the investigation is over. The notary thinks they're going to lift the seals soon.'

Suddenly he seemed serious, preoccupied, almost ill at ease. 'The detective from the city thinks the boom whacked her on the back of the head and sent her overboard. They must be waiting for the autopsy report to confirm the theory it was an accident.'

'I didn't know that.'

He hopped onto the dock and offered me his hand. I took it and disembarked.

'Yves?'

'Yes?'

'I'm going to need your help, down at the Ruisseau-Leblanc wharf. Early one morning. Can you come?'

'I'll be there.'

We walked along the dock in silence.

'Catherine…'

'Yes?'

'That's not how your mother died.'

The sea was glassy calm.

'I'll explain when we go to the sailboat. If you want to know.'

'Yes. When we go to the sailboat, I'll want to know.'

Thérèse must have finished repotting her plants. I didn't see another soul as I walked back to my car.

To say Detective Moralès was drunk when he got home would have been something of an understatement. He must have been at least three sheets to the wind, and – in truth – it was all the doing of Father Leblanc, who had found in Joaquin the charitable soul of a fair-weather drinker whose generosity could easily be milked for a few rounds of drinks, all for the love of women and the Good Lord. The old coroner had also been complicit in their little drinking session by willingly accepting – I ought to thank you – a few generous glasses from, you guessed it, our priceless friend Renaud Boissonneau who – let me tell you – found the inspector was far more amenable with a drink or two under his belt!

It was already getting a little late for dinner when Moralès rolled in, driving his scandalously swaying car into the cedar thicket at the top of his driveway. Jolted by the sight of the trees, he wisely left his car to settle into its new home for the night and continued on foot, stumbling his way through the nettles.

He opened the door, tossed his jacket onto the first stack of moving boxes and patted his pockets. Where the heck was his mobile? He had to call Sarah. Right now. He was going to tell that little minx of a wife of his to put a stop to her charade and get herself down here to the Gaspé. That's right! He left the house, stumbled through the nettles again, found the car, groped around, found nothing. Then he remembered, the phone must be in his jacket pocket.

But where had he put that damned jacket?

The question demanded some thought. He knew he'd seen it somewhere … Joaquin Moralès teetered his way back into the house, found the jacket draped over the stack of boxes in the hallway and, suddenly struck by a flash of genius, thought it might be better to take a shower and gather his thoughts before calling his wife.

He undressed and stepped into the warm stream of water. Was it the drink talking, the heat of the night, or the long caresses of the water sliding over his skin? He found himself getting aroused. Sarah had been sleeping in the other room for months. Months! When he had slipped that into the conversation with the curate, the man of the cloth had emphatically agreed – it just wasn't on. He had even asked for another non-denominational glass of wine to wash away the taste. The coroner had then chipped in and said a woman had to be willing! At that point, Renaud had stuttered and refilled their glasses.

Thus, they all agreed – including Joaquin Moralès himself – that enough was enough. When she was younger, Sarah's warm body used to brim with urgent desire. Surely their wires had just become crossed. Perhaps that dormant desire simply needed to be reawakened.

Joaquin stepped out of the shower, naked in anticipation, like Adam in front of Eve, and hardly towelled himself off at all before taking the phone into the bedroom to call his better half, his voice hoarse, his body tense. Apparently there were couples who did it over the phone … So why not them? He wanted nothing more than to feel desired by a woman – his woman, his wife – and to hear the moans of love. And to come. To come in the beckoning Gaspesian night, to come in time with the frenzied waves rolling in on the horizon.

With one hand, his call; from Longueuil, her response. Why can't we let go of our stiff upper lip and embrace the curved path of desire for once?

Whereas he had fantasised about them whispering sweet nothings and panting each other's names in husky voices, poor Joaquin found himself instead fielding a barrage of 'What are you trying to tell me?', 'Think that's funny, do you?' and 'Will you stop that, I'm trying to talk to you!' Thus began the conjugal conjugations of 'You've never understood me!', 'You never understand me!' and 'You'll never understand me!' The kind of words that snagged in the creases of the bed sheets and shrivelled a man's desire. Like it or not, the familiar ripostes of a lovers' tiff were an easy cliché – long-lasting and thick-skinned.

As Sarah elaborated on the concerns she'd had over the last few days, at last explaining her reasons for delaying her departure and uttering the name of Jean-Paul Lemire, Moralès sprang out of bed, pulled on a pair of jeans and went down to the living room.

'…Because Jean-Paul said they loved my work, how the contrast between the heaviness of the cables and the lightness of the structures suggests both the perpetual impossibility of our escape and our eternal desire for it…'

He just remembered he'd put a bottle of white in the fridge yesterday.

'Are you listening to me?'

'Of course, darling.'

He opened the fridge, looked at the bottle, hesitated, closed the door again. He regretted it. He regretted calling her, he regretted his lonely bachelor soirée, he regretted his lost desire, he regretted all of it.

'Jean-Paul said I really should meet these art collectors.'

Why, at the turn of their fifties, did women who had always seemed so happy, easy-going and faithful harbour such a desire to become artists? To feel fulfilled? Was he really all that fulfilled himself?

'So, I'm going to have to stay here a little while longer, you see.'

'With Jean-Paul. Yes, darling, I get the picture.'

'It's not what you think, Joaquin! I'm going to have to take a step back and rethink my whole career, open up to the international side of things. I'm also going to have to pay a visit to—'

'His bedroom?'

'Please don't be so petty.'

'Petty? Sarah, you've been sleeping in the spare room for months on the pretext—'

'That has nothing to do with Jean-Paul and you know it! I told you, Joaquin, I have to channel my libido into creative energy and—'

'And where am I supposed to channel mine? Maybe you can ask your beloved Jay-Pee and see if he has a theory about that.'

Why did it have to end on that note? When he'd called Sarah, he had been so tipsy and turned on. What had he been hoping for, exactly? A steamy chat, that's what! And she could have at least made an effort! She could have thrown caution to the wind for a second too, couldn't she? Instead, he'd ended up with an earful of … What had happened to them for things to come to this?

'Listen, Joaquin, it's all sorted. The kids are going to help me with the movers.'

'It's not the furniture I want, Sarah, it's you! Listen, is there no way you can organise things from a distance? Your agent could—'

'He's not my agent, Joaquin, he's the gallery owner.'

'Jay-bloody-Pee.'

'I know you don't like him, but he does a great job.'

'He just wants to put his hand up your skirt!'

'Joaquin, you're insulting my art!'

'You've been insulting our relationship for months, Sarah.'

That was when the doorbell rang.

'Expecting a visitor this evening, Joaquin? Not exactly twiddling your thumbs out there, are you?'

'Don't be ridiculous! I—'

She hung up.

He yanked the door open, half-naked, hair sticking up, fire in his eyes.

When Detective Moralès opened the door, I took two steps back.

'YES?'

He looked furious.

'How … how do you do?'

'What do you want?'

'Are you Detective Moralès?'

'Yes.'

'I'm the woman you're looking for.'

He froze and looked me straight in the eye. 'Excuse me?'

'I'm Catherine Garant.'

Sometimes, the unexpected just happened.

'Er, who told you I lived here?'

'This is the Gaspé, monsieur Moralès. If you're looking for ano-nymity, you'd better move somewhere else.'

'Yes. I, er, you're right. Come in. It's a real mess, but do come in. Excuse me, er, I just got out of the shower, and…'

He shuffled off clumsily to put on a shirt. He smoothed his hair down as he tottered his way back.

'I hear you've been looking for me all over the place. I'm not guilty of anything. I came to let you know.'

He took a deep breath, clearly uncomfortable. It looked to me like he'd been drinking.

'Yes, I've been looking for you. I wanted to see you, of course, because your mother died in mysterious circumstances and you're her heir.' He weighed his words, one by one, as if reluctant to hold them out to me. 'What's more, you don't live in the Gaspé. So, what did you, er, Catherine Garant, why did you come here?'

Standing in the doorway of a living room chock-full of boxes, I guessed it was an appropriate question.

'I came to the Gaspé hoping to meet Marie Garant. I said so to Renaud Boissonneau, the day I arrived. He told me she wasn't well liked, so I didn't push it. It's a small village, and I was hoping to run into her by chance. I would have rather seen her alive, believe me.'

'Why did you want to meet her?'

'What a strange question. I never knew my mother. I wanted to talk to her at least once in my life.'

Joaquin Moralès lost his balance, stumbled to one side.

'Are you alright, monsieur Moralès?'

'Yes, yes…'

Gathering his befuddled dignity, he circumnavigated the gaping boxes and leaned pensively on the mantlepiece, the way Sherlock Holmes might have done back in the day, tot of whisky in hand, in an English drawing room with red damask curtains at the window. That said, the obvious and messy signs of someone who'd just moved in stripped away any dignity the scene might have had.

'For now, the most likely theory is that it was an accident.'

I thought about Yves Carle's parting words to me.

'I heard Marie Garant knew the sea far too well to have an accident.'

'That's a naive way to look at it. What does that mean, to know the sea? It's just village gossip. This is a police investigation. The victim had a mark on the back of her neck, probably due to an impact from the boom of the mainsail, as I'm sure the autopsy will corroborate.'

I could tell he was trying to get a handle on the sailing lingo. Savouring every word like an exotic fruit, endeavouring bravely to sound confident.

'Marie Garant came back from down south, proud of all her nautical miles, but old and tired. She wanted to look her best, strut around when she rolled into the village, but it had been a long day, so she decided to spend the night away from prying eyes and sail the last stretch the next day, so she could dance out onto the wharf with a spring in her step and dazzle all the fishermen with her youthful charm. So, she anchored at the Banc-des-Fous. The forecast was light, she knew the area, and there was no sign of any danger. But she had pushed herself too hard on the trip back – her age was slowly getting the better of her – and she was exhausted. Then along came a rogue wave, and when the boom she hadn't properly secured swung around, she didn't have time to duck. It whacked her on the head, knocked her overboard, she drowned and her body drifted until it snagged in Bujold the fisherman's nets.'

'That's a possibility.'

'The coast guard has no record of a call. Her mobile phone records are clean as well. Nobody knew she was coming home. There are no prints on the boat besides her own. Nothing that could warrant any other theory.'

'Very well. In that case, I suppose there's no point continuing this interview.' I readied myself to leave.

'Unless you have any other clues?'

I had my back to him when he said that.

'Clues?'

'Because obviously, there are other theories. Suicide, murder, you name it. And I'm as wary as a fox of any doe-eyed heiresses who might have drowned their estranged mothers in the bathwater or pushed them in front of a train.'

I stopped in my tracks and turned to look at him, my feathers ruffled. 'Excuse me?'

'Not to mention jealous men. Do you know who your father is?'

'No. Do you?'

'No, I don't either. But Marie Garant may have had a string of lovers.'

Moralès regretted the words as soon as they came out of his mouth. Why say all that? Because he was still feeling frustrated?

'I think you've had too much to drink, detective. I'm going to leave you my mobile number and then I'm going home.'

'No!'

Suddenly, he felt ashamed.

'No…?'

At once, he let go of the mantlepiece and the pompous air rushed out of him like he was a deflating balloon, just an ordinary man with the wind knocked out of his sails.

'Mademoiselle Garant, I … Er…' Sweeping a hand of reconciliation over his face, he took a step towards Catherine. 'I'm very sorry. That was crude of me.'

'And foolish.'

'Yes. In fact, ever since I arrived here, everything has been getting the better of me. The move, the investigation … I, er, I was supposed to take my time unpacking boxes, do some jogging, get settled in, relax a bit, but that's not the way things have panned out.'

'I'm sorry to hear that.'

'I was about to eat some lobster. Are you hungry? We can share it.'

What was he playing at? Was he trying to get his own back on Sarah? Not even. He felt old and he felt like a fool, and he just needed a woman to say yes to him for once. To have dinner with him. To accept his invitation. Was it really that foolish to want to please someone a little? Good God, was it too much to ask?

'I have a nice bottle of white in the fridge…'

I hesitated. Me, Catherine Garant, what was I waiting for, standing there in the doorway? It had been a long time since I'd had a dinner invitation, and yes, deep down inside, I wanted to cast away the orderly solitude of my life, watch a man lay the table for me on the ocean sand and let the night envelop us.

With a tender caress, he slipped the lobster into the boiling water. Ten minutes or so of cooking. We waited almost in silence, before sitting outside on the patio to eat. The sun seemed in no hurry to set and the sea at the foot of the cliff embraced the pebbles with its silky backwash. Joaquin Moralès was a bit drunk, you could tell by the hesitation in the way he walked, but he managed to crack the shell without squirting any of the briny juice on me, and soon he was handing me hunks of lobster meat to savour.

'Where are you from, monsieur Moralès?'

'Mexico.'

For the first time in years, he didn't say Longueuil. Without realising. And still subconsciously, as he busied himself picking apart the lobster, he started talking about the sea, the south, Mexico, the noise, which continued throughout the night, the smells of the city he escaped from as a teenager to a Cancún that was much more pristine than it was today, and where there was not a tourist or luxury hotel in sight. He reminisced about the burning sand beneath your feet, the clear blue water, the sun drying your salt-kissed skin. He recalled how the beautiful bronzed women, their laughter as pure as angel wings, would frolic in the waves, sporting brightly coloured bikinis. You could invite them to join you for an evening tequila and they would dance like magic to the guitars in the street.

As he talked about that sea and the pulsing rhythm of the night, a southern accent seeped into his words. It was an accent he had learned to conceal in the chilly suburb of Longueuil, an accent this seaside soirée was now breathing new life into. He found himself rolling his R's like pebbles in the surf, softening the hard French U into a gentler Oo sound, smoothing his every syllable with a silky Spanish sigh.

The alcohol was loosening him up, subduing the detective in him and reviving the high spirits of a man once accustomed to flinging fancy far and wide beneath the setting sun, catching it again for a whirl on the dance floor, and then laying it down gently on the smooth, flat tablecloth. Such tender, generous gestures.

Shades of blue tinged the twilight, the sky calm with the light of a crescent moon. He proposed a walk on the beach as the swell gently, subtly whispered faraway tales in a foreign tongue.

They wandered for a while in silence, then retraced their steps, climbed the steps back up to the patio. Blowing down from the mountains in the night, a katabatic wind wafted a scent of prickly chlorophyll and damp bark under their noses.

'By the sea, between the cliffs and the trees, there's a mist in the air every morning that blankets the leaves. It's like a veil concealing the face of the coast, like a young bride's shy smile. In Mexico, when the sun came up, sometimes I would just go with the flow and let the wind carry me off without a care in the world, caressing the shore, stroking the sand and breezing back out to sea.'

His voice was so calming, it was like an anchor in the night.

'Was that what you dreamed of?'

'Sorry?'

'Moving to the Gaspé – was that what you dreamed of?'

'Not really…'

'Some say a change of scenery can do the world of good. It's a way to take your worries for a walk.'

'Where to, though? I don't know.'

'Why move, then?'

He shrugged his shoulders. Suddenly, the rest of his life, the last thirty years, flashed before his eyes and he held his breath. How could he explain it to mademoiselle Garant? That, at fifty-two years old, he had renounced his own pleasures? That he had lost the ability to make dreams? That he had been racking up humdrum weeks on a monochrome abacus, watching the regular, mechanical click-clack of time and only rarely asking himself why or to what end? That he had been riding his wife's wave because his own had flattened out and run out of steam? That it had all become a habit and it was just less complicated that way? How could he explain that all he wanted was a quiet life, but that the unavoidable had happened, flown in under the radar, because he hadn't been paying attention, and now there was no stopping it? That he had lost the thread of his wants and needs in the knotted spool of days gone by, that he had no idea how to untangle the complications, and now here he was, lost for words?

He turned to look at her. She was beautiful. The sea air made her look almost vaporous. The humid night had teased her hair into little ringlets, which were brushing against her cheeks, and suddenly it felt like a door was opening, just a fraction, between them. It wasn't just the wine that was going to his head; the sweet scent of the young woman in front of him was, too.

'What about you, Catherine, do you have a dream?'

I hesitated. Me? A dream? Looking out to sea, I asked myself the question. A dream? I stood in silence a good while. At one point, Joaquin Moralès leaned against the railing, and I noticed he was looking at me.

'I don't know what dreams are anymore, monsieur Moralès.'

That's when he did it. He leaned in and kissed me. It was an illogical outcome to this encounter, but there are nights when the unexpected can leave you no room to breathe. And the Gaspé was a breathless kind of place.

My hands outstretched in despair, I screamed out to sea and the brittle glass of my silence shattered into a thousand fragments of colour, spreading across the waves.

'The phone … I can hear the phone.'

'What?'

I still didn't know his first name. 'The phone's ringing.'

A messy kind of silence descended on the patio.

'Excuse me, Catherine, I…'

He went inside the house. I sat facing out to sea, taking the time to breathe. I was looking for some excitement, thirsting to rediscover the salty taste of life.

Snippets of conversation floated my way, of their own volition.

'No, you're not bothering me…'

He murmured words I couldn't help but overhear.

'Your career, yes, I understand.'

More words.

'What about our plans, Sarah? Our relationship?'

Right then, for the first time, I knew I'd leave. I knew that I too would set sail towards the horizon and chart my own course. I stood up, skirted around the house, crossed the lawn and followed the hedge towards the driveway. I was furious. How many more times would I keep doing something I shouldn't?

I bumped into a car in the darkness. As I made my way round it, Yves Carle's words came flooding back to me like a wave I just couldn't ignore. 'He chucked the box into the boot of his car like a case of empty beer bottles!' Without hesitation, I opened the driver's door and pulled the lever to release the boot lid. The cardboard box was still there, forgotten in the heat of the moment.

I lifted the lid. The box was full of objects in waterproof plastic bags. My mother's things. And Marie Garant's fingerprints were still on every one of them. Every one of them bore the marks of her touch.

I took the marine GPS. Before I came here, I would never have thought of that. If someone had asked me what the box of my mother's last worldly belongings would contain, I'd never have said a GPS. But what did I know, when all was said and done? What do we really know about other people, about the mothers who cast us off, the married men who kiss us … about ourselves, even?

And what will there be in my own box? A pair of worn-out shoes, a frayed scarf, a handful of childhood photos engraved in the memory of an indifferent hard drive?

Who'll want to work out my story and retrace my lonesome foot-steps? Who'll be there to gather a box of my things when I die? Who'll be wondering where my final miles took me? Would my prints be untouchable too, ordered, bagged and numbered, or thrown out of a window in rage?

And what about Marie Garant? Did I really want to know her story?

I had to say I did. I needed to know, in fact. I needed to know the route that was surely committed to the memory of that GPS, a red line on the backlit screen. Her final miles had to be lurking within that thing. Secret miles, miles that belonged to her, miles her eyes had seen before she sank between two waves.

I knew that in the eyes of the law, I was about to commit a crime. My hands were clammy when I put the GPS back where I'd found it, closed the lid, and picked up the box, but they weren't shaking. I took the whole lot, not sifting through any of it, and put it in my car. Now Marie Garant's memories belonged to no one but me.

My heart beats to the rhythm of the tide. And I clamber aboard. I clamber aboard, I cast away, hoist my sails and turn my back on the shore.

With my mind at rest, I brought the box home, put it on the dining-room table and went to get some sleep.

Chains, cables, tethers

When he opened the file on the table in the overheated kitchenette at the station, he still hadn't called home, despite Sarah's insisting 'Call me back when I can get a word in edgeways!' before she hung up on him. The fact of the matter was, though, the tide was rising in him as well.

That beige cat pinned to Marlène's bulletin board had creeped him out. All the way out of her office, in fact. Anyway, there were too many people breezing in there wanting an update, too many people looking at him. He'd far rather be in the kitchenette.

Last night, he had kissed another woman, and this morning that was all he could think about.

He opened the file. Staring death in the face, he ran a heavy hand through his hair. Marie Garant. Papers, reports, photos of her spread out across the table.

What if the phone hadn't rung? It would have been ... Adultery? How many years had they been married? Going on thirty. Thirty years of fidelity, hard work, fatherhood and compromise. Because that's what it all felt like, all of a sudden. A compromise. Where had all the joy, the pleasure, the exaltation been? And the freedom? This morning, he felt like he was suffocating and about to blow his top, all at once. Was it guilt? When he closed his eyes, he could picture himself caressing Catherine's skin, her hair beading with sweat, her moans, her sweet, sweet song as she rode his wave ... Did it make him feel guilty? Happy? Fulfilled? Manly? What was harder, searching for a suspect or searching for himself?

The autopsy report was in. Alcohol in her bloodstream, severe head injury, cranial trauma that would have been fatal even if she hadn't gone overboard. Because that's what had happened. She had fallen into the sea. Water in her lungs.

Moralès recalled the expression of contentment on Marie Garant's face. What had she done to be so happy? She had lost her husband, given her daughter away and lived a wayward life. Is that what happiness really was? Laying down your head under a different sky of stars every night? Having no one waiting for you, anywhere? Perhaps women had a gift for happiness. They knew how to live with abandon. Last night…

Last night? Her scent … He had forgotten how different women's scents could be, their curves, their rhythm, the way they moved. Their moist kisses, slim waists … The thought of it all made him feel hazy. It was getting very hot in there.

How strange the people here were, maintaining Marie Garant could never have died by the sea's own hand. All the evidence suggested her death was an accident. He leafed through the autopsy report. It was pointless pursuing the investigation any longer. Who would have wanted to kill her if no one knew she was on her way? There wasn't a single suspect in this whole damned affair! Moralès laughed to himself. Typical. Here he was, investigating the death of a woman who many said was too experienced to have had an accident, who didn't commit suicide and whom no one killed. Fingerprints, forensics report. Medical records. Photocopy of the will. Did Marie Garant know her daughter was waiting here for her? Had they arranged to meet?

Perhaps he should give Lapointe another call. He liked hearing Lapointe talk – his speech was so measured. What had he said the other day, about what Catherine was looking for? Comfort, that was it.

Why had Marie Garant anchored out there? What reason would she have had to stop there? Fatigue? Really? If she was meeting her daughter, why delay her arrival? None of it added up. He was forgetting something. What, though? Something important … A witness? An interview?

His mobile rang. He checked the number. It was Sarah. Joaquin didn't pick up. Delicately, so as not to hurt her feelings, he placed the phone down on the table. Last night, he had kissed a stranger.

It made him feel old. Perhaps he should hand the case over to someone else. Conflict of interest. What would he look like if he owned up to kissing and caressing the heiress and sole suspect in his first investigation in the Gaspé? Like a fool, that's what.

'Sergeant! So, this is where you've been hiding!'

Joaquin nearly had a heart attack.

'We haven't had the pleasure of meeting. I'm Joannie.'

There she was, standing right in front of him, coffee in hand, neckline in inappropriate freefall and hips heaving with all the tools of the trade.

'Er, pleased to meet you.'

'Joannie Robichaud.'

His eyes followed the curves up to her face. 'Robichaud…'

'Yes. I'm the coroner's niece. He said you're doing a good job.'

'Er … Thank you.'

'You're from Montreal, aren't you?'

'Yes.'

She moved closer, perched her left buttock on the edge of the table, her uniform clinging to the curves of her breasts, baton and cuffs at her waist.

'I'd really like to work in Montreal. Here, people are so … You know what I mean, right?'

'No. Er, yes. Yes, I see.'

She shook her blonde hair, and it tumbled over the deep vee in her olive-green neckline. 'Do you think there might be any openings for a detective in Montreal?'

'Well … you have to start at the bottom and work your way up.'

'I've already wrapped up my first investigation, you know!'

'Oh, really?'

How were you supposed to look at a woman like that? Back in the day, he would have known how, but now he felt overwhelmed by such volatile femininity.

'Yes, a B & E, up on Fourth Lane. And you know what?'

'No.'

'The guy did it himself to claim on the insurance!'

'It happens.'

'He was furious when we rubbed his nose in it. The Gaspé's a tough place. Everybody knows everybody else. That's why I want to work in the city, you know. Maybe you could help me?'

Suddenly, he felt the urge to see her again. Catherine Garant. To touch her skin, swelter beneath the burning sun of her gaze, be the rock to her sand, the coral against her salt-coated flesh. He stood up. Quickly. Too quickly, but he didn't care. He smoothed his shirt and stuffed the case file closed under the wide, watchful eyes of the young recruit.

'You'll help me, sergeant, won't you?'

'Goodbye, mademoiselle.'

Moralès knew how to sneak out the back. No way did he want to run into Lieutenant Forest. He slipped out and walked around the side of the building. Where was Catherine? He had her mobile number somewhere…

'Sergeant Moralès! I ought to tell you, you're the one I've been looking for!'

With no time to duck into his car, Joaquin had to face the coroner head-on.

'Good morning, monsieur Robichaud.'

'I ought to tell you, sergeant, Langevin's brought Marie Garant's body back to the funeral home in Caplan, so you must have received the autopsy report.'

'Yes. I was just on my way home to work through it, because I don't have an office here yet.'

Moralès tried to make for his car, but Robichaud stood in his way.

'Work through it? Any inklings of a conclusion?'

'An accident. There were traces of alcohol in her system. A glass of wine, one false move—'

'I can confirm the boom was slack when the sailboat was discovered.'

'Yes, I've read your report.'

'I ought to tell you, I'm happy to see an end to this whole affair at last. In a little village like ours, a woman's death really makes waves.'

'I can see that.'

'I had to insist on the investigation, you see, but I was expecting this to be the conclusion.'

'Very well.'

Moralès made another attempt to escape to his car, but the coroner held fast.

'For the funeral, there are no testamentary dispositions. The Garant girl ought to take care of the arrangements. Do you know where she is?'

'No. Do you?'

'No, but she'll need to be told.'

'I'll take care of it.'

Moralès was quick to step up. Too quick. And the coroner sensed it.

'Have you met her? Easy on the eye, isn't she?'

Now he was the one under interrogation. With his back to the wall. *Play him at his own game*, he thought. *Snake around, dodge, avoid. Outsmart your opponent.*

'I ran into your daughter earlier; Joannie.'

'She's not my daughter, she's my niece!'

'Yes, sorry.'

'I ought to tell you, I don't have any children. Been a bachelor my whole life. But if I'd met a beautiful woman like that, I swear I'd have done my damnedest to make her mine!'

Which woman was he talking about? Joannie? Catherine?

'You know what men these days are lacking?'

'No, coroner, I don't know.'

'Courage! Guts! I ought to tell you, when you're in love, you've got to go for it! Men these days just don't know how to chase women the way they used to!'

'I couldn't agree more.'

Robichaud blinked in surprise at such a candid admission, and Moralès seized his chance to step around the coroner, bid him farewell and get into his car.

Victorious and proud, his heart racing, he drove to the sea front, parked in the pullout overlooking the shore, dug around in his pocket, found the number, took a deep breath and dialled the digits. He crossed his fingers. It was ringing.

'Hello, you've reached Catherine Garant's voicemail. Leave a message.' Beep.

'Catherine, it's … er, Sergeant Moralès. I, er … The case file on the death of your mother, er, Marie Garant, indicates the cause of her death was in fact accidental. I'll be filing my report tomorrow. So, that means you're free to collect your inheritance, if you like. Er, the body's back at the morgue in Caplan now. You can, er, dispose of it as you wish. There. That's all I had to say, er, officially. Feel free to contact me if you need to.'

He hung up. *Ouch.* Like a teenager in love, he felt an itch he couldn't not scratch. He dialled again.

'Hello, you've reached Catherine Garant's voicemail. Leave a message.' Beep.

'Hello, Catherine. It's Joaquin. I'd like to … er, invite you for dinner tonight. At my place. I'm going to make, er, a paella. Around seven. I'll be waiting for you.'

He hung up.

He'd spend the day stocking up at the fishmonger's, getting groceries and picking out wine. Going around in circles. Waiting, wanting. He would shave, look at himself in the mirror. Fifty-two years old, and he hadn't lost his touch, he would tell himself.

Around half past four, his mobile rang again. He checked the number. Marlène Forest. Too bad for the lieutenant. He'd be unplugging for a while. She'd have her report tomorrow. Until then, the crises in the world could damn well wait a few hours.

Because today was all about him plucking up the courage to seduce a woman. His marriage had become a burden, and he was tired of it. Why deprive himself of a breath of fresh air? He was still young and full of energy. He worked out three times a week. He still had what it takes, so why not? After all, wasn't that what his wife was doing?

The doorbell rang and Joaquin Moralès checked his watch. Half past six. She was early, but he was ready. He was looking forward to it. He took all the time in the world. Because paella is not the kind of dish to be hurried.

Moralès had prepared the vegetables, the seafood and the shell-fish. He had turned his nose up at chicken and rabbit in favour of crab, lobster, shrimp, scallops, langoustines and mussels. He put some music on while he made dinner. As he loosened up and his movements grew longer and more flowing, he had found himself singing along with the music. And before he knew it, he was dancing. Joaquin Moralès danced as he cooked, and how he laughed!

He had set the table with the white tablecloth and the best Sunday dishes and silverware he had packed in the first few boxes, because they never got used.

He lit the candles before he opened the door.

'Not returning your phone calls, sergeant?'

'Lieutenant Forest?'

She sniffed the air in the hallway like a bloodhound.

'Mmm, dinner smells good.'

What kind of crazy place was this, where your boss could swing by at all hours and dump a bucket of ice-cold water over your hot date?

'Candles, wine … are you expecting someone?'

'No.'

'You're very romantic, sergeant. And discreet. When is your wife getting here, again?'

She gave him a sly smile. She must have seen him talking to Joannie. What else could it be?

'Are you hoping I'll invite you in for dinner, lieutenant?'

'No. I've already eaten, thanks. I came to tell you, since you haven't deigned to show your face at the station or pick up the phone, that I'll be expecting a full report tomorrow.'

'A report?'

'Your investigation report, Moralès. You *are* still a detective, I suppose, even though you're in love?'

'Yes, of course. It's nearly ready.'

'You have good taste in music.'

'Thank you.'

'Who are you expecting for dinner, Moralès?'

'No one.'

'Tomorrow, my office. I want to see your report. Oh, and Marie Garant's body is back at the morgue in Caplan. We should tell the daughter she can go ahead with the funeral.'

'Don't worry, I'll let her know.'

Moralès glanced at his watch. Almost seven o'clock.

'Do you always announce that kind of news over a candlelit dinner? If Catherine Garant is anything like her mother, I doubt you'll manage to get your hands on her.'

Moralès clenched his jaw. 'See you tomorrow, then, lieutenant.'

She shrugged, giving him a sly smile. 'Until tomorrow, sergeant.'

Joaquin Moralès cursed Marlène Forest as she walked out the door. Because, deep down, he knew she was right. Once she was gone, he watched the minutes of his solitude tick by like the notes of a slow, sad song as his paella went cold. How late could a woman be running? He didn't know anymore. Honestly, after so much excitement, now he just felt … past his best. Was that what your fifties were all about? Being past your best?

Maybe it was all in his head. The whispers, the caresses, the gazing into each other's eyes, the gentle arching of their bodies – all in his head. That night of romance on the beach in the bluish light of the moon on the water – all in his head? In his head: that yearning for her, the passion he thought he needed so much, the warmth of her breath on his skin, and something else too, something he silently dreamed of yet didn't dare admit to himself – a burning desire to be loved.

When nine o'clock came around, he picked up his mobile. Wax from the candles was dripping on the tablecloth.

'Hello?'

'Monsieur Lapointe? It's Joaquin Moralès.'

'Sergeant?'

'No. Not tonight. Anyway, the case is closed. Marie Garant's death was accidental.'

Paul Lapointe looked at his watch and poured himself a glass of port.

'Were you expecting Catherine for dinner?'

'How could you know that?'

'It's that time of the evening when dates turn to disappointment.'

Moralès conceded a few seconds of silence.

'I'm old, and I'm a fool. Especially tonight.'

'What did you make?'

'Paella. My maternal grandmother's recipe. She was Spanish.'

'You know, monsieur Moralès, I've spent my life tracing fine lines, but the curves of a woman defy any pencil. Beauty is unattainable. And we haven't even started talking about love.'

'I've been married thirty years. My sons have flown the nest and we bought a house in the Gaspé, but my wife has been dragging her heels about coming out to join me. Last week I was hopping mad. Tonight, I don't know whether I still want her to come.'

'I know what you mean.'

'How old are you, monsieur Lapointe?'

'The same age as you, monsieur Moralès. Or a little older.'

'Are you still in love?'

'Yes. But I'd be lying if I told you I'd never had my doubts. When a beautiful woman walks into my office and turns her back ever so slightly as she slips off her coat, when you catch a glimpse of her neck in the corner of your eye. I do have my doubts sometimes. But every time my wife slips off her tights, I know that's the pinnacle of grace. Perhaps that's what love is, monsieur Moralès, the grace that carries us beyond any doubt.'

Joaquin thought about Sarah. He *had* loved her.

'That grace must have sailed right past me…'

'Don't pay too much attention to Catherine. Women like her, monsieur Moralès, their horizons are too broad. There's no point insisting.'

'I wake up in the middle of this bomb site here, wondering whether this is really what I dreamed of building.'

'Do we dream the right things? I don't know.'

'She never came.'

'Don't hold it against her. She can't be found guilty of just being herself. No more than any woman can. No woman can be found guilty of a paella that's gone cold. Shame, really. Or perhaps it's for the best.'

4

THE SALT OF THE SEA

Alberto (1974)

The first thing O'Neil Poirier noticed as he rounded the breakwater at dawn was his float, bobbing like the sole remnant of a shipwreck down at the far end of the bay. Worried his heart was going to give out, he gave it some throttle, even though it was never a good idea to gun your way into port. He was relieved to see the sloop was still there, sidled up against the wharf.

O'Neil Poirier left his crew to tie up the *Alberto* and made his way over to the sailboat with a familiar shyness. The woman waved him a grand *Ahoy there, give me a second, I'll hop ashore*. He watched her as she disembarked. That hair, those hands … Summer was on the wane, but he hadn't forgotten a thing about her. When she drew alongside him, she explained it all to him. She had returned the night before and cast off the emergency anchor to moor up at the wharf and bring supplies aboard. It was kind of him to have kept a watchful eye on *Pilar*, thank you. She'd had to leave the sailboat here because of the baby. She hadn't been able to pull up the other anchor, you see, it was far too heavy.

O'Neil Poirier listened in silence as she spoke, stuffing those great, heavy hands in his pockets so he wouldn't get all in a lather. She couldn't be sailing with a newborn, you see, it was too dangerous. He watched the way she moved. How old was she? Thirty? A little younger, perhaps. Her hair was in braids and she'd already regained her petite, youthful figure. She'd had the baby baptised here and taken it to the city. Poirier nodded; she'd probably left the baby with her mother, right, just until she could sail the boat home. He could understand that. With tenderness in his gaze, he smiled. He'd be more than happy to take the both of them in under his roof, right here in Mont-Louis, up on the mountainside. There was plenty of room, even, for more children. She told him the rest of the story. She had spent some time in Quebec City weaning the baby (that was where she had planned to give birth, but the baby came ten days early!). Then she had taken it to Montreal, you see, to a generous family. The guy was an old friend from the Gaspé, apparently. People you could trust. O'Neil Poirier hesitated. Should he go down on one knee? Call her miss? How were you supposed to go about those kinds of propositions? She had rung the doorbell, handed them the baby. His wife couldn't have children of her own, you see, so they said 'yes' right away, bought some nursing bottles, signed the papers. That took Poirier by surprise. You put it up for adoption? he asked. No, no, not for adoption – legal guardianship, she explained. That wasn't as complicated, you see. It was quicker, and that way she could keep an eye on the child, step in if ever something happened to the couple. But that was something she'd rather not think about, she explained.

The skipper of the *Alberto* looked down at the water, his shoulders suddenly feeling heavier. No, he didn't know what she meant.

The woman from the sailboat touched his arm. Her warm little hand on his strong mariner's arm. Thank you, she said. The wind was turning west now, you see, so she had to set sail. He nodded mechanically, like a disoriented puppet, as she jumped aboard her sloop, cast off her mooring lines, hoisted her sails, and ever so slowly disappeared from view.

It wasn't yet ten o'clock when *Pilar* faded into a blur on the horizon. Only then, when the white triangle of her sails vanished from the canvas of his silent eyes, did Poirier realise that his hands were still jammed deep into his pockets and he hadn't had the where-withal to ask for her hand in marriage.

Watertight hulls (2007)

Cyrille said that if we chose the sea, she would espouse us – for better or for worse. He said she would slip the golden ring of the sun on our finger, promise the world to us and stay true to her promise. In a whisper, he told me what a gracious dancer she was, what delights she harboured amidst her folds, yet how stormy a night with her could be, how she might blow her top in fits of watery fury. Disarmed, he confided how harsh and demanding she was, but what a privilege it was to kneel before her at dawn.

There was a dog in front of the double patio-door. A husky-mala-mute-lab cross, something like that; eyes true blue in the too-bright afternoon sunlight. The doorbell tolled a heavy, ominous chime.

It was Langevin, or his brother, who answered. I had no idea which one, as they were twins.

'Mademoiselle Garant! I've been looking forward to meeting you. Chins are wagging about you in the village.'

He looked at me with curiosity. 'Came to the Gaspé to meet your mother then, did you?'

'Yes.'

'You must be disappointed.'

I didn't know what to say.

'Oh, how could I forget? My condolences.'

'Thank you.'

I was compelled to fall into step with him.

'This here's the visitation room, but follow me and we'll have a chat in my office. Here, sit yourself down.'

Cosy armchairs, boxes of tissues, a painting on the wall (silk flowers in an auspicious halo of light) and a framed photo of the twins behind his desk, tripling his presence in the narrow beige-and-black room.

'My brother got back last night with your mother's body. I suppose you're fortunate in your misfortune. The autopsy lab in Montreal must've taken a shine to us, because they fast-tracked it, knowing we'd come so far. My brother spent the night in town to be accommodating.'

What was I supposed to say to that?

'We figured you'd surely want to see your mother, so my brother's fixing her up a bit. He must be nearly done.'

'I'm not sure if—'

'Don't you worry, he'll doll her up nicely for you.'

'I don't want to have her embalmed.'

'He's not embalming her! No, no. He's just making the body pre-sentable again, because it's not pretty when they come back from the autopsy, and we wouldn't want you to be disappointed. Especially as you'll only get to see her the once! So, you don't want the embalming then? You're sure?'

'I'm sure.'

'Perfect. In any case, everyone who has their loved ones embalmed, do you know what they say when they see them? They say they don't look like themselves! Of course they don't! The last time they saw them, they were alive! I know the trick, though. When they come in, I say a prayer. It calms them down, then they say their loved ones look at peace! But really, they're the ones who are at peace! The dead are just dead. You, though, since you never knew her, you can't really say if she looks like herself, can you?'

'No.'

'We're going to skip the embalming, then?'

'Yes.'

'We do have a vast selection of coffins, and you know what sells like hot cakes here? Wooden coffins, because people here are so close to nature. We've got steel ones too, if you like. Unless you'd rather have her cremated. That's more and more in vogue, for ecology and all that, and that way you get to put your urn in our new columbarium…

'…You know, the columbarium's something you might want to consider, especially here, because the paths in the cemetery are so narrow. Imagine if you want to go see your mother, one Sunday when you're all dressed up, and you get your shoes all dirty and slip on the wet grass, then it starts to rain, you get cold and you end up catching your death! Not exactly a pleasant visit, eh? Whereas it's always nice in the columbarium. If it's raining one day, you can bring a book and read for an hour or two, beside your mother's ashes. Talk about a nice time to gather your thoughts in some good company!'

'No, thank you. I won't be having my mother cremated.'

'Right, so we're talking about a burial, then. Do you have a family plot here in the cemetery?'

Did my mother have a burial plot? I hadn't thought about it. Marie Garant, buried in a grave named for her father beneath a date carved in stone, surrounded by family – husbands, wives, parents, children – all sleeping soundly in the dense soil. She who had found peace nowhere but on the water, would she rest easy there?

'There must be a communal grave here, isn't there?'

'A communal grave? Wait a second! If she doesn't already have a plot, you can buy one! Actually, if it's not too indiscreet of me, do you have a plot of your own? Because you can always buy one big enough for two!'

'For me?'

'We can take this opportunity to make your prearrangements. You can never plan too far ahead! And as we undertakers always say, your headstone's the last thing you'll ever need! You, me, we all end up poking feet-first out of a big fridge one day, mademoiselle! It's sad to say, but we're all just numbers in the lottery of life!'

Me? Would I want someone to enclose me in a box and bury me? Where would they put me? And for whose benefit? And cremation? Who's going to watch out for my remains when all that's left are my charred bones in a glorified jewellery box? Whose job is it going to be to kneel down and pray for me?

'Leave her be, will you?'

I turned around. Standing in the doorway was the other twin. Just as tall, but slimmer than his brother, he stemmed the incessant stream flowing from the funeral peddler's mouth.

'Well, mademoiselle, looks like my brother's all done with your mother's body. You'll see, funeral directors are true artists of the ephemeral!'

'Alright, I'll take things from here. Go and see your wife, she was trying to get hold of you earlier.'

His feathers ruffled, the salesman stood up. 'How do you know?'

'You left your phone on my desk.'

The phone changed hands.

'Right then, mademoiselle, I'll leave you in the expert's hands! He's not very chatty, but he knows what he's doing. Have a nice day!'

The coffin peddler turned on his heels and hurried off. We could hear the outside door open, hesitate, and close again. Silence then descended on the funeral home.

The dog that wasn't quite sure what breed it was ambled his way into and across the room and plonked himself at his master's feet. Unlike the other one, this twin wasn't the jittery type. It was true, he wasn't very talkative either.

'Are you alright?'

'Yes.'

'Do excuse my brother. He used to be a used-car salesman.'

I rose and moved towards him.

'My condolences, mademoiselle Garant.'

He offered me a strong hand and I took it. There was a quiet air of goodness about him, a slight detachment, and I found it reassuring.

'Do I really have to see her?'

He kneeled to pet his dog.

'You don't have to if you don't want to. But it's better you do, apparently. It's all part of the grieving process. People who have their loved ones cremated without seeing the body first can have a hard time believing they're actually dead.'

'I've never seen my mother.'

He was still petting the poor, mixed-up pooch.

'When the fishermen brought her in the other day, I froze. I don't know if it was my blood pressure dropping, but I couldn't bring myself to go over. It's not that I'm afraid of dead bodies or anything, I just couldn't quite believe it.'

Slowly, he ruffled the back of the dog's neck.

'What brings people to abandon their children, do you think? Do you have any idea?'

He drew himself upright and leaned against the door frame. He didn't place an unduly compassionate hand on my shoulder, nor did he try to console what he couldn't understand with artificial words. With a show of strength, he just looked me straight in the eye and said, 'Let's go.'

We walked out of the office and down the stairs to the basement. The dog ambled happily along beside us. A beige corridor lined with sedate fluorescents. To the left, a window. Behind the glass, a for-est-green Venetian blind with the slats closed. The funeral director stopped, made his dog sit, and turned to me.

'Since the body hasn't been embalmed, you can't be in the same room as your mother. I have to ask you to stay on this side.'

There was nothing I could say.

He went in, turned on a light behind the glass and opened the blind.

I step forward to the bow and look up to the dawn. I stand tall atop the gentle swell, the horizon stretches calmly before my eyes and my body, at last, fills with happiness. I love you, my girl. The only place you'll find me at home is where the sea swirls. My daughter, my love, not a day goes by without you by my side, not one, and when I close my eyes, it's just you, me and the wind in our sails.

He closed the blind again, turned off the light.

I took three steps back until my legs made contact with the edge of a bench, and I sat down. The funeral director came out of the room, then kneeled and petted the dog.

'I want you to wrap her in a big white sheet. Then you're going to lay her down in a wooden coffin, the most basic one you have, just a plain wooden box, and you're going to bury her in the communal grave.'

'When?'

'Two days from now. There's someone I need to tell about it. We'll go straight to the cemetery. I'll ask the curate to come and say a prayer.'

Silently, he acquiesced.

'Monsieur Langevin?'

'Yes?'

The dog gazed at me with its pale eyes.

'I imagine you must know…'

'Know what?'

'Why we live, why we die.'

'Why we live, no. But I do know *when* we die.'

I looked hard and deep into his eyes.

'When our heart stops beating.'

Antifouling

I picked up a ready meal at Sicotte's. I had forgotten there was an adulterous paella waiting for me. Even if I'd remembered, I wouldn't have gone.

I went back to the house that had been hers and now was mine, and heated up my dinner. I unpacked all the stuff as I ate. The letter that had been with the will, the box, the plastic evidence bags. I'd had it with waiting around. Because that was exactly what I'd been doing. I'd been waiting all that time, for what? For a man to come along? For some kind of fate to strike?

I was mad at love for leaving me high and dry, mad at my mother for going off sailing and mad at my parents for being dead. I was mad at my work for boring me, mad at my city for being so impersonal, mad at my life for not living up to my dreams.

My true dreams, though – those that had surely impregnated Marie Garant and seeped into my genes, those that my parents, by teaching me to sail, had nurtured in me – had lost their shine through all my wishy-washiness. I had set out for here telling myself the doctor's orders would bring me out of my shell, but everything was still caving in around me.

There was nothing to tie me down, no family, no job, no boyfriend. No one to wait for, no regrets. And what had I done with all that freedom? Nothing.

Standing in my mother's house, it finally sunk in. While Marie Garant had always taken things into her own hands, I had never known what to do with my life and had spent my time pointing fingers at other people for not keeping me entertained. Through laziness or gutlessness, I had ended up in a complacent vacuum of my own making – my own inner no man's land.

From the west window, I could see *Pilar* brooding on her cradle. Yves Carle had talked about sailing away. To the east, a sailboat at anchor swayed gently on the clear night. Some people just went for it and set sail, come hell or high water. What about me? What was I waiting for before I would sing my heart out, letting my voice ring far and wide? For my heart to stop beating?

I grabbed my mobile. Marie Garant would be six feet under in two days' time, and I figured I'd need three, four at most, to do what I had to do to get ready. This sailboat was no stranger to the seas, and if Yves Carle were to be believed, Marie Garant had kept her shipshape. Drizzle was in the forecast for the next few days, then the skies were supposed to clear.

I dialled the number on the scrap of paper.

'Hello?'

'Yves?'

'Yes?'

'It's Catherine. I'm going to need your help tomorrow morning. Around four o'clock, down at the wharf.'

'You're wanting to put *Pilar* back in the water?'

'Yves … I've always been a wet blanket. I've never had the courage to follow my dreams. And now I want my heart to start beating again.'

'Don't worry, Catherine. I'll be there.'

Boat launches

'Oh, well let me tell you, aren't we the lucky ones, *mam'zelle* Catherine! The last time I saw you, I really did think it'd be the last time I saw you! I'm so happy you're back!'

'Renaud! I'm famished.' I took a seat at the bar. It had been a sleepless night, and an early start to the morning.

'Does that mean you've stopped being angry, then?'

'Yes, I've stopped being angry.'

'Oh, well I'm very much happy to hear that! Because, let me tell you just one thing, our Father the curate didn't half make me feel sorry I'd stuck my nose in, and I shouldn't have. Enough to give you an appetite, all that, isn't it? Here you go!'

He slid a menu in front of me. 'While I think about it, *mam'zelle* Catherine, I saw you've put *Pilar* the sailboat back in the water! Did that bright and early, didn't you!'

Tall, Indigenous Jérémie had stepped up and helped us with his truck, as if it went without saying. And for the very first time, I had set foot aboard my mother's sailboat.

'The dish of the day is a fillet of sole.'

'OK, one fillet of sole, then.'

He jotted down my order on a scrap of paper. 'Yves Carle came and gave you a hand, did he?' He dropped the paper on the floor, picked it up again.

'You don't miss a thing, do you, Renaud?'

Yves Carle had given me a guided tour. We walked around the boat together, trying to clean up the mess the investigators left behind, checking the rigging, the engine and the water supply and making a note of what needed to be done. He was going to come back the next morning to help me with some engine maintenance.

'Let me tell you, *mam'zelle* Catherine, it's because his sailboat was at anchor this morning. *Night Flight*. And I put two and three together when I saw *Pilar* was back in the water too. *Pilar*. Funny things, them boat names, aren't they? Sometimes they're plays on words, like *Seas the Day, Hide and Seak*, that kind of thing, and then other times, let me tell you, you've got people calling their boats people's names, like the *Marie-Sylvie* or the *Marie-Antoinette*. Did she ever really say "let them eat cake," do you think?'

'I don't know, Renaud.'

He twirled off to the kitchen, placed the order, came back and leaned across the counter as if to confide something in me.

'I've given it some thought, and I reckon it wasn't you who killed Marie Garant.'

'Thank you.'

As we walked around the boat, Yves had told me his theory about my mother's death. I could see why Detective Moralès had been put on the case. Because he knew nothing of the past around here.

'And even if you were the murderess, your family's none of my business!'

Renaud drew himself upright and turned on his heels with an air of pomp, donned his cook's helper apron and silly hat, dashed to the end of the bar, yanked open the fridge and grabbed a cabbage, thus sealing its fate.

'Let me tell you, we had our work cut out trying to calm the detective down, didn't we! It was all we could do just to get him to leave you alone, and Guylaine scrubbed all your fingerprints away, as if you'd never slept there!'

He returned, rolling the cabbage on the chopping board with all the tender loving care of a hitman.

'She chucked it all out of the window, so I could see there was nothing in your suitcase that looked like it could be used for killing someone on a boat! And let me tell you just one thing, Guylaine's not that mad at you, really. But you shouldn't go back to the *auberge*, all the same. It's not really the done thing, you know, to sleep at Guylaine's *auberge* without telling her you're the daughter of Marie Garant. But she is softening up a bit about you. She's even stopped shouting.'

He ripped off and jettisoned the outer leaves.

'And let me tell you, you weren't to know because you're not from round here, *mam'zelle* Catherine, but Guylaine and Marie Garant, they used to be great friends. After Guylaine's nephew drowned in the same squall as Marie Garant's husband on their wedding night, though, it was all over. I can't get my head around all of it because I was too young when it happened. And to top it off, Guylaine's nephew drowned in the same canoe as my two brothers, so we had enough of our own folk to cry about without fretting about other people as well!'

'Marie Garant lost her husband on her wedding night?'

'*Oui, mam'zelle!*'

He stopped for a second, suspended in his memories.

'I reckon Guylaine ended up blaming Marie Garant because everyone needs a scapegoat. And it was all such a big shock, her twin sister went mad and tried to kill herself. So let me tell you just one thing, with all that grief floating around, nobody had any time for Marie Garant making a big song and dance!'

He reached out for a knife and pointed the tip of the blade at me.

'I'm so glad you're not letting yourself be swayed by all the gossip, though, because it's hard to believe it could all be true, eh? One thing's for sure, your mother was one heck of a sailor. You know, some say you have to choose between love and boats. Is that true, do you think?'

'I don't know.'

If Marie Garant's husband died on their wedding night, who was my father?

He was on the verge of stabbing the cabbage.

'Renaud ...?'

He stopped with the knife in midair. 'Yes, *mam'zelle* Catherine, what can I do for such a lovely, lovely tourist as yourself?'

'I don't really understand what happened the day my mother got married.'

He rested one hand protectively on the cabbage while he gave me an answer.

'Let me tell you, you're not the only one! But the best person to tell you – that would be Cyrille. He was already old enough that day.'

'He didn't go fishing this morning. The Indigenous fishermen pulled up his traps for him.'

'Ah, well let me tell you just one thing, *mam'zelle* Catherine, Vital can harp on all he likes about them Natives, but it's all thanks to big Jérémie that Cyrille was able to get any fishing done at all this year! Because Vital wasn't exactly falling over himself to help, *non, mam'zelle!*'

The cabbage resigned itself once more to its fate as the cook's helper turned it around and around on the chopping board, trying to figure out how best to plunge his knife into its heart.

'How come?'

'Water under the bridge of jealousy flows for a long time between two men, you know.'

'Isn't Vital married?'

'It's not marriage that's going to stop a heart from loving, *mam'zelle* Catherine! Don't believe any of that!'

By now, the cabbage was enduring a brutal stabbing.

'And let me tell you, if Jérémie wasn't pulling his traps up for him, it wouldn't be long before Cyrille had the fisheries officers circling around him like sharks.'

'What would they do?'

'They'd seize all his gear. His traps, his licence, his boat, his truck, you name it – even the shirt off his back!'

'Is that all?'

Split in half.

'And let me tell you, if you're around, you might get caught in the clear-out too…'

A bell dinged in the kitchen. One little pirouette, and the catch of the day appeared in front of me.

'They're strange folk, them sailors, *mam'zelle* Catherine! Not bizarre strange, mind you, just not quite the same as the rest of us.'

'You think so?'

I dug in with my fork. The sole was good.

'Course I do! And not just your mother, either. Let me tell you, just take Yves Carle for example!'

'Yves Carle?'

Sawn in half again, the cabbage rolled open in raggedy quarters beneath the frenzied blade of its executioner.

'Well, I don't know all the juicy details, because he's older than I am, but I do know he was young when he got married to Thérèse. They had their two boys, and then he found himself a mistress and they got divorced.'

'No, they didn't! Yves Carle is still living with Thérèse!'

'Well, that's what's strange about it. Because they were separated for more than twenty years, and let me tell you, they got back together!'

Now the poor vegetable had to suffer being hacked to shreds.

'What?'

'Thérèse was the one who left him. He had a mistress, and she asked for a divorce. He went off to Percé – that's where he's from. He took the boys with him because Thérèse started seeing a guy who didn't like kids. And let me tell you, at some point, oh, must be twenty years ago, they got fed up with all the divorcing malarkey and they ended up shacking up together again.'

Renaud wiped his hands, took off his silly hat and cook's helper apron and went to take some customers' money as I nervously swallowed the rest of my sole in one go. What Yves Carle had told me about the moorings we couldn't cast off came flooding back into my mind. Did that mean he'd lied to me? Why? Had he loved my mother as well? Chiasson the notary did say Yves Carle had loved Marie Garant *too much*.

I pushed my empty plate aside.

'You're far too serious for such a lovely, lovely tourist!'

Two fifty-something women in cheery sunhats laughed and sang their way out of the bistro.

'I'd like to see Cyrille, but I don't know where to find him. He wasn't at the chalet.'

Pompously, Renaud donned his silly hat and cook's helper apron again, picked up his knife and brandished it over the second half of the cabbage.

'Cyrille? Let me tell you, he lives with his sister. It's that big, yellow two-storey house up on Fourth Lane, just past the bend on the way to Saint-Siméon. You can't miss it. It's right next to the cemetery, and there's only one house next to the cemetery.'

And the blade sliced right through it.

'If he's not fishing, he must be too sick to go out.'

I hardly dared look, the cabbage was suffering such an atrocious fate. Surely it would have rather been sliced with more dignity. Any vegetable would quiver at the thought of being butchered by Renaud's ruthless hand.

'What's wrong with him?'

Renaud stopped his frenzied sawing for a second and looked at me.

'Cancer. It's spread all over. That's why he moved in with his sister last year.'

The blade missed my nose by barely an inch as he pointed the knife towards the invisible house.

'Because, let me tell you, some of them treatments are a real pain in the neck! They had to give radio … is it radiotherapy or chemo-therapy? I don't really know much about that kind of thing, but if they're injecting a liquid into you, it must be chemo, right?'

Unrelenting, the cabbage knife massacre resumed.

'Anyway, it makes him so weak, he can't go out for days at a time. I don't know why they're doing that to him, because, let me tell you just one thing, Cyrille's a condemned man. He doesn't have long left. I don't reckon he'll make it to crab season.'

Mechanically, I pulled the money out of my purse. My heart all askew, I reached out a hand to place the notes and coins on the counter. With a flick of his knife, Renaud beckoned me closer.

'Be careful, *mam'zelle* Catherine. If you go during the day, his sister won't want you to come in; she says visitors tire him out. But I know Cyrille would be happy to see you, so let me tell you just one thing, you'd best wait until nighttime. Walk up the dirt track from the water at Ruisseau-Leblanc. It's a shortcut. Go under the railway bridge, keep on going and you'll end up along the side of the house. His bedroom window is right above the wood pile. Couldn't be easier.'

Choking back the emotions, I thanked him and walked out. On the counter, the poor cabbage had been reduced to nothing more than a pile of lifeless scraps.

That was how I got in the first time, sneaking through the open window after hiking up the wood-pile trail. There was no bug screen on the window. The old fisherman was sound asleep, not moving a muscle. I sat down on the only chair in the room. An old wooden rocker with a shabby cushion. I didn't dare rock because I was worried about the noise. He didn't move, either, but after a few minutes I heard his hoarse whisper.

'Heee … Marie Garant used to call the sea by her first name too, you know.'

Twin tears spilled from my eyes, tracing salty trails down my cheeks. I was crying for my mother, for her solitude and her distress, for everything I'd never know, regret, forgiveness perhaps, and for her death.

'I say that, love, but I don't know for sure. Heee … maybe she never dared to, but she'd earned the right. She could have done, you see. Heee…'

His eyelids were still closed. I sobbed in silence.

'For a long time, people said she was mad. They say she was crazy because she'd go off to sea for days on end and spend her time kicking the kelp when she came back. Heee … it's true she kicked the kelp. There's not a damned strip of kelp anywhere in the marina that doesn't remember the soles of Marie Garant's boots! Heee … she had one hell of a nerve in her feet and plenty of blood in her veins, she did, but she wasn't crazy. Heee … grab yourself a tissue before you start crying your eyes out, love. She had good reason to be irate, you know. The sea had a lot to beg forgiveness for, if you want my opinion. You hear me? Heee…'

'Yes, Cyrille.'

He barely moved.

'Marie Garant lost her men at sea. Two men, love. Heee … I know because those two men, they were my brothers. The first one she never had the chance to marry. And the second, heee … I was barely even at the wedding. I watched it all from a safe distance, like the poor cripple I've always been. But she never had a proper chance to love him either. Heee…'

I gave the world a try, I tried my hand at love. My dress was still white, and my eyes were twinkling from the altar wine.

'They went off on their honeymoon, love. Can you imagine? You've just got married. You lost your first love in a fishing accident, then you marry his brother, heee … because you say to yourself that death won't come knocking for a second son in the same family. It'd be far too unjust and the Grim Reaper's never that cruel, is he? Heee … So you start making a home in which to spend your life together, you paint the rooms one by one, you make a nice little room for a baby, heee … and you hang black-and-white photos of your ancestors on the walls to bless the generations you're going to parent because you have every confidence. Heee … you fill the cellar with jars of preserves and pickles…'

I put fresh sheets on the bed and hung a little bouquet of fresh flowers from the pediment on the porch.

'Then off you go and get married.'

I was barely breathing. That night held the key to my mother's story. And soon my own.

'She hadn't planned to be back so soon. Heee ... Let's go spend a few days at sea, they said. A honeymoon on a sailboat.'

Not long, so the little bouquet wouldn't dry out.

'Just a night or two. Heee ... In any case, it was already October. But the sunshine at the wedding was incredible. They got married early so they could set sail in the late afternoon. Heee ... They'd picked up some fresh mackerel and a bottle of champagne. Marie enjoyed her little extravagances. Let's drop anchor at the Banc-des-Fous so we can enjoy a bit of peace and quiet while we have dinner and gaze into each other's eyes, they said. Then afterwards, we'll make love.'

In my white dress, against all the sea's odds, I latched on to his arm.

Cyrille rolled onto his back and looked up to where the wall met the ceiling.

'They'd barely tucked into their dinner when the wind picked up. It wasn't in the forecast, heee ... but that can happen sometimes. Never mind, they said, it wasn't a big deal.'

We even laughed when the rain began to fall. We hurried to finish the bottle; we swore we'd drink quickly so we wouldn't get caught out if the hail came down.

'Heee ... That's when the squall blew in. Talk about a squall.'

The black curtain thundered towards us through the howling night.

'I never thought they were too drunk to sail. Out here, we sail by sight, even when we're drunk, even when we're stoned, even when we're old. Heee ... the kind of squall you could never imagine.'

He wanted to check the anchor was fast. He was stubborn like that.

'My brother went up on deck. He lost his footing and fell overboard.'

I threw the lifebuoy with all my might. He grabbed hold of it. I saw him grab hold of it.

'Heee ... it took some time for her to kick into action. Marie had to pull up the anchor in the storm and look for him in the dark. Heee ... She looked for a long time.'

I battled with the sea.

'She sent out a distress call, but the radio antenna had been ripped off. Heee … She did everything she could, I'm sure of it.'

Everything I could, I swear.

'I'll never doubt she did a better job than any other sailor would have. Heee…'

He fell silent, rolled over exhausted onto his side, drank a sip of water through a straw and closed his eyes on his convalescent's pillow.

'She rolled up to the wharf half delirious and they went off in search of my brother. Heee … They didn't find him. Nobody else did, either. He never came back.'

In the silence of the bedroom, I gathered my tears. Where was Cyrille the night his brother died? The night Marie Garant sailed in alone to the Ruisseau-Leblanc wharf, who had pulled her together? Who had continued the search at sea? Who were 'they'? I waited for him to go on. Obviously, I was hoping to find out my whole story before I left, but I doubted I'd hear it all. I waited in vain.

'Heee … Since your mother died, the memories have been rushing back to the surface for me.'

Tears filled the pockets behind his closed eyelids.

'Heee … You don't know it yet, because you're young, but as you get older, your heart gets thicker. Heee … And when the memories resurface, they scrape you all up inside.'

I extracted myself from the chair and went to sit next to him on the bed. He opened his eyelids slightly ajar; they were heavy with fatigue and steeped in memories.

'I would have liked to go to sea with you, Cyrille.'

'Heee … Me too, love, I'd have loved to have you aboard. The sunrise here's much prettier than over in Bonaventure! For the sunsets, I won't say otherwise, they do have some spectacular ones. Heee … But it's the sunrises that matter because it's morning and your eyes are still young and fresh, like a clean slate – because you're well rested, you see? Heee … Fishing's not worth what it brings in these days, but when you cut your engine to watch the sun rise and the breeze starts to make a watery fold on the water's surface ... you know exactly why you're there.'

'I put *Pilar* back in the water, Cyrille.'

'You'll never catch me aboard a boat like that! Heee .... you're always leaning to one side. You put barely any soup in your bowl and it looks like it's full! Heee ... I'd far rather a flat bottom to land my catch on, but I can see there's something poetic about wanting to go aboard a sailboat. The kind of poetry you can feel at the end of a romantic film. Heee ... You must've found it more romantic before Marie died, eh? Lost its shine now, hasn't it? I feel old, all of a sudden, love, you can't imagine. Heee ... and it's not just old age talking.'

'Why didn't you tell me you had cancer, Cyrille?'

'Cancer – it's not exactly something a man wants to shout from the rooftops, is it? Heee ... especially when he's just had a shot of chemo.'

'I thought you didn't want to go to sea anymore because...'

'Because that's where she died? Heee ... You don't know me very well, love. The sea is like a woman. When you choose to love her, you know you're giving her your body and soul. Heee ... If you're not alright with that, you don't clamber aboard.'

His eyes were as heavy as an autumn tide.

'The sea, Catherine, that's where I'm going to die. That's why I don't want to sell my boat. Heee ... when my shroud is ready, I'm going to head out to sea, away from the coast and far from any nets. I know some dark places and deep trenches. Heee ... My brothers are waiting for me. It's with them by my side that I'm going to hang up my fishing rod once and for all. Heee ... I'm going to bring some Mary-Jane along for the ride, smoke one last dream or two, and go off and find them. Heee ... And I won't be coming up again. Nobody's bringing me back up again.'

Sitting on the bed, I could see the lines of grey stones in the cemetery outside. I had to tell him, because that was also why I'd come.

'Cyrille ... They're burying Marie Garant tomorrow.'

'Heee…'

'I picked out a coffin yesterday. She's going to be buried here, next to your house.'

'Here or anywhere else, there's just no sense to it, love! Heee … When you've loved the sea, betrothed yourself to her for better or worse and spent your whole life with her by your side, no life after death can take her away from you. Heee … It's just not natural to make us sleep our death away in the ground. The sea should have held onto Marie Garant, chewed her skin and bones, swallowed her up and turned her into sediment, made some pretty coral out of her. Heee … They're always harping on about people being the salt of the earth. Heee … Well, doesn't that make us mariners the salt of the sea?'

I went to lie next to him and placed one arm over his whistling chest. He had a nice smile, the kind of smile that could smooth a clear passage through any waters.

'Now, love, just leave me be, will you? Heee … The treatments are making me sick. I'd rather be sick on my own and stand on my own two feet when there's people around. Heee … Especially with a lovely girl like you looking at me.'

With a heavy heart, I placed my hand on his arm. He closed his eyes.

'Leave me be, love. Heee … Leave me be.'

What became of my mother after that, Cyrille wouldn't be the one to tell me. Cyrille would never have been able to explain how the woman a whole village had once loved and celebrated like the advent of spring, hope and rebirth had ended up being relegated to the desolate cesspool of their collective memory. He, who had loved her in all her glory, might not even have been able to remember all that.

No one else shared those memories of his. They were under lock and key in the drawer of the past and I was having to pick the lock and fill in the blanks, since memory tends to fail us when feelings get involved.

Even Yves Carle had trouble telling me about it the next day, when we gave *Pilar* an oil change.

'It wasn't so much that she was mad, rather, she got under people's skin. You've got to pump the old oil out.'

He handed me the pump.

'Where's the new oil?'

He passed me the containers.

'Then what?'

'Then you change the filters and pour the new oil into the engine.'

'No, I mean what happened with *her*!'

'It's complicated.'

Perhaps I didn't need anyone to tell me what little there was to know.

So off I go again, in spite of everything, in spite of you. And every time I set sail, he watches over me.

She must have screamed her heart out and sailed aimlessly away. People must have seen her struggling, lamenting against the wind and cursing the storms. When she sailed back, she used to bump her boat against the wharf and jump right out onto shore to kick the living daylights out of the rocks, the seaweed and out of the remnants of crabs that the seagulls had dropped onto the pebbles to crack open their shells and feast on their flesh.

She used to go to the bar and drink her cares away almost every night. Sometimes, she used to laugh. She was a beautiful woman, Marie Garant, but I could see now it was the kind of beauty that could hurt. She'd harboured a grudge against the sea, against men and against love.

Watch over me, Cyrille, because I'm drowning.

'People have told me Cyrille protected her for a time. What from?'

Yves Carle stood up and went to sit on the starboard bench.

'At times like that, there's rarely a worse danger than yourself.'

Cyrille Bernard had surrendered his heart to the woman of the seas for a long time, and when he saw Marie Garant suffering, he strung up a hammock in his sister-in-law's sunroom so he could watch over her. He slept there for as long as it took.

Watch over me beneath this sullied sky. Watch over me when the shroud of darkness descends to oppress the night.

The nights she drowned her sorrows at the bar, he brought her home, no matter what time or what state he ended up going fishing in the next morning. He carried her in his arms up the staircase she insisted on descending, until the day he strung up a hammock in the living room, a sturdy hammock in which she could sleep the night away, abandoning the lovers' and child's bedrooms for the rest of her wandering life.

You tell me you love me, so give the stars a rub for me, make the constellations shine bright again so I can see what's left of the ephemerides through the dark curtain of my life, a fragment of Cassiopeia, so I can start dreaming again.

There must have been times when she took her drunken aggressiveness out on Cyrille. With unkempt hair and her body off kilter from the drink, she must have cocked her hip and goaded him to get hard for her. She must have hurled insufferable insanities at him, insulted him as she stripped off. And he, woeful at the sight of her, must have struggled to cover her up again and put her to bed, while she kept getting up again and again – every time putting her back to bed until she finally gave up. Then, and only then, would he slump exhausted into his hammock and cry like a fisherman on his knees, looking on as the woman he loved fell to ruin before his eyes.

I rattled every angel's cage, every night. The fisherman watched over me. Loved me. But I went away again. Because the sea was my oyster.

Other times, though, just as deliriously but in all tenderness, she must have prayed to him like a god, she who had turned her back on the church and would take pot shots at all the saints in Heaven whenever chance roused the monster within. She must have whispered affectionate little orisons in his ear when he wasn't expecting it, as sorrowful and pure as those a young girl murmurs over her father's grave. All of her springtime beauty must have resurfaced in that alcoholic mumbling as the clock struck midnight.

Shelter me from the backwash of the king tides. Lay your hand on my forehead to wipe away my fears. Reach out and touch the water.

The curious poem she had left with her will was helping me rewrite the patchy storyline in my mind. The more I knew, the more the pieces moved around and the more I wished I had the timeline.

She got married in October. Perhaps she was already pregnant. Surely not. Her husband died on their wedding night. Cyrille moved into her house. She screamed. For a week, maybe two. Possibly longer. But she had to take her boat out of the water for the winter, since there was no way she was going to let her perish as well. With the cold store being loaded with fish, here on the wharf, Marie Garant couldn't exactly put *Pilar* into dry dock there. That meant she had to prepare her sailboat for winter somewhere else before the ice set in. She sailed around to Percé, and who did she meet there, that autumn? Yves Carle, who was separated. Maybe he had a mistress, maybe he didn't. Maybe she spent the winter in Percé. With him? Yves was young, enamoured both by the sea and by the courage of Marie Garant. In the spring, he wanted to sail away with her, but Thérèse, maybe to reel him back in, dumped the kids on him, saying her lover couldn't stand them.

'Yves? You were the one who put her boat in the water that spring, weren't you? In Percé, back in 1974.'

No reply.

'Someone must have helped her, because she was pregnant. You knew she was pregnant. That's why the notary sent me to see you. Because he looked at the dates and put two and two together and deduced that you knew. Unseen, she slipped the boat back into the water and was going to sail upriver to Quebec City, where she was probably hoping to give birth at the convent with the nuns. But she never made it that far. Either because the timing was off, or because I came prematurely. She gave birth at sea with no one to witness it, wrote a false name on my baptism certificate, rushed to Montreal, dropped me at my new parents' door and waltzed off again. But after that, Yves? What happened?'

His words were a painful confession.

'She was gone a long time. Cyrille's father sold his quota, and since there was no boat, Cyrille went to work up in Alaska. The Americans were hiring for the ocean liners. It paid well. Anyway, people said he was mad for a good while as well, you know. And sometimes he must have thought he was, too.'

'Where did Marie Garant go?'

'To sea. She cast her mooring lines beyond the horizon. It was years before she came back.'

'Why? Why do we go to sea, Yves?'

He smiled at me sweetly.

'The sea's not a choice you make, Catherine. Some of us are drawn to the Far North and others never want to leave home; some go into politics, and others want to stay home and have kids. You go to sea because it's the only door that opens when you knock, because it keeps you awake at night, Catherine. Every time you step ashore and into the crowd, you feel how different you are. You feel like a stranger. You go to sea because you're a drifter among others and you only feel at home in the silence of the wind.'

He stared at his feet a long while.

'For us sailors, it's not being at sea that's complicated, it's being on land. We live and we die at sea because we're born to chase the horizon.'

We were done with the maintenance and the clock was going on for noon. I had to head to the funeral soon. We sat for a while longer in the cabin, as if we were sealing a secret pact together.

'I don't think love would have made Marie Garant happy.'

She hadn't come back to see the men she had loved, she had returned because the Gaspé was her home. And because she wanted to catch up with me. I always knew she came and went under the radar, but I'd never wanted my parents to talk about it. She must have heard that they'd died and thought she might be able to meet me at last. Time passed. She was sick, and she wanted to explain herself, tell me her story. She wrote me a brief letter from Key West, finally plucking up the courage to meet me, but she died before she could make land.

'Catherine?'

Without realising it, I was playing with my mother's portable GPS.

'What?'

'When were you born?'

'I'm dateless, Yves.'

'Is there a father's name on your baptism certificate?'

I shook my head. 'Why? Are you worried I'm going to claim alimony?'

He didn't reply, but he did look at me for a long moment before he climbed up into the cockpit.

On the wharf, beside where the sloop was moored, a constellation was waiting. Atop the half-rotten boards, someone had arranged a pretty assortment of starfish, seaweed, bits of driftwood, shells – a delicate collage evoking the wind, the shore and the wide, open sea. And a lobster. A gift from the ocean.

Yves Carle set foot on land. 'Looks like you've got an admirer.'

'No, don't be silly.'

He hopped into his tender, and before he rowed off to his sailboat, he said, 'You can say whatever you want, but in all my fifty years of sailing, not a single fisherman's left me a work of art like that.'

I battened down *Pilar*'s hatches and picked up the lobster and a few pieces of the marine landscape.

Tall, Indigenous Jérémie must have gathered it all with his weather-chiselled hands and left it at my door. I looked around for him for a while, but he was nowhere to be seen. I made my way back to the house, where I gently rinsed the starfish, shells, and driftwood and put it all out to dry on the deck. I thought about all those little offerings from the sea that were living on in Marie Garant's house and how I'd first thought they were trivial little things. But they were subtle souvenirs of love.

From the dining-room window, I caught a glimpse of the triangle of sails as *Night Flight* glided past the house, Yves Carle raising a hand to give me a wave.

Fenders and capstan hitches

Did Joaquin Moralès end up eating the cold paella? Of course. Lovestruck or not, Moralès had never thrown so much as a spoonful of paella in the bin. He simply put the wine back in the fridge and downed too many cold beers instead, nursed the knots in his stomach all night and got up on the wrong side of the bed. That morning, he had obediently deposited his investigation report on Marlène Forest's desk, which had bought him a day or two off to get the house tidy and recharge his batteries before Her Highness his wife made an appearance.

Meanwhile, Sarah had rushed a set of keys over to him and she was preparing, like she said, to develop her international profile with the unpalatable Jay-Pee by her side. Joaquin's nose was out of joint, and he still wasn't answering her calls. What else was he supposed to do? He had his pride, after all!

Unsure how things were going to turn out and wanting to give Catherine space to grieve, he kept himself busy by tidying the house. He didn't try to see her again, although he did take advantage of every opportunity to run an errand in the village, just in case. But the problem was, there was no case.

Driven to the limits of his patience, Moralès made up his mind that afternoon to go to the funeral. *Marie Garant, victim of a tragic accident and author of her own misadventure*, he thought.

He took a long shower, reflected on his dark skin in the mirror, picked out a cream shirt and made his way to the church. There, he was given directions to the cemetery up on Fourth Lane (left at the crossroads, right at the stop sign), parked a respectful distance away and got his feet soaking wet in the damp grass.

He was late getting there.

That didn't escape Father Leblanc's attention, who discreetly lifted a nonchalant eyebrow, secretly wondering, before resuming his oration, whether he'd be able to milk Detective Moralès for another glass of wine either in the name of his wife's amorous abstinence or to celebrate the glorious return of their marital libido. There were so few mourners, the list read something like a police report. Yves Carle, Cyrille and his sister, Coroner Robichaud, the notary and all three of his chins, two or three hangers-on from the clergy and a handful of tourists off to the side, somewhat unashamedly peering at the anonymous sculpture erected in memory of the 1922 sinking of the *Wandering Seafarer* and its four crew members lost at sea: Maurice and Émile Thibaudeau, Joseph Bujold and Ernest Hudon, all local men from Caplan.

And obviously, she was there too. Catherine Garant. She had arranged her long, chestnut hair in a chignon. Chic yet understated, she was wearing a light beige-and-blue summer dress with thin straps on the shoulders that had Sergeant Moralès's excitable pulse racing. Joaquin feasted his eyes on every inch of her. In the shadow of a maple tree, his imagination was running wild, like an overexcited teenager's.

She was standing by the grave praying, as pretty as a stained-glass virgin floating on a cloud resplendent with rays of white light over torrents of fury. Was Catherine religious? Who was she praying for? What was she asking for? What might a woman like Catherine Garant ask for? The other night, she was so ... So *what* exactly, Moralès? He sighed.

A big dog that looked like a husky-malamute-lab cross was sitting close to her. In the distance were the men in black and the cemetery workers.

Moralès was regretting having closed the case so quickly. He could have dragged things out, explored more theories, smoothed out the bumps and conducted more interviews. He could have dug deeper, or pretended to. Taken his time and seen Catherine again.

She hadn't returned his calls. Not to thank him for the information nor to apologise for not turning up to dinner. True, she was in mourning, but after the kisses they had shared, he'd thought … Thought *what* exactly, Moralès? Sarah had called right at the moment of truth! He could have not answered

Joaquin remained discreetly in the background.

If Sarah hadn't called, he could have … Could have *what*? Cheated on her? Moralès told himself she was the one who'd cheated on him and bemoaned the dirty tricks his fifties were playing on him, steamrollering his dreams with one betrayal after another that just kept on eating away at everything he had worked so patiently to build.

Something startled him. From across the grave, Catherine shot him a glance that she quickly took back as she pulled herself together beside her mother's coffin. Were there any lovers out there who kept their promises?

Father Leblanc embarked on the final prayer.

Suddenly, they saw a car approaching at high speed. It screeched to a halt in the cemetery driveway and Guylaine Leblanc, the owner of the sewing shop, jumped out. Much to the astonishment of the mourners, she stormed her way over to the grave, stopped a metre or so from the edge and spat onto the rough wooden coffin with all her might. Joaquin Moralès went to intervene, but the old fisherman put a hand on his arm.

'Heee … Let her get on with it.'

In any case, she was already making her getaway, slamming the car door and kicking up gravel with spinning tyres. Father Leblanc resumed the funeral oration and Catherine stared stubbornly at the rough little coffin like a woman who wouldn't be gracing any questions with an answer. They all made the sign of the cross.

Moralès walked back to his car with doubts sprouting in his mind. The seamstress coming to spit on Marie Garant's grave – that was bizarre. He had no inkling whatsoever about what had fuelled

Guylaine's anger towards Marie Garant and her daughter. Just as a precaution, though, he should try to find out.

Moralès slipped behind the wheel and drove back into the village. He had underestimated the bistro as a source of information. A gossip den like that could rekindle an entire investigation.

'Oh, well let me tell you, if it isn't Inspector Spector! You're a bit early for happy hour!'

In the bistro, a handful of holidaymakers were stretching out the lunch hour with a *digestif* while Renaud, always on the job in his cook's helper apron, flayed the living daylights out of a few heads of lettuce that had never so much as hurt a fly. Sitting at the bar, drunk and gesticulating, was Vital, hurling Christs and chalices at Victor as if trying to find some way of containing his anger.

'Christ in a chalice, if it's not the bloody police barging in! Heard we hadn't seen the last of you. Heard you bought a house in the area?'

'Yes, out on the island road.'

'Shacking up right near your victims, aren't you!'

'You weren't at the funeral...'

'Christ in a chalice, that's none of your bloody business!'

Laboriously, the fisherman got to his feet, knocked the rest of his drink back and put some money on the counter. Victor followed suit. Renaud whipped off his silly hat and cook's helper apron and interrupted his tempestuous chopping for a second while he gave them their change.

'Let me tell you, if you've come here to get my customers' backs up, I'll be showing you the door, whatever kind of food inspector you might or mightn't be!'

'I-i-i-it's Vital who's l-l-l-looking for trouble.'

'I'm not looking for trouble, I just want to be left in peace!'

Moralès calmly took a seat at the bar. 'Don't you worry, the case is closed.'

'Badly closed, if you ask me! But that's for the best…'

'Why?'

Not bothering to answer, Vital pocketed his change and made for the door.

'W-w-w-where are you off to?'

'To the boat, Christ in a chalice! To the boat!'

One step behind, Victor ran into Father Leblanc in the doorway. Now that the service was over, he had come to soothe his sermon-parched throat with profane bistro wine. Renaud pulled his silly hat and cook's helper apron back on and resumed his shredding duty.

'Oh, well let me tell you, Father, Vital's been keeping that seat nice and warm for you at the bar! It's your lucky day, inspector. Father Leblanc here's just back from your victim's funeral and he'll be wanting to tell you all about it!'

'She's not my victim!'

Father Leblanc caught a stray scrap of lettuce in midair and put it back on Renaud's chopping board.

'In truth, I don't have much to tell you, because you were there.' He took a seat at the bar.

'Yes. Nice ceremony.'

'Thank you.'

'Not many came.'

'The family kept themselves to themselves.'

'Cyrille Bernard, the fisherman … there was a woman with him.'

'His sister.'

'Was he close to Marie Garant?'

'Yes – he was her brother-in-law.'

'Let me tell you, inspector, I wouldn't be trying to get him to spill the beans before his third glass of red.'

'In truth, I wouldn't say no to a little glass of wine…'

That was all Moralès had been waiting for to get the man of the cloth to open his trap. 'Renaud, I get the feeling I'm going to be buying a glass of wine for our Father here.'

Renaud dropped the lettuce and wiped his hands on his apron. 'You don't mind if I keep my cook's helper uniform on, do you?'

'Keep it on, Renaud. We're used to it.'

Relieved, Renaud grabbed a bottle. 'A glass of red wine, then?'

'Yes. A beer for me and a glass of altar wine for our parched parish priest here.'

'Curate. I'm not a priest, I'm a curate.'

Renaud handed a beer to Moralès.

'Is there a difference?'

'Oh, well let me tell you, there sure is a difference! A curate has the cure – he's responsible for the care of the parishioners, whereas a priest … What does a priest do again, Father?' He poured a glass of wine for Father Leblanc.

'I was never ordained.'

'I'll put this on your tab, inspector…' Renaud recorked the bottle and put it on the bar.

'But let me tell you just one thing, ordained or not, it doesn't make a blind bit of difference to us lot. Blessed or not, so long as you're holding on tight to the cure, Father, we couldn't be happier!'

'In truth, I was just a verger. I used to lend a hand to the old curate, Bujold. Twenty-three years, he held the cure here. Usually the curates are on rotation, but I think the episcopate must have forgotten about him.'

'Either that or they wouldn't have him anywhere else!'

Or nobody else wanted to come here. Moralès kept that thought to himself, though, as Renaud filled bowls with a sad-looking salad.

'The Gaspé's never really been a place for curates. During Prohibition, we used to go over to Saint Pierre and Miquelon to fetch booze. And we were smoking pot long before Montrealers ever knew where Jamaica was!'

Renaud disappeared off into the kitchen with the salad bowls balanced precariously on his forearms.

'In truth, you've washed up here from the city, detective, where everything moves so fast and you're on a schedule that's calculated down to the minute, but time flows a different way in these parts. For plenty of men, an eternity might be no longer than a summer without any fish.'

Renaud wiped his hands on his apron as he came out of the kitchen. 'Let me tell you, it's funny they put *you* in charge of this investigation, eh?'

The detective smiled affably. *Now we're talking*, he thought. 'Why do you say that, Renaud?'

'Because we have to spell everything out for you! Anyone from around here would have understood.'

'Would have understood what? How a verger became the curate?'

'It's because you never knew the old curate! He used to knock it back so hard he'd be sleeping it off for days sometimes! And let me tell you, whenever he'd wake up from one of his benders, he was always so sure it was Sunday morning, he'd start spouting Mass right there and then! Sometimes he was bang on with the timing, but most of the time, he'd wake up on a Monday afternoon, other times a Tuesday morning. And let me tell you, don't even get me started about his sermons!'

Renaud grabbed the bottle, topped up the curate's glass, recorked the bottle and put it back down. 'Let me tell you, a village with a curate who's a drunk, it's no laughing matter!'

'I truth, I started by standing in for him occasionally when we weren't able to wake him up.'

'It was all fine by us…'

'I always wanted to be a priest, but my father had a field up on Fourth Lane, and since I was the only son, he wanted to keep me around to help. When I was twenty, they married me off to the neighbours' daughter!'

Across the counter, Renaud pulled out an unsuspecting box of tomatoes. 'Jumbo Juliette!'

'She was quite astounding. I never wanted children, but she managed to get pregnant four times, and I swear, I had nothing to do with it!'

'Let me tell you, no disrespect to you, Father, but none of the four look anything like you and none of them look anything like each other either!'

'In truth.'

'Nobody can say you stood in the way of the family duty!'

'I just let her get on with it. I used to go over to the rectory, and whenever the curate was snoring it off, I stood in for him. I read the breviary, completed all the parish papers and I started replacing him in office. In truth, nobody ever made a song and dance about it.'

Moralès finished his beer with a smile, and Renaud served him another.

'So anyway, let me tell you just one thing, when the cirrhosis killed him good and proper, nobody made a fuss about anyone else filling his boots!'

'In truth, it did make me feel a bit awkward, except that one night—'

'*Ah, oui!* Tell him about the miracle that night!'

'One afternoon, there were three young lads who went out to sea—'

'Let me tell you, the eldest of the Bernard boys had just got himself engaged to Marie Garant, and off he went with young Jeannot, who was just back from Quebec City. Two friends wanting to celebrate. But what happened? Maybe they were out too late, maybe they drank too much, but they had an accident! You tell him, Father!'

'In truth, we've never really got to the bottom of what happened, but the eldest of the Bernard boys fell in the water…'

Moralès slowed down on his beer. How many men, engaged or married to Marie Garant, had died from drowning?

'But then what? Cyrille, he'd been hiding on the boat, because he was just a teenager green with envy who wanted to go along for the ride as well! So let me tell you, when his brother fell overboard, he came out of his hiding place to help. Tell him, Father, won't you?'

'It was pitch dark, there was a storm brewing, and in truth, he didn't just get caught up in the moment, he got himself all tangled up in the fishing nets…'

All caught up in the events in his own way, Renaud was waving his arms like a windmill, armed with his kitchen knife, which was spattering tomato innards all over the place.

'And you know what? Young Jeannot fished Cyrille out of the water, but he was dead as well, as dead as can be! Strangled in the fishing nets!'

'They came back in about four in the morning.'

'And that was when you came along, let me tell you…'

'I was hunkered down at home with the kids and my Jumbo Juliette. I was keeping an eye on the storm outside, praying for the fishermen.'

'Jeez, let me tell you, it was thundering good and proper off the cliffs!'

'All of a sudden, the Bernard girl came knocking at my door. I opened up, and she came inside in all reverence and said, "You're going to have to come down to the wharf and say a prayer for the dead, Father. For my two brothers." It was her mother who'd sent her. What was I supposed to say to that? The poor girl was in tears.'

'Let me tell you, we can't always be going off to fetch the priest from Bonaventure in the middle of a storm! And what would the priest in Bonaventure have been able to do, anyway? He didn't even know the Bernards! And giving someone the Extreme Unction, that's about as personal as it gets.'

At last, the boss of the bistro let go of the knife and wiped his hands.

'In truth, I never wavered.'

'If they had you giving the cure, then you had it in you to give!' Renaud grabbed the bottle, topped up the glass again, recorked the bottle and set it back down on the bar. He handed Moralès another beer, although he'd barely touched the last one.

'I stopped at the rectory, put on my cassock, grabbed the holy water and the chrism and went down to the wharf. When I got there, everyone went down on their knees.'

'Let me tell you just one thing, you don't want to be trying to find your calling in a piece of paper, no sir!' Renaud scarpered off to the kitchen, apparently to fetch a pot from a particularly noisy pile of dishes.

Father Leblanc raised his voice as he carried on. 'I gave the Extreme Unction to the two boys and after that night everyone took to calling me Father. In truth, I was still expecting somebody to come along and replace me, but nobody ever came. I even went to the priest in Bonaventure for advice, but he told me they were short-staffed in the brotherhood. He went on to say that since I'd made a habit of it, we were all sons of God and I knew what I was doing, I might as well take on the cure myself. I found out that if we'd asked him to, he would have been the one who had to officiate over our parish as well as the parishes of Bonaventure, Saint-Siméon and New Carlisle.'

Resurfacing from the depths of the kitchen, Renaud hadn't missed a second of the conversation. Clearly, his pot was going to be too small. He paused.

'Deep down, it suited him for you to keep picking up the slack. Made for less work for him, let me tell you!'

'Yes. My wife went off Heaven knows where. My kids found jobs and I sold the land. Then I moved into the rectory. In truth, I'm happy. It's a big house, and they're no more trouble than anyone else's.'

'Pretty average, let me tell you.'

'There's only one thing I don't do, and that's confessions.'

Renaud filled the pot. Too small.

'We like gossiping better.'

'I'd rather my flock leave their sins at home. I don't want to be taking their secrets under my wing.'

'We all have our secrets, and the sheep are in good hands.'

Renaud paused, as though thinking about the dishes that needed washing, and threw what was left of the tomatoes in the bin. 'And what would you do if Arseneault came and confessed to fathering your kids behind your back? You'd never be able to forgive his sins and you'd have a conflict of interest, wouldn't you?'

'I'd rather not know.'

'Let me tell you, him and Dodier, no doubt about it! And your youngest, he must have been Ferlatte's, what with no hair and his teeth all wonky! Ferlatte should've been the one to pay the orthodontist's bill, let me tell you!'

'Family business is always complicated.'

Moralès took a swig of his beer.

Renaud put the pot down. Rag in hand, he wiped the dripping counter dry. 'Speaking of family, Guylaine hasn't been in for her coffee. I hope your sister's not poorly, Father.'

Moralès looked the curate up and down. 'Guylaine Leblanc's your sister?'

'In truth, yes.'

'The seamstress who spat on Marie Garant's grave is your *sister*?'

'Before God and the grave.'

'Why would she do that?'

'We all have our tics, detective. My sister is no exception.'

'But ... why did she hate Marie Garant so much?'

'I might be a bit of a tippler, but I'm not a bigmouth. You should be asking her, not me.'

Renaud picked up the bottle and drained the dregs into Father Leblanc's glass.

'Let me tell you, your bottle's empty, inspector. What say I open another one for you?'

But Moralès's mind had drifted elsewhere.

'You said Cyrille Bernard was strangled to death in the fishing nets that night, did you not?'

'In truth, no. They took him to hospital and he ended up pulling through.'

'Let me tell you, it was quite the miracle, eh?'

'A year and a half he was in the hospital, and he's never been able to breathe properly ever since. But he's very much alive, believe me!'

'If he wasn't, the cancer couldn't be killing him!'

'Did they find the other brother's body?'

'No, but let me tell you, there's nothing unusual about that. Dead folk from around here, they always get carried out to sea, and there's no bringing them back!'

'Such a sad story,' said the curate. 'The poor young man was going to be married just a few days later.'

'And Marie Garant was far from amused, let me tell you!'

Here was the window Moralès had been waiting for. 'So he was Marie Garant's first fiancé, not her husband?'

'That's right. He fell overboard. Too drunk, he was.'

The curate shook his head, either too drunk himself or sincerely sorry. 'Jeannot told me he did everything he could to save him, but let me tell you one thing, I'm far from sure of that!'

'Who is this Jeannot? A man from these parts?'

Renaud and Father Leblanc clammed up in a heartbeat, clearly ill at ease. Having reached the bottom of his glass, the man of God stood up suddenly, as if in a hurry to trot away and up the steps of his rectory.

'In truth, I have things to do. May the rest of the day treat you well, detective. See you, Renaud.'

The boss of the bistro cleared away the empty wine bottle. 'Let me tell you, inspector, don't be forgetting to settle your tab before you go, will you?'

I didn't put on a spread after the funeral. Who would I have been feeding, anyway? Cyrille went home tired and heavy-hearted. Yves went home to his wife; they were expecting the children for dinner that night.

I went to pick up some spare parts from the chandler's in New Richmond before making my way down to the wharf. I had to get the boat shipshape and make sure I was ready to set sail soon, either the following night or the next.

I was thirsting to hoist my biggest sails, fill them with the prevailing winds and drive Pilar *through the swell.*

Jérémie was working on Cyrille's boat when I arrived. I slowed my pace, he waved.

'Thank you,' I said.

He bowed his head without a word and I recalled how the first time I had seen him, he reminded me of a tall wooden mast. It struck me how he could have just as easily been a landmark, a lighthouse on the rocks.

Intimidated by his presence, I kept walking towards the sailboat, where I busied myself unpacking the spare parts, putting the canned food away and finding a spot for a few things I wanted to hang on to. I glanced at the time. The day was getting on and I felt like having a nap. I battened down the hatches on the boat and set off towards my car.

'Oh, well, Christ in a chalice, if it isn't Marie Garant's daughter herself coming to see us! To what do we owe the honour?!'

He was standing in the middle of the wharf, blocking my way. 'Didn't shout it far and wide, did you?'

I hadn't seen Vital since the day he snagged Marie Garant's body in his nets.

'I see now why you wanted to meet Cyrille so much! Why you were always on about Cyrille this and Cyrille that—'

'Oh g-g-g-give it a rest, Vital!'

The harder Victor tried to calm him down, the louder Vital shouted.

'And Guylaine, Christ in a chalice?! Did she tell you why she chucked you out?'

'Y-y-y-you're scaring her.'

Slowly I recoiled, feeling unnerved by the situation.

'What's going on here then, Vital? Fish bit you, did it?' said Jérémie, who had glided over silently to my rescue. It struck me what a gentle, almost lulling voice he had, for such a big man.

Now he had an adversary his own size to unleash his anger on, Vital cranked his aggression up a notch, swaggering dangerously close to the Indigenous fisherman.

'Christ in a chalice, now the bloody Indian's poking his nose in! Can't say I'm surprised, 'cause *she* was a bloody savage as well!'

'You'd better cool your jets, Vital, because you're the only one acting like a savage here.' Jérémie held fast, oozing as much menace as the fear I harboured and the anger Vital had unleashed, all of it coming from that place we all have at our very core that can turn our bodies into a solid brick wall. He stepped in between the two of us, blocking my view of Vital completely. All I could see was Jérémie's back, a broad back carved out of solid wood that I felt like running my hand over to give me courage.

Vital lowered his tone a touch, just slightly, but he still said it. He spat it out like a filthy gob of hatred, planting it like a battle axe in the ground between us.

'Christ in a chalice, your mother was nothing but a crazy bitch! Guylaine chucked you out 'cos your mother was a fucking whore!'

In one sweep, Jérémie took a step towards Vital, lifted him off the ground and threw him into the water. I recoiled from the fisherman's words, which reverberated through the air like a shock wave. That was all I could bring myself to do – get away from all of this. I retreated one step at a time, tracing an arcing path for myself around the edge of an imaginary circle, at the centre of which Vital was wallowing. Vital, the man I had thought so handsome the morning after I arrived. I ran to my car.

I didn't see Robichaud the coroner coming out of the Café du Havre, nor was I aware of him asking what had happened. But I did hear Jérémie answer him from a distance.

'It's Vital, coroner. He said the tide was too low to go to sea. See, though, Vital … if it's deep enough for your big mouth, it's deep enough for my boat!'

I hazarded a glance in the rear-view mirror. Facing out to sea, Tall, Indigenous Jérémie, a true rock of a man, stood firm on the wharf, unaware he was washing an indelible layer of bitterness over my chart of the Gaspé coast.

Nestled into the cliffside, the quiet cormorants were hesitant to spread the wings they had kept folded all night. The wind ruffled their feathers a little as it whistled its way along every inch of the grey rock, swaying them on their perches. It was the kind of morning that gave free reign to the sea.

Moralès was teetering on the edge, hounded by delirious images scrolling through his mind.

Marie Garant, lying thin, blue and lifeless on the bottom of the fishing boat, opened her eyes, her pupils as hypnotic as empty sea shells. As her features began to blur like footprints in the sand washed away by the west waves, her face morphed into Catherine's, whose soft lips whispered, 'The sea would never have done that to her!' Sarah's voice echoed, 'What are you doing to me?' and the image of his wife slowly vanished, her heart deflating like a balloon. He tried to hold onto her, reaching his arms out to save her, but Sarah's body was nothing but water now, her hands dissolving into the sea, her fingers melting like salt into the waves.

That was when he woke up. Five in the morning and his sheets were sticky with sweat. The wind was howling like crazy, whipping at the solid rock cliff.

He got out of bed and had a coffee. The more he thought about it, the more he doubted the accident theory. He felt sheepish admitting it though, since it was embarrassing how he had let the locals pull the wool over his eyes. That morning, he wondered what it was he hadn't grasped. Or rather, what *had* he managed to grasp in this whole affair?

Why did Marie Garant drop anchor on the Banc-des-Fous? Why did Vital harbour such a strong dislike for her? Because she made such a big song and dance about things? What could get under a woman's skin so much it drove her to kick the kelp? Why was the seamstress so keen to obliterate Catherine's prints and spit on Marie Garant's grave? Yves Carle and Cyrille Bernard had both told him

Marie Garant's death was no accident, so why hadn't he asked them any questions? And there was something else … something else he had missed, he was sure of it. What? *Dig deeper, Moralès. What is the wind hiding from you?*

Like a freediver resurfacing from a long time in the depths, squinting at the sun with deadened eyes, Joaquin Moralès suddenly caught his breath, overcome by the sense he had let the whole investigation slip through his fingers, glossed over interviews and botched the whole thing like a tired old detective. Was that what he had become? An old fool of a detective who tried to seduce despondent orphans?

He stepped out onto the patio and looked out at the sea in contemplation. Ashamed, he felt the urge to run away from himself. He started down the staircase on autopilot. Faster and faster. Put his mug down. Faster still. Broke into a run. He jogged along the shore to the west, parallel to the breakers. He knew he'd have to dredge it all up again. Rethink the whole investigation from the beginning, re-examine everything with fresh eyes. The land and the sea, the men and their secrets, their defeats. And confront them all.

As he approached Ruisseau-Leblanc, it struck Moralès that the sailboat was back in the water. Of course, it was there yesterday, he recalled. Who had done it? Catherine? He slowed his pace as he drew near the wharf. He could see a fisherman busying himself in the wheelhouse of one of the boats. *Probably just back from fishing*, Moralès thought as he walked over.

'Excuse me…'

The fisherman turned his back on him.

'You're Cyrille Bernard, aren't you?'

The thin old man looked sunken and drained.

'Heee … yes, I am.'

'The other day, you told me I was wrong about the Marie Garant case.'

'I've not changed my mind.'

'Would you have any new information to share with us?'

'What about?'

With his back still turned, it looked like he was hiding something he didn't want the detective to see.

'Marie Garant's death.'

'Heee … I don't know what you're talking about.'

'You're sure you don't have anything to say to me?'

The old fisherman finally turned around.

'Heee … now you listen to me, Sherlock Holmes. Heee … I've just buried my best friend and I'm not far from my own death bed, heee … so I've no time for your beating around the bush. If you've got a question, then either ask me straight up or get out of my face! Heee…'

Moralès took a step backward, shocked by the man's abruptness. 'My condolences, monsieur Bernard, for the death of your friend,' he conceded.

The fisherman nodded, turned away to check something and eventually came out of the wheelhouse. He looked exhausted as he climbed onto the wharf.

'Hard time fishing?' Moralès asked.

'We're all done now until crab season. Heee…'

Cyrille carried on walking towards his truck, as if trying to shake a stubborn Moralès off his heels.

'Monsieur Bernard, the other day you told me Marie Garant's death was no accident. Why are you so sure? If you know something, surely you can help me shed light on the circumstances of her—'

'Heee … I've no time for that.'

'Marie Garant was your sister-in-law and you have no time to wonder how she died?'

'No.'

'Am I to understand you didn't care for her much?'

Cyrille whirled around. In spite of the difference in age and strength between them, Moralès recoiled from the tall fisherman.

'Heee … That's right, I've no time for her death! Heee … You know why? Because I loved Marie Garant alive! Marie Garant with her laugh and her temper! Marie Garant who sailed the seas solo, heee … in spite of everything people said about her. Marie Garant with her heart-shaped mouth, her eyes trained on the horizon and her tangled hair … Heee … Do you know what your problem is, detective? Heee… Do you know why you're never going to find whoever did it?'

'Why?'

'Heee … Because you don't want to know who she was, how she lived her life or what she loved … heee … none of it! You're so caught up with her dead body, you've lost sight of the fact she was a living, breathing woman! You were looking for a conclusion for your files, heee … and you jumped headfirst into one. It wasn't the right one, but who's going to get their nose out of joint because of it? Who cares?'

The old fisherman carried on walking to his truck.

'I do!' Moralès retorted.

Cyrille didn't even bother turning around.

'You're a poor liar and a poor detective! Heee … That must be why they lumbered you with this case. An old woman dead on her sailboat in the depths of the Gaspé isn't exactly the kind of stuff that calls for an expert, is it? Heee … They only sent you along because they knew it wasn't rocket science, it was right on your level. Heee … And you still screwed it all up!'

'You don't know what you're talking about!'

Cyrille yanked open the door of his truck and whirled around to face Moralès, who was still snapping at his heels.

'Don't believe me? Heee … Ask Yves Carle, he'll tell you you jumped too quickly to conclusions and let the wool be pulled over your eyes. He'll tell you there was no way the boom could have knocked Marie overboard! Heee … you wanted to offload the investigation because you were too scared to accuse the real culprits.'

'If you know who did it, why don't you tell me?'

'Me? What do I know about all that? I'm not a detective … Heee … I'm just a fisherman. An old, tired fisherman.'

Cyrille was already in the driver's seat. Instead of driving up to the road, he turned onto the dirt track under the railway bridge, the one that ran along the stream, and vanished into the woods.

With Cyrille Bernard gone, Moralès walked back to the wharf and made his way over to the sailboat, only to find it battened down and deserted. Catherine had cleaned away the marks left by the crime-scene technicians when they came to dust for prints. Moralès opened his notebook and took the phone out of his pocket.

'Hello?'

'Yves Carle?'

'Yes.'

'It's Sergeant Moralès.'

'I'm on the water, sergeant. Can we make this quick?'

Joaquin felt silly asking, but he had to take a firm line.

'Is there any way the boom on the sailboat, *Pilar*, could have hit Marie Garant on the head and knocked her overboard?'

Yves Carle gave an ironic laugh on the other end of the line. 'Marie was at anchor. The mainsail was furled, and the cover was on it. To furl the mainsail, chances are she hauled the sheets in, so it's unlikely the boom wasn't secured.'

'I don't really understand all of that.'

'To fold the mainsail down over the boom, the boom can't be swaying loose.'

'But even then, is there no way she could have forgotten something or somehow made a mistake?'

'No. The boom could easily have knocked you overboard, but not her.'

'You're going to try and tell me the boat would never have seen her come to any harm now, aren't you?'

'Listen … even with her hair up, Marie Garant can't have been any taller than five foot one. Just ask Catherine, she had to size up the coffin for her. The boom was five foot ten above the deck, so the boom couldn't have hurt her even if it had wanted to!'

Moralès turned his eyes to look at the sailboat. What an idiot he had been!

'Excuse me, sergeant, I have to go now.'

Yves Carle hung up, and Moralès ran back home to take his second cold shower of the day.

The full extent of his ignorance having sunk in, Moralès tried to pull himself together by putting away a solid breakfast and then tidying the boxes in the living room. As the seasoned detective carried his own boxes from one room to another, the memory of another box – the one containing evidence gathered aboard *Pilar* and that he'd forgotten about – came flooding back to him. He hotfooted it over to the car, only to find that the boot had been relieved of its precious cargo. When had he last seen the box? Not since his impromptu lobster dinner with Catherine, he realised. Shortly after lunch, he went to knock on Catherine's door, but she wasn't answering. Then he stopped in at the station in Bonaventure before washing up at Renaud's bistro.

'Oh, well let me tell you, inspector, if you keep this up, the bistro's going to be your new police headquarters!'

'I saw Lieutenant Forest's car out front. Is she here?'

'In the window, there. Twist your arm for a beer?'

But Moralès was already over at his boss's table.

'Sergeant Moralès, you must be happy to have this time off, I imagine? How's the move coming along?'

'Lieutenant, I need a word.'

'I'm expecting someone.'

He couldn't help but notice she was decked out in an elegant lace-trimmed blouse and a delicate glass-bead necklace.

'It'll only take five minutes.'

'I'll give you two.'

'I want to reopen the investigation into Marie Garant's death. I think the waters were muddied by my unfamiliarity with the lay of the land, or rather, the ins and outs of the water. I have reason to believe that Marie Garant may have had a clear motive for dropping anchor by the Banc-des-Fous – that she met someone there and that her death was no accident.'

'Smells to me like you neglected to follow up some leads.'

That was when Robichaud the coroner made his entrance, clean-shaven with a hint of cologne.

'I ought to tell you, I wasn't aware the sergeant was dining with us,' he said, standing with his hands on his hips a little distance from Marlène's table.

Moralès was still standing, and hadn't realised he was blocking the coroner's way. 'No, I won't be dining, thank you. I just came to ask Lieutenant Forest for permission to reopen the investigation into Marie Garant's death.'

'Looking for a reason to call the heiress again, are you?'

'Sorry?'

'I ought to tell you, we know all about your little flight of fancy…'

Moralès felt his cheeks redden, but he carried on.

'Listen, lieutenant, the boom was too high to have hit Marie Garant—'

'Marie could have been standing on one of the benches in the cockpit, as sailors often do.'

'I have reason to believe someone is trying to stand in the way of this investigation.'

'I ought to say, we have reason to believe someone's standing in the way of us having a nice, quiet lunch, sergeant, and you've spouted on enough already!'

Moralès refused to drop it. 'A box of evidence gathered aboard the sailboat was even stolen from my car!' he persisted.

Marlène Forest cleared her throat before she delivered her verdict.

'I don't think there are grounds to reopen the investigation, sergeant.'

'Listen, lieutenant—'

'No, Moralès! You listen to me! And listen very carefully.'

She pointed her index finger so firmly and menacingly at Joaquin that Renaud Boissonneau, who had sauntered over with the menus, found himself standing to attention.

'You dropped the ball with key witnesses on the fringe of the investigation, you neglected to follow up on technical details that a rookie would have picked up on and you misplaced evidence. In spite of all that, the findings of the investigations hold together and it's clear this was an accident. I'll give you the go-ahead to reopen the investigation only if you bring me evidence that's relevant enough for me to do so. Otherwise, if you keep blurting out your blunders to me, I'll be very happy to write a note in your file about the sheer negligence you've shown. Is that clear?'

'Let me tell you, it sounds as clear as a bell to me!' Boissonneau slid the menus onto the table and scurried off behind his counter.

Moralès retreated a step.

The coroner seized the opening to pull up a chair and sit down, sure of his place. 'You ought to cool it with the heiress, you know ... Anyway, aren't you married?'

Seething, Moralès stormed out of the bistro, got into his car and drove down to the wharf. The boats were empty. The fishing was done. What should he do? His investigation was a washout and it was clear that turning it around wasn't going to be easy. Still, he'd find a way. He started off towards home, but just before he got to the paved road leading up to Highway 132, he slammed on the brakes. What was down that dirt track Cyrille took earlier that morning?

Moralès decided to find out for himself – only rarely did curiosity kill the cat. He turned left onto the track.

After a couple of miles or so, the track came to an end between a house and the cemetery. There was a man in the cemetery. Moralès recognised him as one of the undertakers who had been at Marie Garant's funeral. The detective stopped the car, got out and made his way over. Clad in boots, the man was levelling the earth around a headstone with a spade.

'Can I help you?' he asked.

'Do you work here?'

'Langevin Brothers, your one-stop shop for funeral services of every kind; eternal satisfaction guaranteed for you and your loved ones,' he quipped, shaking the detective's hand and handing him a business card, which Moralès pocketed without looking at it.

'We're running a special at the moment – thirty percent off all crema-tions, and that extends to prearrangements too. You know, cremation's really the best way to go, especially if you choose to store your ashes in our new columbarium. Take a day like today, for instance, it's raining on and off, and the grass is all wet. Off you go to gather your thoughts by a loved one's grave and before you know it, your feet are soaked through! That's what I try to explain to our clients: nothing beats the columbarium if you're wanting a comfortable, hassle-free visit.'

And on he went. 'Especially since the groundhogs have been causing a ruckus all over the place! Can you imagine? You're just paying a visit to your mother's grave to say a little prayer and what do you see poking its head up out of the ground? A cheeky little marmot pilfering a few flowers from the next-door neighbour's bouquet to feed its young right under the blooming headstone! It's beyond a joke, I said to my brother. So, I'm out here setting some traps. Might be overkill, I know, but we have to get rid of them. I'll be back tomorrow. I reckon we should catch them fast enough. Don't worry though, I don't think they've been digging over Marie Garant's way.'

'What makes you think I'm here to stand over that grave?'

'I saw you at the service. It wasn't the nicest of burials.'

Langevin – or his brother – seemed keen to elaborate and Moralès encouraged him. 'Why do you say that?'

'Because I don't understand why the daughter buried her mother in the communal grave. Come have a look-see…'

Langevin led Moralès a few steps away.

'See, the Garants have a family plot right here. I checked, and there's still room for more of them! I tried to tell Catherine Garant, but she wouldn't hear any of it. A plywood coffin in the communal grave! My brother said we should just respect her decision, but I find it strange all the same. Why bury your mother in a dark corner by the woods when you can come and see her right here? Follow the gravel path and you won't even really get your feet dirty! It wasn't the practical choice!'

Langevin was right. Moralès examined the headstone, which was just slightly off the path. Why had Catherine made that choice?

'Have you been back to the communal grave today?'

'No. I was going to head over to check. Although I'm fairly sure the groundhogs won't have been there.'

'I'll come with you.'

'Are you family?'

'No, I'm with the SQ. I was the detective in charge of investigating Marie Garant's death.'

'Don't worry, she's well and truly dead.'

Moralès remembered what a morbid sense of humour undertakers tended to have.

'Oh, no!' said the undertaker as they reached the communal grave. 'See what a dog's breakfast the gravedigger made of this job? He must've still been drunk when he did it!'

Moralès could see how roughly the grave had been filled in. The ground was uneven, and the grass was full of dirt. In a heartbeat, Langevin grabbed his spade and set about evening out the ground.

'See what I mean about the columbarium? Like I say—'

'Wait! What if someone's desecrated Marie Garant's grave?'

The undertaker stopped what he was doing and looked up at Moralès. 'What are you on about? Desecrating a grave? In our cemetery!? You're out of your mind! Nobody would dream of doing such a thing! Not here! Just let me smooth it over with the spade, and—'

'Stop right there, monsieur Langevin! Don't lay another finger on that ground!'

Langevin turned to Moralès. 'Excuse me?'

Moralès dug his phone out of his pocket. This was the perfect opportunity to convince Marlène to change her mind. 'I'm going to see about reopening the investigation…'

That wasn't the way Langevin saw it, though, and suddenly he was at it again with the spade like there was no tomorrow.

'Stop!' Moralès insisted.

'No, detective! I'm not going to let you stir up any trouble in my cemetery! Nobody opens up a grave here! Nobody. Not even you!'

With a quick step, he was trampling all around the edges of the grave.

Moralès glared at him, feeling sick to his stomach. Then he paused for a second. Maybe the undertaker was right. Calling Lieutenant Forest, requesting the case be reopened, disturbing the grave – those were all good ways to make longstanding enemies in such a small village. Not to mention Catherine … There were better ways to seduce a woman than to unearth her mother's body. He put his phone back in his pocket.

'You're right, monsieur Langevin. How silly of me to even entertain the idea.'

'In any case, there's rain in the forecast tonight and tomorrow. Things will clean themselves up.'

Moralès gave the undertaker a wave and walked back to his car. Along the way, he noticed a curtain twitching in a window of the house next door. The fisherman's truck was parked in the driveway. *I'll be seeing you tomorrow, Cyrille Bernard*, he thought. In the meantime, Moralès decided he would pay Catherine another visit. And this time he wouldn't take no for an answer.

I rocked for a long time on the veranda that evening, keeping pace with the gentle rhythm of the waves. The south wind was veering west, and the eye of the sun, half closed on the dark horizon, hinted that rain was on the way. The skies were forecast to clear the day after next.

I thirst for the horizon. I long to hoist my heart to catch the west wind.

My days in the Gaspé were numbered. I had finished the maintenance work I needed to do on the sailboat, retraced my mother's steps on the GPS and revisited my sailing manoeuvres with Yves Carle. The things I had to do here were drawing to a close. There was just one question that was still niggling at me, though, and I had given myself twenty-four hours to find the answer. Then, answer or no answer, I was going to cast off my moorings.

Sleeping between sea and sky, sandwiched between a hundred and eighty degrees of waves and a hundred and eighty degrees of stars, in the rumbling belly of the hull, with the deep breathing of the wind in my sails.

I drank my herbal tisane and then, weary from the last few days, I found myself falling asleep.

Joaquin Moralès left his car at the top of the driveway and walked the rest of the way down to the house. There she was, on the veranda. He realised something terribly disconcerting was happening. The closer he approached, the weaker he felt at the knees, and the more he forgot what he had come here to say.

She was asleep in the rocking chair. He climbed the five steps and contemplated her. How were you supposed to touch a woman, anyway? Reach for her hand? Stroke it gently? Touch her hair? His heart was tied in knots. He had been dreaming about this for days and now. He who had no qualms confronting criminals day in, day out, was now afraid to approach a sleeping woman. That's right, he was afraid. She might wake up, push him away, reject him – or scream. This sleeping woman was like a detonator.

His whole being was begging her. Don't say no to me, Catherine, not today, because my life is such a mess, and it's so silent and hollow and empty, I've latched on to your hope like a buoy. You're sleeping, and as you rest easy, I'm drowning, my head held under by my absent wife, by this investigation that's made a fool out of me, by my loneliness, by your presence. You're the one who buried your mother, but I'm the one on my knees. I'm touching your shoulder, gently, let me come closer to you, don't say no, I'm begging you, let me clutch your young, womanly curves to my ungainly middle-aged body, draw you near and lay your head against me.

She opened her eyes and woke from her slumber.

'Detective Moralès?'

'Joaquin.'

He was crouching down in front of her.

'You put the sailboat back in the water, then?'

'Yes.'

He stayed right there. Hesitated.

'Did you, er … Did you get my messages the other day?'

'Yes.'

'You didn't come to dinner.'

'No.'

'I was waiting for you.'

He looked deep into her eyes, searching for the spark he so desired. 'The other night, Catherine, when we kissed…'

I shivered. 'The other night, Joaquin Moralès, you kissed me, yes, and after the kisses, the caresses, the seagulls' calls, you went inside and told your wife you loved her!'

'No, listen—'

'You pretended it was nothing, that she was nothing!'

'That's not true!'

'I held my body to yours, Joaquin Moralès, and three minutes later I heard…'

That was when I had made up my mind to leave. And now the decision seemed the right one.

'Listen, I … er—'

'Detective Moralès, you closed the case on my mother's death. You've no business being here anymore.'

He stood up, looking ill at ease.

'Catherine—'

'Joaquin Moralès, I yearn for my heart to start beating again, but not in the arms of a man who lies!'

'Lies?'

'Yes!'

He leaned over me again. 'What do you know about lies, Catherine Garant? And while we're at it, what do you know about love, eh? How old are you? Thirty-three years old, no children, no stable relationship! You don't know what it is! When a man asks his wife whether she still loves him after thirty years of marriage, and she answers, "Yes, of course, darling…" while she's thinking about what's for dinner – and, anyway, what a ridiculous question! When you try to catch her eye and brush your lips against hers and she says, "Stop it, I've got things to do!"; when your arms are empty, day after day, and your body's crying out … what does fidelity really mean? Perhaps it's my marriage that's become a lie!' He straightened up as he spoke.

'That's not my problem.'

'Yes, it is! You can't just show up at my door one night, tell me "I'm the woman you're looking for", ask me what my dreams are made of, let me touch you and then wash your hands in all innocence!'

'Have a nice evening, monsieur Moralès…'

I stood up, sending him a signal to leave, but I mistimed the movement and found myself pressing against him.

'It's time to stop running away, Catherine…'

5

TETHERED TO THE HORIZON

Archimedes' principle

Cyrille always said the sea could take care of itself, so it could take care of us. He said that lies would always ebb in the undertow of truth, and they'd end up sinking like a stone. Only determination would save us, he added, when the wind picked up and filled our sails with knots.

That morning, I finished packing my bags and went down to the wharf to load the last of the things onto the boat. The skies were forecast to clear by the end of the day and I was hoping to sail away under the watchful eye of the full moon.

The fishing was all over, but Tall, Indigenous Jérémie was there, as patient as the sand turning over on the shore. He helped me carry the bags over to the boat.

'Are you going away?'

'Yes.'

'For a long time?'

'Yes.'

There was tenderness in his eyes. His hands remained rock steady as he spoke. At peace. 'Maybe I could wait for you?'

I didn't know what to say.

Jérémie nodded his head slowly. 'When your mother went away, Cyrille waited for her. That's what he told me.'

'Marie Garant didn't want anyone to wait for her.'

'He loved her.'

'No. He liked waiting for her, and he liked the idea of loving her, but he didn't really know my mother. I doubt anyone truly knew her. Since the day I got here, it's struck me how no one truly knew my mother. Everyone has painted their own picture of her to channel their anger at, their failures, their lost love, but no one knew who she was. No one knew she had a child, no one can tell me who my father was, and no one knew where she was going or when she was coming back. It's easy to fall in love with a dream, an elusive fantasy of a woman, but perhaps from one day to the next, caught up in the daily grind, Cyrille, just like any other man, would have grown tired of her feistiness and her insatiable thirst for freedom.'

'Perhaps he wouldn't.'

'I don't know what love is, Jérémie. I never learned to love. I don't know how they do it, you know, those couples who've been together thirty years and still gaze at each other with eyes as big as saucers – who met when they were young and made promises they know they're going to keep.'

'Don't you want to give it a try?'

I turned and gazed out to sea.

With open eyes, I watched that powerful, faithful sea stretch far and wide, beckoning me in; I heard the whisper of the waves, like a mermaid's song, and what little hesitation was left in my pendulum of a heart dissolved into the moist saltiness of the morning.

I wanted to leave the Gaspé. The people I'd met here were living in the past, in the nostalgia of a bygone era they had all conspired to revere as it had been. The only beauty in the present was the memory of yesterday, and nothing else would ever compare. No bumper summer catches, wharves filled with sails, windfalls of tourist dollars or even resplendent sunrises would ever be anything like those of old.

If I stayed, the past would forever haunt me, whereas I was looking for a new dawn that would harken to the future.

'I'm going to sea, Jérémie. I don't want anyone to wait for me.'

'Not a soul who waited for your mother ever asked permission...'

He gave me a wave and I watched him walk away. Then I clambered aboard to put away my things.

Meanwhile, Moralès was going around in circles.

There was no news from his wife, but he preferred not to give that too much thought. He was still essentially living in an empty house with just his few boxes for company. It suited him. Not that he was especially minimalist, no, but housework wasn't his strong suit. As such, it was best not to dwell on the current state of the living room.

He piled his dirty breakfast dishes in the sink, on top of those from the last few days, then made his way up to the cemetery, feeling like a has-been fairground carousel that keeps clunking up and down as it goes around and around in circles.

Moralès ended up at Cyrille Bernard's window, spying on the old man inside.

Cyrille looked up and saw the detective standing there.

'Can I come in?'

'Heee ... Remind me to put a lock on that window, will you?'

Moralès ducked and climbed in through the window. 'I need to talk to you.'

'How so? Your case is closed!'

'I filed a report because I was asked to. But you were right the other day. I wouldn't be a detective worth his salt if I didn't get to the bottom of who killed Marie Garant. That's why I've come to see you.'

'Heee ... You make me laugh, you do!'

'Why?'

'I tell you you're wrong, so off you go looking for another conclusion to jump to! Heee ... You're like a weathervane in a storm that points any which way and can't put its finger on the true wind. Heee … The birds always know which way the wind is blowing, even though their brains are only yay big.'

'I have some questions to ask you, monsieur Bernard.'

'Do you, now? Heee … Now you're going to ask me to answer your questions, and I'll answer them. Heee … But then what? Then you're going to compare my version against everybody else's and you're going to decide which one of us is lying. Whoever fills in the most gaps in your story chock-full of lies, eh? Heee … I'm too old for all that malarkey.'

'If everyone else is lying, then tell me the truth! What do you have to lose?'

'Me? Nothing! Heee … But round here, nobody's going to tell you the truth about Marie Garant. Not for lack of wanting, but because our memory's failing and our memories are misleading. Heee … Time is a bare-faced liar and emotion blurs the picture. Heee … all we have left is a bunch of old, discoloured photos and hard, condensed feelings all dried up by years on the kitchen counter and now your kettle's hell bent on washing them away with hot water. Heee … You came a long way to cause us so much pain and suffering.'

Visibly tired, the old man closed his eyes. Moralès wasn't sure whether he should say it, but he did anyway.

'Tell me one thing, Cyrille. Just one. Who was with you on your father's fishing boat the day your eldest brother died? The day of your accident?'

Cyrille Bernard raised his head. Sitting up on his elbows in bed, his every bone in agony, the fisherman tried to deter the detective with an angry stare. But Moralès refused to back down.

'Listen, Cyrille—'

'No! You listen to me! Because I've been asking myself questions too, you know. Heee…' Cyrille sat up in bed. 'The woman I loved is dead, killed by a man in my village. Maybe it was an accident, maybe it wasn't. Heee … But everyone suspects it was him. Because in this neck of the woods, you wear your secrets like a party hat. Heee … All his life that man's been dragging around a sack full of regrets I'd never want to carry myself. The kind of sack that keeps getting heavier with every step you take, that trips you up when everyone's looking, a burden only you can shoulder. Heee ... he knows we know it. What are you hoping to achieve by arresting him? To take our pain away? See justice done? Who for? Marie's not coming back. Justice is something your conscience hands down, and your reports have nothing to do with it! Heee ... that man won't do any more harm to anyone but himself. Your investigation is pointless.'

Taken aback, Moralès turned away. The heaviest burdens we carry are those no one else can see. He was conscious of that. We all carry a burden, with every step we take and even when we're sitting down. So why keep at it, why insist on finding and punishing who did it? What would make less of a fool of him – letting it all sink away now or hauling the truth to the surface?

'Marie Garant died and you swooped in to investigate. Heee ... Why? What good can it do to fill out one report after another? Who's even going to read your damned reports? Nothing but paper, they are! Heee ... Why keep at it? Surely not for the love of the Gaspé? Heee ... And even less for Marie Garant herself!'

Joaquin looked outside. The morning had cloaked the cemetery in a stubborn mist. 'For Catherine...' he admitted.

Cyrille frowned inquisitively.

Moralès was still looking outside, but he couldn't see a thing. 'For her. Or for myself. I don't know anymore.'

Somewhere in the stillness, between the bed and the door, a night light on a timer clicked off, making the misty cemetery appear a little clearer by contrast.

'I'm fifty-two years old,' he went on. 'Fifty-two, you know what that's like. You go to the doctor's – because all of a sudden you need a doctor – and they bend your ear about your cholesterol, your liver, your heart and everything else that isn't as good as it used to be. You're told not to drink too much, to stop smoking, to get more sleep. Not to mention the prostate exam.'

In spite of the rain, the mist twinkled with the light of the rising sun.

'As a man in your forties, you still have what it takes, and women still find you attractive. By your fifties, though, you've lived half a century and old age begins to set in, with all the wrinkles and the lines no number of caresses can iron out. Oh, the caresses! After thirty years of marriage and two children, it takes a strong will to look past the Tupperware parties and hairy legs and put the moves on your wife. Or get hard as a rock whenever she snaps her fingers. I can't do it the way I used to, you know. I need a little time now, a bit of preparation, a splash of wine … and what's a man who's aging supposed to do about his skin, anyway?'

Joaquin Moralès turned towards Cyrille, or, at least, the thin contour of him there was beneath the covers. 'I envy you for loving one woman your whole life long.'

The old man didn't move a muscle.

'As long as I've been here, I've been dreaming about another woman. About cheating on my wife. You talk about regrets. I should feel unfaithful, but unfaithful to what? I don't know who I am anymore. A middle-aged man who's screwing up his marriage and his career? Since I arrived in the Gaspé, I've had nowhere to hide. I'm making a fool of myself. I'm like a ringmaster standing in an empty field after the circus has packed up and moved on.'

Cyrille was still watching him.

'That's why I want to close the case once and for all. You're right, I'm not doing it for Marie Garant, you know. I'm not even doing it for Catherine, and it's not about finding the truth. I'm doing it for myself, monsieur Bernard. To prove to myself I'm not completely over the hill. To show I'm not an old fool.'

Joaquin Moralès lowered his eyes, either in shame or because he'd suddenly relieved himself of it.

'Heee … Open the cupboard there to your left. There's a bottle and two glasses. I think you and I should have a wee dram of whisky, Detective Moralès. No ice. Heee … Let's have ourselves a little chat…'

Marine forecast

Yves Carle hit the nail on the head when he said the more you put it off, the less you're likely to leave. The doctor's orders were nothing but a distant memory as the only thing beckoning me now was the sea.

That day, I climbed in through Cyrille's window one last time.

'Heee … make sure you look both ways on your way in, because that window's becoming a real motorway!'

'The ladies just can't help themselves, can they, Cyrille? You're going to end up spooning with one of them sooner or later, if you keep this up!'

'Heee … not just the ladies! The detective came in that way this morning as well!'

'Moralès?'

'He's falling over himself to sleep with you, and I'm not talking about spooning! Heee … He couldn't be more head over heels with your pretty blue eyes!'

'He's going to have to get back on his feet, Cyrille, because I'm leaving.'

Long and hard I held the deep blue of his watery gaze. I'd had enough of turning away from it. From now on, I'd have the sea in my sights and everywhere I looked.

'You're strong like your mother, young Garant. A whole lineage of women breaking men's hearts! Heee…'

'It's not like we do it on purpose!'

'I know, love. Heee … You might not mean to do it, but you still scoop out little mouthfuls of our hearts with a teaspoon!'

I sat down on the bed next to him.

'Heee … It's all alright, love. Loving you is something we take to heart, like a bunch of madmen. Heee … And we're prepared to wait for you, like a bunch of fools.'

'I don't know why my mother went away. But I think I know why she kept coming back.'

When he finally spoke, water pooled in his eyes and sadness oozed from his throaty voice.

'Heee … The Gaspé's a land of empty, love. We've bled the sea dry and we work the soil for nothing. Heee … There's the tourist trail that channels them all to Percé. But the rest of it's just old and washed up, love, heee … and we're all living in the past. Leaving's the right thing to do. This is no place for a pretty young girl like you.'

'I'm going to miss you, Cyrille.'

'Heee … No, Catherine. Don't be like that. Live for what's there, not for what isn't.'

There were no waves to mark the silence.

He spoke slowly. 'Heee … My breathing's going downhill. I'm sucking in less and less air, and more and more water. It's the tide rising in my lungs. You see, love, heee … when my lungs are done breathing air, I'll take my boat and go out to sea. A long way out. Further out than the Banc-des-Fous. I won't be dropping the anchor. I'll turn off the engine, heee … so I can listen to the waves creaking against the hull. If it's daytime, I'll watch the sun splash its colour all over the place. If it's nighttime, heee … I'll get to see the stars settling into the troughs of the waves on the horizon all around. Heee … See, I won't be sticking around for them to kill me with morphine. I'll hold my mother's medallion of the Virgin in the palm of my hand, heee … and I'll take off my boots. That's important, you know. You don't go knocking at the pearly gates with fishing boots on your feet! Heee … some go up to Heaven when they're six feet under. But I'll be dripping with seawater on my way up there. Heee … I can't swim, but it doesn't matter, Marie will be there. She's waiting for me. Heee … And you know what I'm hoping for, love? I'm hoping the tide'll be high. Heee …. That's all, a big spring tide, even though it'll be autumn, that'll carry me far, far away on its way out.'

He looked deep into my eyes.

'Me too, Catherine, I'll soon be going out to sea. Heee … So we'll be seeing each other again.'

He had such a nice smile.

'Go, love, heee …. it's time.'

'Cyrille … I have one more question.'

He nodded. He'd known it was coming. We all want answers. It's hard not to.

'Go and see Vital, love. Heee…'

'Vital?'

'Moralès went to see him, but … heee … he must be down at the station by now. Heee … Go and see Vital before you leave.'

I kissed Cyrille on the forehead with all the tenderness that should have been my mother's. He sank down into his bed. I straddled the windowsill and emerged into the drizzle and gloom of the cemetery. I plucked up my courage. If I was leaving, I would have to accept that nothing would be the same if I ever came back, and that I was beholden to no one.

Vital's first reaction was to storm out onto the porch and poke his right index finger into the detective's chest.

'Christ in a chalice, what are you doing here?' he spat.

Moralès was undeterred. 'Monsieur Bujold, I have a question to ask you.'

'Isn't your case closed?'

'The day you found Marie Garant's body, you said in your interview that you hated the woman. You did everything you could to dodge my questions.'

'What do you want?'

A thin, warm drizzle was falling. Vital didn't invite him in. Moralès stood tall on the front porch.

'I've been wondering why you hated Marie Garant. I was thinking, you don't hate a woman just because a woman makes a big song and dance about something. Every woman makes a song and dance about something one day or another.'

Vital didn't say a word.

Moralès went on. 'And another thing I found strange was how your wife's twin sister, Guylaine Leblanc the seamstress, feels the same kind of hate as you do for Marie Garant. Then I assumed it must have something to with the death of your only son, Guillaume, who drowned along with Renaud Boissonneau's brothers in the almighty squall that also took the life of Marie Garant's husband on their wedding night.'

Vital retreated a step.

'I figured that Marie Garant's whole song and dance about losing her husband must have brought memories flooding back for you both. Not just of your son's death, but also your wife's reaction when she tried to—'

'I had nothing to do with Marie Garant's murder. Nothing!'

'I know that.'

Vital took a deep breath. Staring out to sea, he folded his arms across his chest. 'What was your question, then?'

'The night of Marie Garant's murder, Clément Marsil had his safe stolen up on Fourth Lane. The investigation concluded he'd done it himself to claim on the insurance.'

'Christ in a chalice, I doubt that! He was at his sister's place in Gaspé!'

'The next day, they found the safe in the ditch behind his place, along with your sledgehammer.'

'I often lend my tools to folk.'

'The police officer who was investigating the crime neglected to make a note of whom you'd lent your sledgehammer to the day before.'

'She was too busy strutting around with all that stuff hanging off her belt to think about asking me!'

'That's what I'm here for now.'

Vital sighed. 'Christ in a chalice! It's about time…'

Weather report

It was in the patchy afternoon mist that I knocked at Vital's door. There was no answer, but the door was unlocked. So, I turned the handle.

I meant to call out to him as I crossed the threshold, but I couldn't. I froze as soon as I laid eyes on the scene inside. The house was impeccably kept and exuded such a feminine, old-fashioned charm that didn't fit at all with the picture I'd painted for myself of the fisherman. I was struck by the lace curtains, flowery tablecloth, braided rag rugs, laughing children in photo frames, rocking chairs, stained-glass ceiling lamps with floral motifs. But most of all, over by the west-facing window, I was struck by *her*. The woman, a lifeless replica of Guylaine, was rocking gently in a chair, holding idle knitting needles in her hands. Her eyes stared without seeing.

I called hello to her twice. No response. I moved closer. Her lips murmured something, and she started knitting again. I retreated towards the door. There he was, standing in the doorway. Vital.

'I knew you'd come.'

His voice was so low, it seemed he had risen from the earth. My whole body started to shake. My mouth opened for no reason. He moved back, motioning to me to step outside. The silence was broken by the regular, repetitive click-clacking of the knitting needles. We sat down on a long wooden bench on the deck. My hands were shaking so much, I had to press them against the slats to calm them down.

'Christ in a chalice! All this is going to end up driving me mad.'

As I focused all my energy on breathing, the fisherman's voice drifted towards me through a slowly dispersing fog, gradually gaining clarity as I came to terms with the strangeness of the situation. The clicking of needles knitted the air a little tighter as the waves rolled in at the foot of the cliff.

'I don't dwell in the past. I know I keep saying there's no money in fishing anymore, and I can see the sea's been drained of all the fish, but I don't do nostalgia. For me, the past is all about suffering. The suffering of my mother, who died too young, and my father, who got screwed over by the government and their bloody *Gaspésiennes*. Too many slaps on the back of the head! I've never known any different. Christ in a chalice! There's nobody here who's known anything different! Fishing never lined the pockets of any French-Canadian, only the bloody English! Anybody wanting to try their hand at something else ended up at the pulp and paper mill. Christ in a chalice, what a place that was! Do you know why they shut it down? Because three quarters of the men got cancer! They close the mill, the bosses bugger off, and who are the cancer patients going to complain to? And where are they going to go? And what would they end up with anyway? Ten thousand bucks at best, and what would they do with it? Pop their clogs in a private room at the hospital? Might as well die in a room with four beds, at least that way they won't die alone!'

One wave, two.

'The Gaspé's a land of poor folk whose only riches were in the sea, and now the sea's on its death bed. It's a mish-mash of memories, a place that keeps its mouth shut and won't bother a soul, a land of suffering only the open sea can bring any comfort to. And we latch on to it like no-hopers. Like fishermen who need consoling.'

The needles were still clicking away. He let two waves roll by, then glanced over at me.

'Did you come here because of the will?'

'No, because of Cyrille.'

He twitched with surprise.

'Cyrille ... Cyrille, what is he, five, six years younger than me? It's not a lot, but it's enough for us to not have biked around the village together as kids. We weren't friends when we were young. Later, when Marie Garant grew into her beauty, we were this close to being enemies. Christ in a chalice! Of all the men that were around, I'd be hard pushed to tell you which one of them she truly loved.'

'Maybe she loved them all.'

He threw me an indecisive glance. 'Maybe. She married Lucien because her first fiancé was dead. It was Jeannot who killed him, on a fishing trip. Cyrille was there, hiding on the boat. He nearly died as well, and he's been handicapped ever since. He'll never say so, but I'm sure the guys were fighting over her. I reckon Jeannot even tried to kill Cyrille. He must have thought he was dead, to bring him back to shore. They said it was an accident, but Cyrille's never been able to talk to Jeannot since. If it's nothing but an accident, you don't fly off the handle like that at someone! But it's the cancer that's going to get the better of him. Cyrille I mean. And before crab season comes around, at this rate.'

Three, four waves.

'I was drunk, the night of their wedding. I used to drink like a fish when I was younger. Marie and Lucien set sail in the late afternoon. They'd had their wedding early in the day, so they could set out to sea on their honeymoon.'

Resting his forearms on his knees, he rubbed his hands together, the rest of his body in stillness.

'Irène, my wife, was sulking because I'd been drinking. Something happened, I don't know what, but she tore a bit of her dress. Guylaine told her to come up to Le Point de Couture and she'd fix it. So, she came over to me and told me to keep an eye on Guillaume.'

He took a deep breath.

'My son was ten years old. It had been a difficult birth and the doctor said we couldn't have any more children. My wife and her sister were mad about the little kid. Guylaine was only young, but she'd always been a bit of an old maid, so she had nothing better to do than look after the kid and spoil him rotten. Christ in a chalice! I loved him too – of course I loved him like crazy – but whatever else could I have done for him? The women were always on his case with their "Guillaume, do this, Guillaume, don't do that! Guillaume,

come and try on the trousers your auntie Guylaine's sewn for you!"
So I wanted to do the opposite, you know, stay off his back and teach
him manly things so he wouldn't turn into a big softie.

'But no matter what I did, it was never the right thing. Never.
What should I have done? How the heck should I know? What more
could I have done? I wasn't allowed to take him fishing, I could
never take him swimming, I wasn't allowed to take him anywhere!
The women used to tell me off like I was a child myself. "Don't tell
him that! You're upsetting him, he's a sensitive soul!" and all that.
Sometimes I even wondered whether I had the right to be his father!
Christ in a chalice! It's not that I didn't want to be all trendy and talk
to him about philosophy and all that kind of stuff, but that's just not
my thing. I can't rattle on about that! You can't ask me to go on about
something I never knew anything about, can you? All I ever knew
were fish that never brought home the bacon, my unemployment
cheques every winter, little jobs under the table here and there and a
bunch of slaps on the back of the head! So no, I never did know how
to talk to that boy of mine!'

He bowed his head.

'I'd already had too much to drink. We were partying. I can't
remember whether Guillaume came to ask me if he could go out
for a paddle in the canoe with the Boissonneau brothers. What was
I supposed to say to him, anyway? "Don't play down by the water"?
Christ in a chalice, we live by the sea! I wasn't going to tell him
twenty times a day it was dangerous, was I? And the women were
always brooding over him too much, anyway.

'I must've said yes. I imagine I said yes, I can't remember.'

The rain had stopped, and the sun was starting to burn off the fog.

'The women were taking their time, and I kept on drinking. I
don't know what time it was when the wind picked up. Someone
told me the wind was picking up. I thought I'd better go and check
the mooring lines on my boat. Why ever did I think that? Maybe I
was just looking for a reason to go down to the wharf and see where
they'd gone off to after their wedding…

'So, I went down to the boat and smoked a joint. The weather turned heavier, and it kept getting worse and worse. I shut myself into my wheelhouse, stretched my legs out on the seat and fell asleep.

'It was Marie who woke me up. She was banging on my boat like a crazy woman, like she was going to smash it all to pieces. She was still in her wedding dress, but it was filthy and torn. Her hair was dripping wet and sticking to her shoulders and her makeup had run, giving her these big, ghostly eyes. I'd never seen her look so beautiful...

'She was shaking and screaming that she hadn't finished looking, that we had to get back out there. There wasn't another soul on the wharf! Nobody except me. Marie Garant, in her dirty wedding dress, asking me, just a poor fisherman, to help her find her husband who'd gone overboard! What else could I have done, Christ in chalice? So I took her aboard and off we went...

'We looked as long and hard as we could. I did alert the coast guard, but they had so many calls to deal with it took them hours to get there! It rained for three days solid. Three days! You could have cut through the fog with a knife. If he were still alive, my old man would have told you all of us guys wore ourselves out trying, day and night, and you should have seen the Bernard boys' father crying when we brought the lifebuoy back to shore, empty of his son. Christ in a chalice! We never found him.

'The night of the third day, when we came back from looking, Marie gave me a great big hug. I'd lent her some clothes, and she was floating in them. She was still beautiful. She was always beautiful! Victor was waiting for us on the wharf. He said I had to get home as quick as I could. He looked at Marie, and he never said a word, but that didn't mean he agreed. All it meant was he knew when to keep his mouth shut.

'I left Marie down on the wharf. Victor said he'd drive her home. When I drove off, she screamed the place down. She was kicking and screaming so much, it took three men to hold her down. That's how she started kicking the kelp. And Christ in a chalice, did my little Marie ever kick the kelp!'

He straightened himself up. The needles were no longer beating time, but the waves were still battering the solid rock at the foot of the cliff. He leaned against the side of the house.

'And then I went home.'

He paused.

'When I came in here ... You ever heard the sound of silence? True silence ... like something clicks, and you know something's happened? It's the beginning of a nightmare you know you're never going to wake up from.

'I called out to Irène. No answer. I never even took off my boots. I ran up the stairs. The bedroom door was open. My heart was pounding in my throat.

'She never was the world's greatest wife, and I haven't spent my life going down on one knee for her like you read about in books, but I loved her. She had her faults. She was too overbearing, and her sister was annoying, but she was a hardworking woman who was where she belonged and she could be really nice when she wanted. She thought I drank too much, but she never said no when I snuggled up to her. There was tenderness in her. That's it, tenderness. You won't find much of that around here, and deep down inside, I knew I was a lucky man.'

Three waves, four perhaps, passed slowly.

'The bedroom had been turned upside down, as if she'd been taking out her anger on everything she could find in there. She'd knocked over a little table and broken a glass ornament, and she'd got cuts all over her stomach and wrists from that. There was broken glass all over her hands and her belly. She was barely breathing, not much at all. Christ in a chalice! Now I might not be a thinking man, but I knew when I should take my wife to the hospital! I lifted her up off the floor, carried her to the car and drove her to Carleton as quick as I could. I lifted her out of the car and took her into Emergency, grabbed the first stretcher I laid eyes on then I shouted so loud, doctors came running from all over the place. Then they took her away.

'The whole time they were messing around with her, I stayed at the hospital in the wedding suit I'd had on my back for the last four days, that stank of fish, the smell of another woman and the blood of my wife. My wife's blood! Christ in a chalice, it was everywhere! On the floor in the hospital, outside on the road, and all over the car. If I'd been rich, I'd have set the car on fire, it was that bad. But I could only just afford to clean it up as best I could and live with the stains.

'At some point in the night, a doctor came to fetch me. He had bags under his eyes and he looked exhausted. The waiting room was empty, so he sat down next to me. Him in his clean hospital pyjamas or whatever they're called, and me in my filthy, stinking wedding best. He pretended he couldn't smell me, but there's no way he couldn't have. Maybe he found it refreshing after the smell of all those cleaning products. He leaned his head back against the wall, he looked up at the ceiling with big, wide eyes and he had his hands on his thighs. I remember his hands, because I thought they were the hands that had just been ferreting around in my wife's wrists and in her stomach, and even just the thought of it made me want to cry like a baby. He didn't move a muscle. The whole time he was telling me, he didn't take his eyes off the ceiling once, and I reckon it was for the best, because I couldn't have held myself together if he'd looked at me.

'He told me she'd tried to kill herself and that she'd lost a lot of blood, but that wasn't the worst of it. He said she'd gone into nervous shock that had caused serious injury to her brain, and that I'd have to be brave. I wondered what he meant by "serious injury", but I didn't ask any questions.

'I also found out I couldn't take her home with me because they wanted to keep her under observation. He told me I could see her, but not for long. He said, "After that, you should go home and have a shower and get some sleep. You're going to need all your strength." Christ in a chalice! I remember those words, because I've never had any bloody strength ever since!'

He was staring at the bottom of the ramp, straight in front of him. He could have been looking anywhere, because he wasn't seeing a thing. I could still hear the sound of the sea, and the rain clouds were dispersing.

'It must've been three in the morning when I went into the room. She was asleep, all pale in those white sheets. There were a bunch of machines all around her. I was so filthy I didn't dare touch her. I was worried I'd make her dirty. Worried she'd be cold to the touch, or dead. It's stupid, I know, all those machines going beep, beep, beep, but Christ in a chalice, I was afraid she was dead!

'I sat down next to her, and I spoke to her. I didn't know what to say. I told her all about my last catch. I told her about the music we were playing on the boat and I told her about Victor's cheesy jokes, how big the fish were and how much I got for them. I had nothing else to say. Christ in a chalice, what makes us so brainless when life shakes us up like that? My wife was slipping away through my fingers and all I could talk to her about was the bloody price of fish!

'At some point, a nurse came over and crouched down in front of me, the way you'd talk to a child. She told me to go home and get some rest. That snapped me out of it. I remembered I was a man after all, so I got up and I went back home in my car full of blood.

'It must've been five in the morning and everything was still such a mess. The blood had dried in the bedroom and it stank of mould in there. I was all alone. So bloody alone! I thought I'd better clean it all up before my boy came home, but he never came back.'

Those useless hands of his.

'The week after that, I buried my son and I brought my wife back home. My wife who'd lost her mind and would never find it again. Who spends her days knitting socks. Toasty warm fucking Christ-in-a-chalice wool socks for her dead son!

'And me, while my son was being swept out to sea in the squall and my wife was going crazy to the point of wanting to kill herself, instead of watching over my own, I was scouring the sea with Marie Garant...'

He turned to me. The blue of his irises lining up with mine. A few waves passed. I didn't bother to count them.

'Maybe I just can't forgive myself, and that's why I harboured such a grudge against your mother…'

His voice was breaking up.

'You know, I'm not even surprised she came and threw herself into my nets! I loved her too much for her to leave me be. She always did that, she always brought it all right back to the surface. Christ in a chalice, she'd never let anything drop! No danger she'd ever stop screaming and kicking the bleeding kelp! No, she wouldn't let go of us. She was so full-on, it hurt. And we should be allowed to forget. We have the right to want to forget it all…'

He stared so hard at me I thought he was going to tear his eyes out of their sockets.

'What date were you born, Catherine Garant?'

'I don't know. Sometime between the twentieth of May and the twentieth of August.'

'Ah.'

'I wish I knew, but my baptism certificate was faked. There's no way it could have been early September. Where my father's name should be, it just says "Alberto Garant". I've looked into it, and he doesn't exist. It's a made-up name.'

'Alberto … Sounds like the name of a boat.'

He stood up, looked at me one last time, and then he leaned down and planted a tender kiss on the top of my head.

Then he disappeared inside. Through the window, I could see him go over to his wife, gently take her by the arm and ever so slowly guide her up the stairs.

I made my way down the steps on the tips of my toes and closed the door of the day behind me in silence. As I looked ahead, the sea was still counting the waves and my sailboat was waiting for me.

Letting it all go

Moralès parked his car to the side of the house.

'Heee … Why don't you come in through the window, it's open!'

He clambered his way in. 'You're in better spirits, Cyrille.'

'Heee … There are days you get used to dying, detective.'

Moralès reflected on that in silence.

'So? Shuffled any papers recently? Heee…'

Moralès pulled up a chair by the bed and sat facing the window. He had spent the afternoon at the station in Bonaventure causing an almighty hullabaloo, strong-arming the case open again, checking alibis and finding the holes in them, confounding false witnesses, turning findings upside down and reminding himself there was nothing stranger than people. Now he had worked it out of his system.

Outside, the dusk streaked the sky with lines of red and orange. A car came into view in the corner of the cemetery, and stopped. Langevin the undertaker stepped out, smoothed his hair down and gave his trousers a shake.

'Quite a few, yes.'

'And did you find the answers you were looking for?'

'Some of them. If I'd taken the time to check Marie Garant's medical records properly, I'd have seen she wasn't well—'

'For the last three years.'

'—and I'd have seen she needed medication.'

Langevin crossed the cemetery at a diagonal.

'Anyway, her prescription was running out and her stockpile was running low. Her doctor – who wasn't just her doctor – knew she'd be coming back soon for a check-up. He also knew that whenever she was heading out for warmer climes or back in from them, Marie Garant would always make a stop by the Banc-des-Fous to say a prayer for her late husband. So he knew there was a window of a few days when he'd be able to intercept her on her way back if he waited around a while in that remote spot.'

Langevin bent down, perhaps to check one of the groundhog traps he set the other day, and stood up again with a look of triumph.

'Why intercept her, though? Because he was in love with her, and he had been for a long time. When he was twenty-three years old, he found out your brother was engaged to Marie Garant and it made him crazy with jealousy. They went out to sea together, and your brother didn't suspect a thing because they were friends. But things soon turned ugly. They had a fight and he tipped your brother overboard. Maybe he tried to catch him, or fish him out, but the weather was too heavy. You were on board too, that time. You must have had to fight him too, but you were younger and he was stronger than you. He tried to strangle you with the fishing lines, and make it look like you'd tangled yourself up, trying to save your brother. He was hoping to silence you once and for all, but you survived. I know who Jeannot is, Cyrille. Why didn't you blow the whistle on him?'

Moralès had finally pieced it all together; it was time to untangle the knots.

'It was nighttime and I'd been drinking beer on the sly. I wasn't sure what I'd seen. Heee ... My brother was dead. People would have called me a liar.'

'Is that why you have such a hard time breathing?'

'The cancer can't be helping either.'

Moralès nodded, keeping an eye on Langevin, who was on his way back to his car.

'Marie Garant wasn't getting any younger,' he continued. 'She needed care and he figured, after a lifetime of waiting, maybe she'd agree to marry him. You knew her doctor was the coroner, didn't you? Jeannot Robichaud – the same man who killed your brother.'

'Marie never loved Jeannot Robichaud. Heee... She was sick, but

she wasn't out of her mind. She'd never have had a change of heart
for him! Heee…'

Langevin opened the boot of his car and dug out a spade. He
returned to the trap.

'Here's what I suspect happened: That night he went out to the
Banc-des-Fous and she was right there, at anchor, as he'd hoped.
She'd just arrived. He pulled up alongside her sailboat, offered her
a glass of wine and started spouting on about love. She laughed at
him, because she always had a sharp tongue, did Marie Garant, and
he went for her. She fell backwards, cracked her head, lost conscious-
ness and slipped into the water. It was dark. Coroner Robichaud was
an old man; he knew he couldn't save her. And what would it look
like if he called the coast guard? Like an old fool of a man had lost
his temper in a lovers' tiff and killed a woman. Perhaps accidentally,
perhaps not.'

Langevin bent over the trap and put the groundhog out of its
misery with a solid whack of the spade.

'So, he set about wiping the boat clean. Surgically clean. Because
he's tall, he banged his head on the boom and that gave him the idea
to loosen the mainsail sheets and make it look like an accident. But
in his haste, he failed to see the boom would have been too high to
hit Marie Garant.'

'You're not bad at this when you put your mind to it. Heee…'

Langevin freed the animal from the trap, picked it up and carried
it off to the edge of the woods.

'He sneaked back home in the middle of the night, hoping he
wouldn't be seen. But as fate would have it, he ran into his neighbour, Marc Lapierre the fishing guide. Lapierre was sneaking back
home himself – from Clément Marsil's place up on Fourth Lane.
One just as sheepish as the other, they darted indoors without so
much as a wave.'

Langevin dug a hole.

'The next day, when the coroner heard Marsil's safe had been stolen,
he put two and two together and figured it must have been Lapierre.

More importantly, though, Lapierre gathered it was Robichaud who killed Marie Garant. So, he made a deal with him. The two men gave each other an alibi: they'd say they were playing cards together that night. Meanwhile, the coroner persuaded Lieutenant Forest, who fancies her chances with him, to put his nice Joannie in charge of the safe heist so he could lead her to his own conclusion.'

Langevin dropped the animal into the hole and proceeded to bury it.

'As for the sailboat, Robichaud had been planning to bring it in the next day, but Yves Carle beat him to it overnight. Robichaud brought it in all the same, and he seized the opportunity to smear his fingerprints all over the place. That way his prints would be excluded when the case was examined.'

'Heee … Now you're talking like a real detective…'

Using the back of the spade, Langevin patted down the mound of earth before returning to his car with a satisfied smile.

'They're searching Lapierre's house right now. Robichaud has stepped down, young Joannie is beside herself and Lieutenant Forest doesn't know whether she's coming or going. They're bickering over the details, but if you ask me, we should be hauling the coroner in for questioning. I'm still new around here though, so I'd rather let them all air their dirty laundry together.'

'Heee … Sometimes I tell myself a man's worst punishment is a life without love.'

Langevin started the car and drove away from the cemetery. The moon was rising.

Moralès turned to Cyrille. 'I don't know who stole the box of Marie Garant's things that were evidence, but I think it was Catherine.'

'Heee … if the investigation's over, they're not much use to you anymore.'

'I do still have one question, Cyrille.'

'Heee … What's that?'

'Who pillaged the grave?'

'What grave?'

'Someone dug up and made off with Marie Garant's body.'

'I don't know what you're talking about, but surely it can't have been me! Heee … I wouldn't have the strength.'

Moralès spent a while contemplating the shadow of Cyrille on his death bed.

'You were right, Cyrille. Marie Garant deserved to go back to the sea.'

The old man arched an eyebrow.

Moralès cut to the chase. 'You did the right thing, the two of you.'

Cyrille Bernard nodded, then closed his eyes.

Beyond the window, it was a clear night. A night for will-o'-the-wisps and ghosts to rest in peace.

That night, Joaquin Moralès didn't go to Catherine's house. Nor did he go to Renaud's bistro. He went home and let the clock tick around until daytime. Sarah tried to reach him, but he didn't answer. He just needed some time to firm up his decision.

He dined alone on a marinated salmon fillet, reflecting on the fine balance between the grace of love and the craving for comfort. The clouds had parted to reveal a bright, pure sky awash with stars, and Moralès settled down with a glass of red wine on his patio overlooking the sea. He thought about Paul Lapointe again, so he picked up the phone and gave the architect a call.

'Sergeant Moralès? How are you doing?'

'I've had to review the findings of the investigation. Marie Garant was killed accidentally.'

'*Accidentally?*'

'Yes, it appears a spurned lover pushed her over the edge.'

Sitting on the edge of his bed, Lapointe was sipping a glass of white port. The door to the ensuite bathroom was ajar and he was watching his wife take off her makeup with delicate, airy strokes.

'A spurned lover? At her age? Marie Garant must have been a real stunner.'

'Like her daughter.'

She started with her foundation. She used a damp washcloth to wipe away the colour, laying bare the contours of her face.

'Catherine is a lure, monsieur Moralès.'

'I don't think so.'

'The beauty of a young woman is always deceiving. When my assistant, Isabelle, walks into my office, I know my clients are going to sign on the dotted line. She entraps them with her beauty.'

Moralès wanted to tell him he had taken Catherine in his arms, swept her off her feet, carried her into the house and showered her with kisses and caresses; he wanted to say how young he had felt, like he was riding a wave. A whole new wave! Instead he settled for saying, 'I remember, you talked to me about the grace of love.'

Paul Lapointe's wife took a corner of the washcloth, opened her lips wide and wiped her rouge away.

'It's real, monsieur Moralès. And when she takes off her makeup in front of you, it's smothering.'

'Sorry?'

'Does your wife wear makeup?'

They didn't take it any further. Catherine had rejected him, delicately. She'd said no. She'd gone on to say she'd had enough of all the lies and the deceit and only had eyes for good deeds and a clear horizon. He'd understood.

'I'm getting a divorce.'

There, he said it. That was why he'd called Paul Lapointe, to say it out loud. To hear the words come from his own lips so they'd feel real when he told Sarah the news.

'Is your mind made up?' In the sliver of light, Lapointe could see his wife gently rubbing her eyelids.

'Yes.'

Joaquin had even planned out in his mind what he was going to say to Sarah, tomorrow. A torrent of reproaches about the extended urban sojourn she was sharing with the insufferable Jay-Pee, followed by him giving moving testimony about his yearning for youthfulness and passion. Because he wanted to feel the same fulfilment she did. He had sacrificed it all for her, and now it was time for him to take care of some 'personal things' of his own. He was ready for his second wind in life and in love.

'You should sleep on it, monsieur Moralès.'

Paul Lapointe's wife rinsed her face with running water, patted it dry, noticed her husband was watching. She smiled. The architect hung up.

A southwesterly wind had risen over the Baie-des-Chaleurs, and it heartened Moralès to see a sailboat in the distance, its wake slicing a right angle with the sliver of moon on the water. He finished his glass, went to bed and drifted into the impatient sleep of a young man in love.

Hoisting the sails

No, he didn't get much sleep. He got up early, being in such a hurry to change his life. He tried to call Sarah, to get these conjugal formalities that had been nagging at him over and done with as soon as possible, but he got the answering machine. She must be otherwise occupied with the insufferable Jay-Pee, he thought. Joaquin left her a curt message – 'Call me back.' – and went down to the wharf.

Pilar was absent, but he wasn't concerned. Catherine must be out for a quick sail. He wandered over to the Café du Havre to await her return. When she docked, he would go over and invite her to dinner. She would understand.

He pushed the café door open.

'Let me tell you, she's only gone and done the same as her mother!'

'In truth, she has.'

Renaud Boissonneau and Father Leblanc were fretting over their half-eaten veggie omelettes.

'Inspector! You'll never guess what!'

The cook's helper from the bistro had tears in his eyes. Moralès smiled. Boissonneau did have a gift for drama.

'What's up, Renaud?'

'It's Catherine Garant!' He choked back a sob. 'Let me tell you, she's gone! Just like her mother!'

Moralès froze. 'Gone? For a stroll?'

'In truth, no.'

'She came in to see us at the bistro yesterday and said it like it was a drop in the ocean. Over a mouthful of her *coquilles Saint-Jacques*!'

Renaud Boissonneau hazarded a bang of his fist on the table, only to knock over his coffee, spill half of it on the table, right his cup and pile a stack of paper napkins in the dark puddle. The red-haired wait-ress came over and mopped up the mess, then she turned to Moralès.

'Take a seat, I'll bring you a coffee.'

But Moralès couldn't bring himself to sit down. He stood rooted to the spot, uncomprehending, while Renaud and Father Leblanc drank their bitterness away one sip at a time.

'Let me tell you, I even turned in my cook's helper apron to the boss!'

'In truth, departures can be upsetting.'

'Because we loved her, didn't we, our lovely, lovely tourist? And you just don't do that, do you? Go off forever, I mean!'

Forever? Moralès looked to the horizon. Pools of sunlight danced across the sea as a stiff breeze whipped crests of foam atop the swell.

'You must be mistaken—'

'She set sail last night.'

'Let me tell you, our hearts were in pieces all night long!'

'It was a clear night. We watched her boat cross the bay.'

Like a knife to the heart, it suddenly struck Moralès how he had watched the sailboat gliding through the sliver of moonlight. So that had been her? Setting sail forever?

At that very moment, because the Gaspé was such an unrelenting kind of place, his phone chose to ring. Moralès picked it up with a mechanical reflex, taking three steps off to the side.

'Hello?'

'Joaquin? It's me.'

'Me?'

'Sarah. Your wife.'

The silence fell flat as a pancake. For the first time in thirty years, he hadn't recognised the sound of his wife's voice. Because he was somewhere else entirely, on that boat with its back turned and the wind in its sails.

'Joaquin? Are you there?'

Moralès was lost for words.

'You left me a message.'

He stepped outside the Café du Havre.

Why hadn't he gone to see Catherine last night? Why had he waited before telling her what he had decided? She had no idea he was going to get a divorce. She left without knowing! How was he supposed to get hold of her now?

'Why aren't you saying anything? We've not spoken for days…'

He took a step towards the sea. Towards Catherine. With her, he felt so … young … He was so…

'Joaquin?'

Sarah was insistent.

'Yesterday, I met with the collectors in New York and I … I'm going to let Jean-Paul take care of it. I'm sorry, Joaquin. I regret my … my hesitations, my doubts. I miss you.'

It was now or never. He had to tell Sarah. To stop any wishful thinking, to stop things getting out of hand. So, Moralès let it all out. He told her he was in another place. He felt lighter, uplifted, swept away. It was too late. Could she understand? His life was shifting too, embracing new possibilities. He explained all that to her, but only in his mind, because she was the one doing all the talking.

'If you like, I can hit the road today. I can get the boys to finish up the move. I … I'll come and join you in the Gaspé.'

Possibilities? Who was he kidding? If Catherine had known he had been plotting a divorce, would she still have left? Moralès gazed out to sea. Stared. *Pilar* was out there, somewhere beyond the horizon.

'Joaquin?'

In spite of himself, he knew his name when his wife called it.

'Yes, Sarah. I'm listening.'

'I … I know we don't make love often enough…'

She went on to say how old and graceless she felt, struggling to keep pace on the day-to-day treadmill, what a fool she had been. She insisted how handsome she found him. Even more handsome than before. And she was still attracted to him. Here or elsewhere. Anywhere. Out there, why not? Down by the sea.

'What about you?'

As she was talking, Moralès realised he was not alone. Over on the wharf, a tall, Indigenous man had his eye on the horizon. Rooted to the shore like a lighthouse, he too was casting his gaze far offshore.

Suddenly, Moralès felt … old. Past his best. Over the hill. What a fool.

He bowed his head.

Down by his feet, his reflection stared back at him from the watery mirror of a puddle. Yes. Even if she'd known, Catherine Garant would have gone. Forever. She was a lure. Admit it, Moralès, though you know it hurts. And you do feel hurt, Moralès, in all that hurt can mean. A pang at the pit of your stomach, a hole, a void.

'I still love you, Joaquin.'

He closed his eyes and, in spite of himself, he saw age-old images emerging from the depths, scrolling across the slate of memory. His wife slipping off her tights, stripping away her makeup, wiping off her lipstick, rubbing her eyelids ever so gently. The grace of love.

He took a deep breath and opened his eyes.

'Me too, Sarah. I still love you too.'

And he turned away from the sea.

Daughters of the sea

Cyrille said the sea was like a patchwork quilt, that our pure morning gaze was a clean slate for the splintered light of sunrise to make a mosaic of us. Cyrille was right. The rising sun fanned its rolling colours over the Baie-des-Chaleurs, washing the hull crimson, drawing me ever deeper into the coralline canvas of the open sea.

I stole away in the dead of night, because I wanted to sail my first nautical miles of freedom under a sky full of stars. I cast off my moorings with neither sorrow nor regret. Happy. I glided out to sea with the wind on my side, in the same regal style as the great tall ships.

Around one in the morning, *Night Flight* drew alongside me. Together we traced parallel wakes at close quarters. Suddenly, Yves Carle veered course slightly to bring our hulls abreast. He pointed to a bay.

'Look, it's the Banc-des-Fous!'

'I know!'

Our voices echoed on the water.

'Who told you?'

'I was here the other night.'

He gave me a grand send-off as I steered my course offshore.

The other night had been moonless. Pitch dark. I was dressed in black. The sky was heavy with clouds, and the will-o'-the-wisps were as still as could be. I didn't make a grand entrance through the wrought-iron gate with the letters of eternal repose – RIP – embraced in a tangled wreath of flowers; rather, I crept along the edge of the wood.

There was no need to count the rows. I knew exactly where the earth had been freshly churned up, where they had buried my mother's old, drowned and butchered body, in the shadow of the tall trees. Slow, solid steps carried me forward. I skirted my way around the grey headstones of others, engraved with indifference, and I stood before her, asking her forgiveness for my dirty clothes, my work boots, the spade breaking the surface. I dug into the soft ground. I could feel the tears streaming down onto her grave. The sacred site of our missed rendezvous.

My daughter, I am willing Pilar *to you, and the horizon is your oyster.*

This was no sacrilege. I pried the wooden coffin open. There she was, pale in the funeral director's sewn-up shroud. Though it was light, I toiled to lift her body out of the hole. I laid her down on the grass and smoothed over the grave as best I could. Then it struck me they'd know what I'd done anyway, and I wouldn't get away with it. But never mind. I hid the spade in the woods before returning to her side, while she sagely waited with eyes closed, horizontal in the nocturnal dew. Mother.

I had sworn I wouldn't love her, but it was stronger than me, this urge to take her in my arms, forgive her, carry her body back to the waters where she deserved to rest in peace – beyond my fears, beyond the promises I had made to myself and cemented so they became stumbling blocks in the way of my own freedom.

I tore open the cloth of the shroud. I lifted my mother's cold, blue body to my chest – Marie Garant's body there in my arms – and I carried her to my car.

He emerged from the shadows as I drew near the edge of the cemetery.

'If you take the sailboat, they'll know it was you. Heee … Let's put her in my truck and we'll take my boat. Heee … It's safer that way.'

I checked the route on the GPS as the sun continued tracing its southerly circle. Out to sea, I spotted a fishing boat. I grabbed the binoculars. It was a trawler, the *Delgado*. And somewhere, invisibly, I knew Jérémie was watching over me. I put the binoculars down and turned my gaze north one last time.

Who was my father?

I didn't know. I had put a name on all those whose paths had crossed Marie Garant's and traced their timeline. But too many men had loved my mother. I was missing the date of birth that would reveal my true patronym. The date that would give me a name. Without knowing that first day I had come into the world on the water, I could only drift between those who had fluttered their sweet blue eyes at me. But if Marie Garant hadn't left me any clues, perhaps she didn't want me to know. There would be many fathers' faces on the watery undersides of my eyelids.

And why would it ever matter where I came from? The beauty of the day was stretching out before me, over the sea. I would always be an intriguing collage, a splintered stained-glass window. The light of the rising sun illuminated the revolving kaleidoscope of my path. I might not have the answer, but the horizon was all mine.

Delgado (2007)

Half past five in the morning. Aboard the *Delgado*, O'Neil Poirier and his sons were just getting the day started. This year, they were fishing in the Gulf of Saint Lawrence. O'Neil looked on from the wheelhouse as his sons – grown men! – hauled up the traps they'd thrown overboard the night before to slow the trawler's course.

The rising sun traced a white sail of a triangle on the sea. Without thinking, he picked up his binoculars, twisted the lenses into focus. *Pilar*. He rubbed his eyes to be sure of what he was seeing, then had another look. There she was. *Pilar*, with the silhouette of a woman in the cockpit! Sixty-five years old and widowed too young, his heart caught in his throat.

It was her! The woman he never did marry.

He grabbed the VHF transmitter. Hesitated. What would he say? 'Ahoy there, fair skipper, remember the day I helped you give birth? I had another trawler, the *Alberto*, back then!'

He stopped short of placing the call. What would he sound like? Because O'Neil Poirier had never had a knack for words. What's more, the men of the *Alberto* had never said a word about that birth. Not to a single soul. What happened on the water, stayed on the water. They had long memories though, you mark their words! Poirier checked the calendar. That little girl would have turned thirty-three last month. The twelfth, to be precise. She should have been born ten days later, that's what her mother had said, but she was in a hurry to live!

He took one last look at the sailboat.

Loving a woman of the sea was nigh on impossible. There were women whose hands you should never ask for. Women you could never marry. He for one knew he was happier on the water than anywhere else. Deep down, he knew the ocean was a selfish soul.

And so, O'Neil Poirier put the VHF transmitter back in its cradle. For a second, he stuffed those big, useless hands of his deep into his pockets, and then he got back to his fishing.

THE END

Acknowledgements

Sailing the sea comes with a slow learning curve. I consider myself lucky to have had such generous partners in crime. Sylvain Poirier and Marlène Forest, and your *Douce Évasion*, I have a lot to thank you for.

Thanks to the sailors for showing me the love of sailing: Tom and Marie-Sylvie, Jean-Phylip, Michel, Yvan and Sylvie, Caroline, Diane, Dave and Caro, Bine, Stéphane and Julie. Thank you to everyone at the Club de voile de Berthierville (especially Claude Milot and Yves Carle), the Club de voile de Bonaventure and the Marina de La Grave (Luc, Sylvain and *Le Pistorlet*). To name but a few.

Thank you to the locals in the Gaspé who welcomed me with such open arms: Michelle Secours (Frëtt), Guylaine, Renaud, Lancelot, Laurie, Cyrille and Jack in the Baie-des-Chaleurs; Michel Chouinard in Sainte-Flavie; O'Neil Poirier in Cloridorme; and Rob, Bob and Jérémie in Gesgapegiag.

Thank you to detectives Jean-Yves Roch and Serge Caillouette, and to the inimitable undertakers Landreville. Thank you, Lieutenant Jean Joly.

Thanks for your input, Mathieu Payette and Gilles Jobidon. And a huge thank you to my literary editor in French, Jean-Yves Soucy, whose keen eye helped to turn a detective into a hero. Thank you to Rogé for the wonderful cover art on the original French edition and to the publishing team at VLB (including Myriam, of course).

Thank you to the Conseil des arts et des lettres du Québec, the Canada Council for the Arts and SODEC. No words can ever express just how essential a role literary and translation grants play in encouraging the creative process.

Special thanks to my English publisher, Karen Sullivan of Orenda Books, for believing in me and bringing *We Were the Salt of the Sea* across the pond. Thanks to West Camel for his eagle eye in the editing suite, and to Mark Swan (Kid-ethic) for the intriguing cover art. I am especially grateful to David Warriner for his extraordinary work on the English translation and for his dear friendship as we embark on this adventure together. Most of all, thank you to my one-and-only Pierre-Luc, who keeps the light on the rocks burning on even the stormiest of nights.

Finally, thanks to you, my readers, for sharing your thoughts and fishing stories with me through my website, roxannebouchard.com. I'm always happy to hear from you.